W9-AUS-747

# THE VAN GOGH CONSPIRACY

## J. MADISON DAVIS

**ibooks**

new york
www.ibooks.net

DISTRIBUTED BY PUBLISHERS GROUP WEST

"The Van Gogh Conspiracy" is copyright © 2005 to ibooks, inc.

An ibooks, inc. Book

All rights reserved, including the right to reproduce this book
or portions thereof in any form whatsoever.
Distributed by Publishers Group West
1700 Fourth Street, Berkeley, CA, 94710

ibooks, inc.
24 West 25$^{th}$ Street
New York, NY 10010

The ibooks World Wide Web Site address is:
http://www.ibooks.net

Printed in the United States of America

Cover Art: Courtesy of The Scala Group

ISBN: 1-59687-102-4

First ibooks printing July 2005

10 9 8 7 6 5 4 3 2 1

# Contents

# THE VAN GOGH CONSPIRACY

ONE

# A Murder on Game Day

Esther Goren had no memory of her father. No photographs, no artifacts, no stories from relatives, nothing.
To her mother Rosa, Samuel Meyer was less than a
sperm donor. He was an accident, a man who deserted his
wife as soon as his child was born and deserved no forgiveness for his self-imposed exile. In the rare instances in which
Rosa *had* referred to Esther's father, her lips pursed. Her teeth
clenched. Uttering his name was such an exertion, like lifting
a grand piano, that Rosa always failed in the attempt. She
never used his name. She never called him "Esther's father" or

9

"my ex-husband." Rosa spat the words: he was just "the Pig." Always, "the Pig."

"The year the Pig left, I went to work in a shoe shop."

"The Pig was strong. That's why you're strong."

"You've got ten times the brains of the Pig and more character in your toenail."

"Stop asking! The Pig didn't love me, so he couldn't have loved you, either. That's just the way it is. Who needs him?"

Was there any real reason to travel halfway around the world to meet the Pig? But here Esther was on a street in Chicago. Why? To see if he could redeem himself? To find out who Samuel Meyer was? To find out who *she* was? What did he have to do with who she was?

She felt torn, dizzy, physically ill. She tried to blame the sensations on jet lag but knew that the vertigo had come upon her the instant the dreadlocked cab driver had said cheerfully, "Here you go, ma'am."

Samuel Meyer's home was just an address to him.

The Mossad had trained Esther to conceal her feelings, but she had never found it more difficult. The danger wasn't physical. Twice in her career, she had been in deep cover, once in Tehran, once with Hamas. Once, in a firefight in Gaza, she had been shot at by the Israel Defense Forces. When she had served in the IDF at the age of eighteen, a Syrian machine gunner had pinned her down, his gun blazing. The boulder she was hiding behind spewed sharp blades of rock all around her, but she rolled, leveled her rifle, and took him out with a single shot. She had looked into the barrel of his Soviet-made Kalashnikov to do that, but at this moment she couldn't bring herself to look directly at Meyer's house.

Across the street, a wall loomed. A roar rose from behind it. "What is that?" she asked. "American football?"

"Why, Wrigley Field, ma'am!" The cabbie shook his dreadlocks. "The Cubbies!" His white teeth flashed. " 'If dey don' win, it's the *same*,' " he sang.

Esther didn't respond to his chuckle but listened to an organ sounding a charge as she read the meter: $39.80. With a shaking hand, she offered a fifty-dollar bill over the seat. She tried to calculate how much tip was fair by converting dollars into shekels, then gave up and waved off the change. The driver seemed pleased. She slid her carry-on bag to the sidewalk, stepped out, and the cab screeched away. She took a deep breath, turned away from the stadium, then looked at the row house in which her father, "the Pig" she could not remember, lived.

Doubt paralyzed her. She was a few meters from a door that, once opened, would change her life in a totally unpredictable way.

Oh, Esther had fantasized about him many times, particularly when she was a teenager. She imagined her father was a secret agent working with Simon Wiesenthal to hunt down the men who had tortured her mother. She had told this to a childhood friend, but the girl hadn't believed her. It was too obviously only a desperate wish that would swing to despair and then to hate and then back again.

In Esther's kibbutz, there were children whose fathers had been killed in Lebanon or during the Intifada. These men had been torn from their children unwillingly. There were images in these children's minds of a pilot or an artilleryman who had given them life and then died to protect it. Samuel Meyer had willfully slammed the door in Esther's face. Once or twice when she had pressed, her mother, Rosa, had said that the Pig had run off with a blonde shiksa. But she said it in a way that meant: "If you've got to have a story, how about this one?"

Whatever painful memories Rosa Goren had nurtured—Kristallnacht, Auschwitz, her rape by Soviet troops—these things she could haltingly speak of. But not Samuel Meyer. Now Rosa's memory was dissolved by Alzheimer's, and her shell stared serenely at the Mediterranean. Unless a medical miracle occurred—a hope Esther clung to despite herself and against all odds—Rosa would never be able to tell Esther anything more about her father.

A beer-bellied fan wearing a baseball cap passed, looking up and down Esther's lean body. She was suddenly aware of her conspicuousness, standing on the sidewalk, her bag at her feet. She instinctively glanced all around her. In her line of work being conspicuous meant a short, painful life.

She picked up the bag and climbed the stoop of her father's house. Her heart pounded as she pressed the doorbell and heard its shrill ring. Loudspeakers squawked in the stadium. Setting down her bag, Esther listened, but the words smeared and she couldn't make out what was being said. She pushed the doorbell again. She caught the blink of a movement behind the lens of the peephole, but when no one answered she passed it off as the reflection of a passing truck.

"Come on, Meyer!" she said, ringing the bell again. As before, it faded into the interior of the house without a response.

Esther imagined him too embarrassed to open the door. She imagined him too ill to rise from his bed. She saw him dead on his sofa, sprawled on his floor, lying in his bathtub. She had seen the dead many times. Nursing mothers. Children. Terrorists. All they had been, all they had meant, translated into bloated flesh and blood-caked hair. How different would it be to see the body of a father you had never known and never loved? What were you supposed to feel about that?

The relief she felt from the unanswered rings made her uneasy.

She climbed down the stoop and peered up the narrow alley between Meyer's house and the next. The alley smelled sour, like rotting melons or stale beer. She thought for a moment, took a breath, and walked between the buildings in an effort to find a rear entrance.

"*Sie ist gegangen, SS-Standartenführer Stock.*"

At first, she wasn't sure she'd heard it: "She's gone, SS Colonel Stock." The pounding of her heart seemed to echo off the walls.

Then, a second voice. "*Ich bin nichts der Standartenführer!* No more games, old man! Where is it?"

Esther looked up. Several feet above her was a tiny open window.

"Where is what, SS-Standartenführer?"

There was the crack of a hard slap and a wet cry.

"*Wo ist es? Wo ist es?* Where? I will shoot!"

Esther tensed like a cat, every nerve alert, but there was no shot. The second man laughed at the threat. "And I will be dead! You think that scares me? Ha! Thank you. I should thank you!"

Esther sprang down the alley. This was the kind of situation she had been trained to deal with and *had* dealt with, often. The fear didn't disappear but was channeled into deadly energy. When she reached the end of the building, a six-foot wooden fence blocked her way. She flipped herself over it and landed in a tiny backyard beside a small porch. The door was protected by a barred metal storm door, but to her left was a cellar entrance. The padlock hung useless in a torn hasp.

She paused at the edge of the opening, heard nothing below, then scurried down into the musty air. It was like diving into cool water. She spun to the side to avoid being sil-houetted against the sky. Cobwebs clung to her face. The water heater clinked as it switched into its normal heating cycle. She closed her eyes to adjust them to the dark as a spi-der scurried across the wired glass of a narrow window. She made out an old workbench, dusty and neglected. The tools on it were coated with rust, but she had killed men with much less. Esther considered the pipe wrench, then plucked up a long screwdriver. An old can of spray paint caught her eye. A quick push told her it was still charged.

Wooden steps led up from the cellar. Any one of them could scream out her presence. She clung to the wall and mounted like a cat moving into attack position. As she eased up to the closed door, the voices grew louder.

"More? You want more? Where is it?" There was a thud. One of the men had been knocked to the floor.

"Maybe it's in the mail. Maybe you're too late."

"Who has it? *Wer?*"

The man coughed and weakly laughed. "You think you know what pain is, Standartenführer Stock? Jews know what pain is. *I* know what pain is."

The man on the floor must be Meyer. Esther peered through the keyhole. Wallpaper gone brown. The edge of dark wainscoting. She needed to know if the man called Stock had his back to the cellar door, but she couldn't see.

A shot cracked so loud it was as if someone had slapped the door. She nearly fell back. Meyer screamed in agony. Esther went through the door, the screwdriver low and the spray paint high. In a glimpse she saw Meyer on the floor of his living room clutching a bloody knee, his face twisted. Astonished, the man called Stock spun his Ruger toward her, but she had come upon him so quickly, the screwdriver and pistol whacked against each other. She pressed the button of the paint can, and a splutter blossomed into a plume of battleship gray.

Stock fell back against the fireplace, covering his eyes with his sleeve and flailing the Ruger. Esther drove the screwdriver toward his belly, but in the collision with the gun, the handle had slipped through her hand and she held only the long blade. It struck his belt and popped through her grip, dropping to the floor. Immediately she brought up the heel of her hand to drive his nose cartilage into his brain, but the flailing Ruger cracked her across the wrist. She winced at the pain but kicked into his groin. Stock bellowed, clinging to the mantelpiece, shaking his head like an angry bull.

She leaped at his throat, thumbs extended, but she slipped in Meyer's blood and fell harmlessly against Stock, who flung her across the room with his thick arms. The doorpost struck the back of her head like a club, and she was momentarily paralyzed. Stock, blinking, raised his pistol, trying to aim, his gray face streaked with tears from his burning eyes.

"Esther!" Meyer shouted. "My girl!" He clawed at Stock's leg, clutching him around the calf, but Stock kicked him away. Stock turned to face Esther, but Meyer had given her the chance to recover. She flung herself at him again.

He caught her full in the face with a meaty forearm. Again she was flung back, this time spinning off the door jamb and tumbling down the dark basement stairs.

As she lost consciousness, she wasn't certain what she experienced. The cool concrete of the cellar floor. The metallic taste of blood. Or was that paint? Was that a siren? Or screaming? Her arms didn't work. Did she roll on her side to see the silhouette of Stock at the top of the stairs? He leveled his gun. Did it fire? They say you don't hear the one that gets you.

Shots. Certainly there were shots. They slammed into her body like penalty kicks smashing the nose of an inept goalie.

Thump. Thump. Thump.

She had two simple thoughts before the darkness closed in:

*My father knew me.*

*My father fought for me.*

# TWO

# The Secrets of Samuel Meyer

The sharp thunk of knuckles on the steel door raised Esther's head from the exhausting task of tying her sneakers. She thought it would be another doctor; nurses didn't seem to knock. Instead it was a thin, square-jawed man with short, sandy hair. *Detective*, she thought. A better-looking suit than usual, but copper to the bone. She dropped the laces and sagged back in the low vinyl chair.

"How many times?" she asked.

"Excuse me?"

"How many statements do you take?"

"I'm not here for a statement."

"What then? Move me to another room? No more. I've

changed rooms six times in three days. I'm out of here. The way I've been moved around in this place, I should get frequent flyer miles."

"Do you mind if I come in?" the man asked. "I can help you with those."

Esther looked up at him as if she expected him to launch into a sales pitch for a new weight loss program. But everything was so tiring since she'd been shot.

She shrugged indifferently. "If you like."

He smiled a sheepish boy's smile, then knelt on one knee as she turned toward the window. He quickly finished one shoe, then gently cradled her heel to slide the other over her toes. Sunlight streaming through the window flashed off his plain gold wedding band. She glanced down to see if he ogled her legs, but she saw only the top of his head. He felt her stare and raised his eyes.

"I'm Martin Henson," he said. "Are you feeling better?"

"Like someone has been beating me with a rubber hammer for twelve years."

"You're making a full recovery, they say."

"Who says? I was lucky. He threw bullets all around vital stuff, but he didn't win the prize."

"Better lucky and alive," said Henson, "than talented and dead."

Esther shifted uneasily. She thought he might be wondering about the bullet that had passed through her breast. Was that kinky to this guy?

"Hurt much?" he asked.

"Being sore means being alive. Slightly. They can give you Percocet."

He stood. "Have you ever been shot before?"

*Shot at,* she thought. *Never hit.* "No. Why would I be? I'm just a travel agent."

He nodded. "Do you mind?" He crossed to the door, glanced both ways into the corridor, and closed it without waiting for her to agree.

She tensed slightly but sensed that this Henson was too relaxed, almost too goofy, to be a physical threat.

"I hate hospitals," he said. "Don't you?" He didn't seem to be making conversation when he said it. "You know," he whispered after a pause, "much could be made of a Mossad agent operating clandestinely in the United States. The diplomacy could be nasty. It could mess up whatever peace talks we might be having with the Palestinians and who-knows-what."

"Mossad?" Esther laughed. "Talk all you want. What's the Mossad got to do with it? I'm a travel agent."

"You think we don't keep track of intelligence agents coming into America?" Henson said quietly. "Especially these days. And then, of course, your government notifies us. The Chicago police were quite intrigued by an Israeli national stepping off a plane and two hours later getting shot. They called the FBI, who called your embassy, who then called State, and so on. They assured us that you were not here 'in a professional capacity.' They also assured us you would cooperate completely."

"I went to visit my father. A burglar shot me and left me for dead."

"That's what Yossi Lev told me," said Henson. "That you'd cooperate."

Esther stared, trying not to show that the name had startled her. The painkillers weren't that strong, but she didn't feel confident that her expression wasn't telegraphing every thought. Who was this Henson? A mind reader? "Excuse me?"

"Yossi Lev. I talked with him this morning. Major Lev says *shalom*. He said after all you'd been through he couldn't believe this would happen on vacation. At first they suspected Hamas, you know, but that's been ruled out."

"I don't know who or what you're talking about."

"No," Henson said, smiling, "of course you don't. Listen, I'm not up to anything. Let me just explain what our interest is."

"I've got to be at the airport in ninety minutes."

"There's no hurry." He removed a notepad and a Montblanc fountain pen from his inner jacket pocket. An expensive pen was not the usual accessory for a cop. Was he from the State Department? Henson did not open the pen, however. He just used it as a pointer to scan down his notes. "According to Chicago Police Detective Thomas," he asked, "you said your father telephoned you to say that his prostate cancer had metastasized and he had only a couple of weeks at most."

"Yes." Esther turned to look out the window. "Maybe days."

Meyer had called her half a dozen times. He had begged. He had wept. He told her he had spent thousands of dollars on international telephone calls to keep track of them over the years and knew that Rosa had never remarried, but simply reverted to her maiden name. Didn't this show he cared? He had never remarried, either. He still loved Rosa, he sobbed, and he still loved Esther.

How could he call that "love"? All this did was fuel Esther's anger, and she had remained adamant. She had no desire to see him. He had abandoned her mother not a year after Esther was born. How could that be forgiven? She winced, recalling how she'd shouted that she hated him and slammed down the phone. He called back. She had listened to him bawling and begging in crude Hebrew and even worse Yiddish on the answering machine. He said he had something to give her, something that might make up for what he had done. Her mother would understand, he had said. His life had been worthless. This was his last chance to do anything for his only child.

Esther had been torn. What he wanted to give her meant nothing to her. She wasn't even curious about that. But no matter what Meyer had done, she wanted to know who he was, to look him in the eyes to try to understand what her father was like. She needed her mother's advice, but Rosa was far beyond understanding anything. A year ago she sometimes mistook Esther for her aunt Pola, who had suffocated in the train to Auschwitz. As Rosa's thought processes melted away, she was mentally reliving the horrors of her youth. Now the woman stared from her wheelchair without confusion, a pale ghost finally freed of all nightmarish memories. Rosa Goren was alive only in name. Esther asked herself: had she agreed to see Samuel Meyer merely to fill the void she was facing, to re-create some kind of family for the brief time Meyer had left?

One sleepless night, Esther had driven across Tel Aviv to consult Yossi Lev. He listened patiently but as usual answered bluntly. "See him, don't see him. Follow your instinct," he said. "Your instinct has served you well in a thousand terrible situations." But what *did* her instinct tell her? She didn't know. Her emotions pelted her from opposite directions like stones flung by an angry mob.

As she walked home, she remembered an orthodox rabbi she had met at her mother's nursing home. She had never been particularly religious, but this rabbi had always seemed kindly and particularly wise. The next day she called for an appointment. He told her she mustn't let what she imagined to be her mother's feelings decide the matter for her. Her mother was beyond feelings. Esther, he advised, might never feel at rest until she had confronted her father. Visiting him, perhaps offering him forgiveness if she could bring herself to it: that would be a mitzvah, an act of charity to a dying man, no matter what wrongs the man had committed. Charity was a more important good than punishment and would redound to her.

"So you flew to Chicago," said Henson.

Yes, she nodded. Meyer had not known she was coming, however. She had bought the ticket thinking she could back out at the last minute. Perhaps she knew she couldn't, but this is what she'd told herself.

"You called him from the airport, then, and he gave you the address."

"He gave me what he called the 'grid numbers.' So many hundred north, so many hundred west. I didn't know what he meant exactly, but the cab driver knew."

"They use a grid. The crossing of State and Madison is the zero point," explained Henson. "It's a handy scheme. It's so easy to get lost in a big city, especially in the Old World: London, Damascus, Cairo. Those ancient streets."

"I wouldn't know," she said.

Henson smiled. "As a travel agent?"

"I arrange trips."

"Oh, you get around."

She remembered the quavering of Meyer's voice on the phone. She momentarily considered if Stock had been there, already holding a gun to him, but she knew that it was emotion she had heard—gratitude that she might forgive him. "My father gave me the address and the city grid code when I called from O'Hare. And then I walked into—Well, all that."

Henson studied her for a minute. "The man called Stock must have been an expert to handle you. I mean, your training. Lev says you are one of the best."

"Training? I don't know what you are talking about."

Henson looked down at his notepad but said no more. He was so smug she wanted to slap him.

"Look," she whispered angrily, "why is the Company interested in this? The Chicago police have a murder to solve. I gave them the description, told them all I know. They need to find the man who killed my father. Murder is their problem, not yours."

"The Company? Who said anything about the CIA?" Henson smiled. "I don't know what *you're* talking about."

*All right,* she thought. *Throw it back at me.* "I've got to get a cab."

"Detective Thomas initially thought you had killed Meyer."

"Me! I was shot three times!"

"It was his theory. I'm not kidding."

"Meyer shot me three times, then put two bullets in his own face? Or I shot him and then shot myself to make it look like—"

"Crazy, isn't it? But when he first got Meyer's background he thought—"

"Background?"

"Why your mother left him."

There was a silence as if the universe had shuddered. What was this man saying? "Meyer deserted us! My mother didn't leave him!"

"You really don't know?" Henson tipped his head to one side. "Excuse my saying so, but that's hard to believe. I mean, you could have found out if you had wanted to. But you didn't want to, did you? I suppose that's understandable."

"He left my mother for a shiksa. A blonde shiksa."

Henson's expression was blank. "No."

Esther's heart seemed to stop. She had refused to see her father, even when he was dying. Then, when she had finally acquiesced, he had been snatched away from her just as he might explain why he had abandoned her and her mother. No, it wasn't possible there was a sufficient explanation. Why hadn't he tried to contact her for the past thirty-five years? The hurt in her mother's eyes whenever Esther had asked about her father—that didn't come from nothing.

"You were born in early 1966," Henson said. "About the same time, Immigration and Naturalization was looking into some of the cases of Jews who had asked for asylum around 1951. They were less concerned about finding Nazis than possible deep-cover Soviet agents. In any case, there were a number of things about your father that seemed to match up with a thug named Stéphane Meyerbeer."

A cold sweat broke out on Esther's forehead. Her mother had said nothing about this. "And?"

Henson summarized. From the time of his arrival in the United States, Samuel Meyer had led an undistinguished life. He had settled in the Chicago area and taken a job in a machine shop, occasionally driving a cab on the weekends for extra money. He saved his money and, with Rosa Goren, eventually bought the house that he died in. There were two times his name appeared in any police records. In 1959, he was the witness to a white on black mugging outside a jazz club. The case never came to trial as the victim never showed up to press charges. In 1963, he was arrested during a strike while picketing along with a dozen of the other machine shop workers. The charges were trumped up to harass his union and were dropped within hours. Meyer quietly lived his life working, attending synagogue occasionally, and playing dominoes with some of the Italians at work. Early in 1966, Esther was born. Samuel Meyer and his wife, Rosa, were living out the American dream.

A few months after the baby was born, however, Samuel Meyer went into a pawn shop near the Loop with a silver snuffbox decorated with crossed cannons and fleurs-de-lys. The pawnbroker recognized it as being much older and more valuable than Meyer said. There had been a break-in at one of the mansions in Lake Forest a month before and several antiques had been stolen. A snuffbox was not on the warning list the pawnbroker had received, but he notified the police nonetheless. Detectives found Meyer at his taxi stand and questioned him. He said a man had given it to him during the war when he was in Holland, and he'd carried it with him in his pocket as a good luck piece until he emigrated. Examining the snuffbox more closely, the police found a monogram and a hallmark on the bottom and discovered it was one of five snuffboxes made for Philippe, the gay brother and chief military commander of Louis XIV, to give to his friends. Three of the boxes were in museums, one was unaccounted for, and one had been stolen from a Jewish banker in Nice in 1943 by a French Nazi named Stéphane Meyerbeer.

Meyer was hauled in. The fact that he could speak French and could not verify his whereabouts from mid-1940 until he surfaced in Avignon in 1947 seemed to match with the history of Meyerbeer. In the puppet regime of Pétain's Vichy France, Meyerbeer had helped round up Jews and loot their possessions. When the Germans exerted more direct control in the south of France, he set about proving his loyalty. A former German army officer had been willing to testify that he had seen Meyerbeer kick a pregnant woman to death. Two survivors of a slave-labor camp had seen Meyerbeer gouge out a boy's eyes with a soupspoon. Both were certain they could identify Samuel Meyer as Stéphane Meyerbeer, even though the former army officer was nearly blind. Preparations were made for a hearing to consider revoking Meyer's citizenship and deporting him back to France for trial. The hearing was set for November 1966.

Esther's stomach dropped. Her mouth was so dry she could hardly speak. "Did—did my father admit to being Meyerbeer?"

"Not to anyone in the government. He continued to insist that as he had fled south a Dutch refugee had given him the box somewhere near Maastricht to pay for a meal and some clothes. Things got crazy late that summer. Around Labor Day, your mother slipped out of Chicago carrying you in her arms and flew from New York to Tel Aviv. On landing, she asked for sanctuary for both of you as Jews and later renounced her U.S. citizenship. She refused to explain her suspicious behavior and continued to say she knew nothing about Samuel Meyer's background, just that he was—excuse me—a pig. Even when Israeli authorities threatened to block her entry and send her back to the United States if she didn't say what she knew about her husband, she continued to say nothing."

"Sending her back would have been against the law of return!"

"Perhaps it was just a threat," said Henson. "But later the Israelis kept out Meyer Lansky, the gangster, despite the law of return, didn't they? A week before the hearing, sudden news came from a small village, Chantèrie, near Geneva. The accusations against your father had appeared in the *International Herald Tribune* and were noticed by an engineer, who remembered something his father had told him. A man claiming to be Stéphane Meyerbeer had slipped across the border from France in 1945. Normally such men were immediately deported. The Swiss had even sent a number of Jews back to certain death in Germany in previous years. However, this man claiming to be Meyerbeer was in terrible health. He tried to bribe the village officials with a crucifix, which they later discovered to have been looted from a collection in Avignon. At the time he arrived in Chantèrie he was coughing up blood from a beating and running a high fever. He died after about four days."

Henson leaned closer to Esther. "The villagers thought this man might have been the victim of a crime or had been beaten in revenge, as was happening in most of the liberated countries, so they took a photograph of the man lying in his bed. They buried him with the paupers, and he would have been forgotten except for the crucifix and the engineer's memory of his father's story. Facing the substantial evidence that Meyerbeer was dead, the authorities dropped the case against your father. Most of them were quite clear that they thought Meyerbeer's death was faked, perhaps with the collusion of sympathetic Swiss, but they had nothing to confirm their suspicions in a court of law. Der Spinne, the Odessa group, all the groups of Nazis-in-hiding were good at trumping up 'deaths.' In any case, it all seemed less important to confirm that Samuel Meyer was Stéphane Meyerbeer when Vietnam was heating up and the superpowers had their fingers near the button."

Esther's eyes flashed. "You believe my father was Meyerbeer!"

Henson did not try to avoid her hot glare. "Yes, Miss Goren, I'm afraid I do."

She shot up from her chair and paced in an awkward motion to loosen up the stiffness of her bruises. "It's idiotic."

"Why? What did your father tell you?"

"He told me nothing. He never had a chance to tell me anything. I traveled thousands of miles for—for this! Do you think my mother would have allowed a war criminal to live free? My mother was fourteen when she was beaten on

Kristallnacht. She survived Auschwitz only by becoming a commander's plaything. After the liberation, she was captured by Soviet troops and raped for three days. And she would let Meyerbeer get away with it? It's insane."

Henson had winced at the details of Rosa Goren's story. He seemed uncertain what to say. "We believe she wanted to keep it from you."

Esther's agitated pacing stopped immediately.

"What would it have done to your life in Israel to be known as Meyerbeer's daughter?" Henson continued. "Would you keep such a secret to protect your daughter? I mean, if you had a daughter."

Esther turned back to the window and gripped her chair for support. "No," she finally said. "No. I would have to turn him in. My own father. I am not as strong as my mother. As my mother was."

There was a long silence, then the normal sounds of a hospital gradually surfaced in her whirling mind. They were paging a doctor. A wheelchair squeaked as it moved past.

Henson spoke cautiously. "I think you underestimate your strength. You went up against a man with a gun armed only with a paint can and a screwdriver."

"And he shouldn't have had a chance. I should have taken him."

Henson looked into her wide, dark eyes. "I think—tell me if I'm wrong—that you want to know the truth about your father, one way or the other."

"I'm supposed to be at the airport by four," Esther said numbly.

"El Al flies every day," said Henson. "It's a small world, after all."

# THREE

# "It"

Ten days had passed since Esther had first stood on the stoop across the street from Wrigley Field. Henson pulled aside the yellow tape warning that the area was a crime scene and unlocked the door. He stepped aside and waited for her to enter. She hesitated, then stepped across the threshold, stopping in the foyer to listen to the row house's strange silence. A smell like old, hot wool lay heavy in the air. She peered up the long staircase from the foyer. The small window at the upper landing emblazoned a triangle of multi-colored light on the fading wallpaper. Unsteady, Esther closed her eyes.

"Are you all right?" Henson asked, taking her elbow.

"It was a worse fight than I remember," she said, taking a

deep breath and looking into the living room.

"Uh-oh," said Henson. "Two-legged rats. It wasn't like this."

He took her upper arm, gently moved her behind him, and stepped gingerly into the living room. Someone had systematically and thoroughly ransacked it. Meyer's old sofa and loveseat had been overturned. The cushions had been slashed and gutted. Pictures had been taken from the wall and their frames pulled apart. The end tables were overturned, and their drawers lay scattered in front of the radiator under the tall window curtains.

Henson squatted and reached under his pants leg, pulling an automatic pistol from an ankle holster. "Stay by the door. You hear anything, you get out of here and press star one for backup." He handed Esther his cell phone.

She watched him shimmy along the wall, take a look down the cellar stairs, then move toward the back. *I'm better at this than he is,* she thought. She stepped back so as not to be an obvious silhouette in the doorway. The haze of her convalescence snapped off as if it operated on a toggle switch. Her senses were alive to every sound in the old house. The boards creaked like an old man's bones as Henson moved through the back rooms, but there were no sounds that warned of another's presence.

"The kitchen's the same," he whispered quickly. "Trashed." He lifted his gun high as he moved up the stairs to the second floor. She listened to his footsteps above her, her wounds throbbing in time with her heart. After several minutes, Henson appeared at the top of the stairs, the gun hanging limply at his thigh.

"Upstairs, too?"

"Oh, yeah. The boy was thorough," he said.

She looked down at the quiver in her hands, startled as if

she had just discovered she had them. "How do we know it was him?"

"This wasn't a bunch of gangbangers tearing up a place for the hell of it."

Esther knew he was right. Things had been tossed aside but not destroyed randomly. Nothing that might have hidden anything had been neglected. Cushions had been slashed, but the fireplace tools hung undisturbed on their rack. Vandals would have used the poker as a tool. Vases were smashed, but there were no random holes punched into the walls. "Do you think he got what he came for?"

"I don't know how he could have missed it," said Henson.

She stepped closer to him. "It could have been someone else. It could have been a group. The yellow tape could have attracted someone."

"It must be the same guy," said Henson.

"You know who did it?"

"Not exactly. But a big guy showed up outside the emergency room."

"What? Looking for me?"

Henson met her eyes. "Maybe to finish you. But maybe just to find out if you had 'it,' whatever 'it' is. He was scared off by something. Major trauma centers like Cook County have pretty good security. A lot of wannabe masterminds want to finish their sloppy handiwork. When someone comes in and asks questions about a patient, they pay attention. They tried to find out who he was, but he bolted. The tape of him outside the emergency room is blurry, but we've got a vague description, and he seems to be your boy."

"When do you think he searched here?"

Henson shrugged. Esther bent and ran a finger along the overturned telephone stand, then held it up for Henson to see. "No dust since it was turned over," she said. "A day at most. Last night maybe."

"Well, let's see if he missed anything."

She nodded. "What are we looking for?"

" 'It,' " said Henson. "The man your father called Colonel Stock wanted 'it.' They didn't say anything else?"

"Don't you think I've asked myself that? Over and over?"

Henson nodded. Esther gripped the baluster post for support and looked up at the small-wattage foyer light. An old man saving a few cents on electricity, she thought. He gently touched her upper arm. "You want to sit down?"

She pulled away. "I'm fine. Where do we start?"

"Bottom to top or top to bottom."

She tried to think quickly which alternative would keep her out of the living room longest, then summoned her nerve. "The hard part first," she said, turning toward the murder site. Henson opened the curtains. A large, dark stain of blood covered one corner of the fireplace hearth, then spread in an oblong loop across the oak floor to the edge of the flipped oriental carpet. She remembered skidding in her father's blood. When she turned away from the stain she saw blood spatters on the arm of the settee.

Stock had shot Meyer first in the knee, reputed to be the most painful nonfatal wound a bullet can inflict. He had done that to cripple him, maybe, but more likely to get him to talk. That was when Esther had attacked. After knocking her down the cellar stairs, Stock had fired three shots into her. One slid along her third rib and flattened against the concrete. Another passed through her left breast at the base and ripped a flower-shaped exit wound just below her armpit. "No worse than a bad cut," said the bleary-eyed surgeon. The third shot had hit her in the upper part of her chest. This might have been the serious one, but it took an upward route and settled behind her collar bone, having missed anything vital. It might have been slowed by the adjustment clasp on her bra strap, the doctors speculated. The clasp had been pushed into her chest cavity and lodged to the side of the wound. The surgeons nearly missed picking it out. After evaluating the X-rays, they had been more worried about the bang on her head from the concrete floor than the bullet holes. "In gunshots, as in real estate," Esther remembered one of her army instructors saying, "location is everything."

Leaving her for dead, Stock had then silenced Samuel Meyer with two shots in his face, fleeing out the back gate as Chicago police officers battered open the front door. If the hacky-sack players two buildings away hadn't heard the shots, Stock might have climbed down the stairs to check Esther, found her unconscious but alive, and finished the job. He would also have tortured Meyer until he got what he wanted: the mysterious "it."

Warily stepping around the dried blood, Henson yanked up the torn sofa cushions, squeezing and poking each in succession. He set the sofa up and felt in the cracks. He came out with a section of newspaper with a half-finished crossword puzzle, some loose change, and a red comb labeled "Pep Boys." Esther picked up a ceramic milkmaid that had been knocked off the mantel or the coffee table. One of the figurine's blue milk pails had broken off. One of two candlesticks remained on the mantel, but they were of a cheap leadlike metal coated with something silvery. There was nothing in the hollow at the bottom.

A number of things had been tossed toward the radiator: a chipped ashtray with the Sears Tower on it, a book of coupons, a menorah. The menorah was solid brass, but one of its arms was newly bent. A surface crack exposed clean metal. There were no hollow compartments that she could detect, but there was a mark on the bottom, a hallmark and the engraved script words "Steinitz, Nîmes."

She was about to set it aside when she thought, *It's a menorah. From the south of France.* Was this further evidence that Meyer was really Meyerbeer? Could Meyerbeer have been so cold that he kept a menorah stolen from one of his victims? Psychopaths often kept trophies of their "accomplishments." He could have looked at it, touched it, remembered when he had power over people, could beat them and send them to their deaths. Ironically, he could then have kept it to demonstrate his Jewishness, as a means to help conceal his own identity as a traitor to the Jews. It could have been an evil joke to him to display it, *if* he was Meyerbeer. If he was Samuel Meyer, refugee, it might merely have been an emblem of his faith. Esther sat the menorah on the windowsill, thinking she would take it with her.

Henson was going through the magazines caught under the capsized television. " 'Dr. Elihu Winston.' 'Charles Goldman, MD.' " He looked at Esther. "Meyer stole magazines from his doctors' offices. Maybe they can tell us more about him."

She felt an urge to defend her father and then was ashamed of it. Why? What kind of father had he been? She didn't say anything but bent to look at a large group photo lying on the floor. The glass was splintered, and the frame had been broken open at one corner. She peered around at the old walls to see if she could make out where it had hung, then bent and carefully pulled the glass shards away. " 'The 1929 Chicago Cubs,' " she read. " 'National League Champions.' "

"It's been a long time since they were champions of anything," said Henson, shining a tiny flashlight into the back of the television.

" 'Carl "Driver" King,' " she read. " ' "Spider" Woodsprite. Ernest Brown.' "

"Ballplayers had colorful names back then," said Henson. He picked up a similarly shattered frame holding a picture of ducks paddling among cattails. "Old-timey baseball. Foxx with two *X*s; Cobb with two *B*s."

On the back of the team photo a set of twenty numbers had been penciled in uneven rows, each proceeded by letters. Usually three letters, sometimes four, preceded three numbers. "What do you think of this?" she asked. He glanced over.

"Batting averages? That's what it looks like."

"Averages?"

"The percentage of hits a batter makes in baseball. One twelve," he said, noting one. "Pretty lousy. Hmm. Five seventeen."

"There's a *P* in front of it. In front of a couple."

"Oh, it must be an earned run average. *P* for pitcher. No one can bat five seventeen. It's not a very good ERA, though. Bet they traded him."

"Do you think it could be some kind of code? Bank accounts or something like that?" Esther ran her fingers over the picture and its cardboard backing to see if anything else had been in the frame behind it and perhaps bulged it out.

"Keep it, if you like," Henson said, "but it just looks like baseball stats to me. Baseball fans have always been nutty about stats. We'll check it out." Henson was more interested in the etching he was holding, squinting at the vegetation by the ducks. "Ever see Al Hirschfeld's drawings? He hid his wife's—daughter's?—name in every drawing. Nina."

Esther nodded, though she didn't know what he was talking about. She put the Cubs photograph on the radiator, then laid the menorah on top of it. "He smashed everything that could be smashed."

"You might have sold the stuff. You're the only heir."

"Me? I don't want it! I wouldn't want it if it were in mint condition!"

Henson was startled by the sharpness of Esther's words and watched as she looked along the baseboard. She set an unbroken wine glass on the sill, then from under the radiator fished out a dusty mousetrap with a lump of bait dried hard. Oh, yes, this was all hers. All of these things were what Samuel Meyer had wanted to give her. A legacy of cheap furnishings. Mummified cheese. A heritage of betrayal.

She remembered now how her mother had often narrowed her eyes and said that the worst man was one who betrayed his own people. She knew the generalization was really about Meyer, but she had thought Rosa meant only Esther's father's betraying his wife and child. Had Rosa meant that she knew Samuel Meyer was actually Stéphane Meyerbeer? Was she unable to bring herself to turn him in? Did she remain silent to protect Esther?

"I'm going to the back," Esther said.

"Hold your nose," Henson said.

The kitchen was as sparse and lonely as the living room. Under the smell of garbage and thawed frozen dinners scattered and rotting on the floor, she smelled bargain soap. Meyer kept empty mayonnaise jars. He used them for storage. Sugar had been dumped from one, flour from another. Could Meyer have buried one in the backyard? That was a possibility. A trash bag, which had been waiting by the door to be taken out, was shredded as if a Saint Bernard had been at it. Six or seven cans lay in the rubbish: three for pork and beans. Meyer hadn't kept kosher, she noted. A prune juice bottle. Old newspapers.

The cabinets were as depressing as the rubbish, though

most of the food hadn't been broken open. Herring in wine sauce. Macaroni and cheese in narrow boxes. Spaghetti in cans. Ramen noodles, mostly beef flavored. On the counter, Maalox tablets, several kinds of laxatives, and a bottle of prescription tablets labeled "MS Cont, for pain."

Henson checked the freezer compartment of the old round-top refrigerator, which was unplugged.

"What is this?" asked Esther, holding up the tablets.

"Morphine," said Henson. "I see. That would mean this break-in wasn't a drug robbery, wouldn't it? Good thinking."

"I wasn't thinking of that," she said, "but you're right." *How strong is this medicine? How much pain was he in?*

Henson read her expression as she studied the label. "He was in bad shape," he said sympathetically.

"At least he didn't lie about that."

"No," Henson said, lifting back a newspaper covering a lump of gray meat. "It was all through him. He didn't lie about that."

Esther took a quick look under the sink and saw scattered aluminum pans. The broiler pan drawer was half pulled out. There were streaks of burned grease on it. She straightened up and looked around the room. "This is wrong," she said. "A man wouldn't hide something important in his kitchen. A woman would, but not a man."

"Your father lived alone for over thirty years."

"I'm going to the cellar," she said.

"Suit yourself."

Esther opened the door and looked down at where she had lain when Stock had fired three shots into her. She had been saved by the poor lighting, the curiosity of the hacky-sack players, and the plume of blood that spread on her chest when the shot passed through her breast. It must have looked like a heart wound and cracking her head on the pavement had kept her still. She had been sideways to the bullet's line of flight, so it had passed through. The bullet would have passed directly through her heart except for her position.

She raised her hand to her face. What was she doing, reliving those moments of terror? The instant she asked herself the question, the answer appeared as well. She was doing exactly what they did in each Mossad debriefing. It was automatic. Every detail was reviewed and examined to understand the success or failure of the mission: Why weren't the weapons hidden where the informant had said? How did the boy get caught in the crossfire? How did the secret police get onto the way they were passing the money? The difference this time was that Esther had been the target. Well, no, put vanity aside. Meyer was the target. Esther had merely been a nuisance. Stock would not have left Meyer until he got his answer or killed him. That meant that whatever Stock was after was also in Meyer's head and that killing Meyer could possibly end someone's problem. On the other hand, Stock had clearly been after something. Stock must have weighed the comparative dangers of leaving Meyer alive and failing to get whatever it was that Meyer held. Perhaps Stock had panicked, but possibly he had determined he could get whatever it was later—hence, the break-in. Was it possible that what Stock was after was the same thing her father had wanted to give her? Had he found it?

Esther felt the throbbing in her wounds increase again as her pulse raced. She saw herself at the base of the stairs, her head bloody from the fall, struggling to maintain consciousness, raising herself on her arms to look up at the dark figure at the top aiming his pistol.

Stock had not dared to climb down the stairs. He couldn't leave Meyer alone, even though the old man was crippled by the knee shot. In an odd way, her father had saved her life.

She ground her teeth. *Damn him!* She wanted nothing from Samuel Meyer. Nothing. Not even her life. But the frustration was that she had no choice in that. He had given her life, run away, then, years later, perhaps saved it.

Esther gripped the rail and slowly made her way down the stairs. At the bottom she stepped around her own bloodstains and fumbled for the light cord. Dust lay thick on everything: tools on the workbench, cans of paint, boxes of nails, screws, a few hinges, scraps of leather from some sort of project. The old furnace, converted from coal to gas, loomed in the corner like a tank. There was nothing behind it but cobwebs. Stock hadn't searched the cellar thoroughly or there wouldn't be so much dust. There were signs he had gone under the work-bench and rooted around in the toolbox. The dust had been disturbed along the tops of the foundation. Perhaps "it" was down here? Esther slowly examined everything that Stock had not disturbed but eventually gave up and went upstairs. She heard Henson's footsteps on the second floor.

The bedroom seemed filled with possibilities, but in the end it, too, revealed only that an old man had lived there. Clothes that Meyer could not have worn for years had been flung from the closet. A half dozen umbrellas leaned in the corner behind the hanging clothes. The tossed bureau drawer still held a couple of broken watches. She kicked at worn-out underwear. Odd cufflinks. A mayonnaise jar of pennies.

Dumped boxes of papers filled the corner. Twenty-year-old paycheck stubs. Tax forms. Meyer had worked for the city water department and had retired. He had been operated on last March and then received radiation and chemotherapy. A pamphlet told him that there were many ways to "find relief from the aftereffects of male surgery." Beneath these papers were a few coupons and a small rectangle of browned paper.

"He wrote a letter to the editor," said Esther, gently lifting the newspaper clipping.

"About what?" said Henson, reaching deep into the closet and coming out with a handful of worn paperbacks, all Westerns.

"He complains about the lights being installed. They keep him awake. The noise was bad enough during the day, but now they have to put up with it at night."

"Wrigley Field? They put the lights in years ago. They held out for quite a while. It was the last stadium to do it."

"Well, he didn't like it. A 'silly game' he calls it."

"All games are silly," said Henson. "What's the point?"

Esther flipped past a few more coupons, all outdated, and a calendar from 1985.

Henson crossed to the nightstand and opened the drawer. "Did you see these?" He lifted out two old photographs. One was dated on its border "Jul 1966." A fat-faced baby was sleeping with her fist crushed into her mouth.

"You?" asked Henson.

"That's my blanket. My mother still has it in a cedar chest."

"He must have kept this picture by his bed."

"He must have kept it when my mother emigrated." Esther quickly put it into her dress pocket. "What's the other one?"

"A woman."

This photograph was much older. A thin woman with a wan smile stood with her gloved hand on Meyer's forearm. Meyer, wearing a double-breasted suit, his dark hair combed back, beamed.

"Your mom?" asked Henson.

Esther nodded. She looked in the drawer and saw another old photograph. It was also of her mother. Rosa stood in front of a barbed-wire fence, an Italian policeman to her right, two men to her left. One of them was a near skeleton, emaciated to the point that Esther wondered that he could stand and smile. The other man was elderly but looked healthy. Rosa was smiling, too. Her black dress seemed incongruous in that setting. Esther remembered that her mother had often said that the Italians had been kind to her and had given her a dress to replace her louse-ridden clothes. On the back of the yellowed photograph was written "Trieste, 17 März 1946" in the style of cursive known as the Italian hand. Esther slid it into her pocket alongside her baby picture.

"Don't you want the wedding picture?"

"You keep it," she said.

"You know," said Henson, clearing his throat, "these seem to be the only photographs in the place."

"The 1929 Cubs," said Esther.

"I meant personal photographs."

"The 'silly game' must have meant more to him than we did."

"That's hard to believe. Maybe the bad guy took them all."

"This has nothing to do with anything," Esther snapped. "I should have flown home."

Henson studied Esther for a moment, decided to say nothing, then toed the other objects on the floor. Pennies. Paper clips. Nasal inhalers. Morphine. Anonymous orange tablets. A money clip with seven one-dollar bills. "There's no sign of tape on the drawer bottoms," said Henson, "so he wasn't hiding things that way."

Among the coupons, Esther spotted Hebrew lettering. An Israeli stamp on a small envelope. Flipping it over she saw it had been air-mailed from her mother to her father in 1973. Her hand shaking, she tugged the letter from inside.

"What is it?" asked Henson.

Esther did not answer. She sat on the bed and read the short message.

Do not ever write again. Do not ever try to contact me or *my* daughter. Please understand I cannot look at you without remembering. You say you love us. Let Esther have a life. You can only cause her pain. If you do not care about me, *please* think of her.

Rosa had not even signed the note.
*"You can only cause her pain."*

# FOUR

# The Attic

"**A**re you all right?" Henson asked Esther. He glanced down trying to see what had upset her, but Esther quickly jerked the letter back.

"We are getting nowhere," said Esther sharply. "What is it you expect to find?"

He studied her for several seconds, as if considering whether he should ask about the letter and envelope. When he did speak, it was cautiously. "Who knows?" said Henson. "The man called Stock was after something." He knelt in front of her and touched the back of her hand. "Look, if this is too much for you—"

She pulled her hand away and stood. "This is my father! My

father! I am here looking at all this minutiae in his life, every damned little detail, and it tells me nothing! Nothing! Who was he? Who was he?"

She tore the note from her pocket and threw it at him. Suddenly tears formed like a great bubble that rose up from her belly until it burst past her choking throat and poured out from her eyes and nose. She covered her face and fled into the corridor. Henson pursued her, but when he placed a hand on her shoulders she flailed at him. Helpless, he glanced down at Rosa Goren's note on the floor, then stood back.

"I'm sorry," he said. "We'll find the truth. No one knows for sure he was Meyerbeer."

"Oh, stop it!" she said. "You think he is! You're just looking for proof!"

Henson had nothing to say.

Esther gripped the baluster and composed herself. Her wounds throbbed unmercifully. She was grateful for the physical pain: it took her mind off her father.

"Why don't you wait outside?" Henson suggested.

"There's one more room," Esther said.

Henson watched her go in. The second bedroom was as dusty as the cellar. The walls hadn't been painted for years. There were no clothes in the low white dresser, only a roll of picture wire. There were some men's clothes tossed from a corrugated box by the door, as if they had been shoved in there for storage. There appeared to be another large box in the corner under a dusty sheet. When Esther lifted the corner, she thought at first she had discovered a wooden cage. When she realized that she was looking at a crib, she sensed that this little room had been her nursery after she was born. Even though she'd slept in that house for less than a year, for over thirty years Meyer had kept her baby furniture. If she hadn't already broken down, this would have done it. But she had gone numb now. She looked at the stained ceiling, the empty dresser, and the closet bare except for a few wire hangers. Could this really have been her room? Shouldn't she be able to remember something, anything? *You can only cause her pain.*

"Any luck?" Henson stood in the door.

Esther shook her head.

"The attic's all that's left. I can do that."

"No," she said, "I'll go, too."

Henson opened a low door, revealing a narrow and steep wooden staircase. He twisted the old-fashioned Bakelite switch, and a yellowish lightbulb came on above them. With the pale color of the wood, Esther was reminded of some of the ancient stairways in the old city of Jerusalem.

In the attic, the rafters stretched overhead like the ribs of a beast that had swallowed them. The crude plank flooring covered only part of the attic space. Beyond it, the joists were open to the ceilings of the rooms below.

"A few boxes," said Henson. There were only three, actually, opened and overturned on the floor.

"More dust," said Esther, looking at the spiderweb across the iron vent screen on the eyebrow window. "He wasn't up here much."

Henson just missed stumbling over an enameled metal bowl. "He had a leak," he said, squinting toward an outdated and long disconnected light fixture shoved up under the eaves.

Old electrical wires, insulated with cloth and held in place on raised ceramic posts, stretched across the rafters.

"Don't touch them," Esther warned.

"Surely they're not live," said Henson. He gestured to their left. A closed umbrella hung from one of the wires.

"I don't see anything back here," Henson said, reaching the

end of the planks and gingerly stepping along the joist toward the eyebrow window. "He had bats once."

Esther knelt to examine the contents of an overturned box. Several simple dresses. She dragged another box under the single light and saw dozens of reel-to-reel tapes. Names were handwritten on the boxes. "Ever hear of someone named Reinhardt?" she asked.

Henson paused, then shrugged, bumping his head on a rafter. "Damn!"

"Be careful," she said. "How about Bixby—no, Bix Beiderbecke."

"Germans?" asked Henson. "Maybe he taped things. Did you see a tape recorder downstairs?"

"Just the radio in the kitchen and the television in the living room."

"We'll take those with us." He started back toward her, still rubbing his forehead where he'd hit it. He was stepping awkwardly along the joist, coming out of the dark.

" 'Tex Beneke,' " read Esther. " 'Jimmie Lunceford.' What sort of Germans are named Tex and Jimmie?"

"Shoot!" said Henson. "Those are all big band guys. Django Reinhardt. My dad—" Henson lost his balance and lurched to the side, but somehow managed to stay on his feet. He reached out and snatched the umbrella off the wire, then used it to keep his balance.

Esther started to say that he was lucky not to have been electrocuted, but Henson had stopped on the edge of the planks, giving the umbrella a little shiver. "Hey," he said, hurrying under the light. She could see what had excited him. Brown paper had been wrapped inside around the umbrella shaft. He peeled the top edge back and saw more paper, thick paper. No, it was canvas, heavy and stiff.

Henson shouted, "Ha!" and frantically tried to slide the roll off the shaft. The handle got in the way. He twisted it until it unscrewed, then dropped the roll onto the flooring.

"What is it?" asked Esther.

Henson knelt and tugged up his sleeves with immense satisfaction, then slowly began rolling out the canvas. The textured paint of the top became visible, then the yellowish red of a man's hair. When it was finally all spread, Henson sat back on his heels. "I'll be damned," he said. "Damn!"

"A painting?" Esther asked. "Is that what it is?"

"Unless I'm very much mistaken," he said, "it's a Van Gogh."

Esther heard the words but couldn't for the life of her grasp their meaning.

She was stuttering for a question that might help her understand what this meant when a loud cracking noise was followed instantaneously by a blast that sounded like a combination of *whoosh* and *whomp*. The entire attic floor seemed to rise two inches and drop back into place like an airplane skittering over turbulence. The effect was unearthly. Henson rolled back from his kneeling position and flailed like a dying cockroach. Esther fell forward, landing on all fours, and momentarily thought of her head wound.

"What the hell!" shouted Henson.

She remembered the sound. "Was the gas on?"

Henson scrambled to his feet and uneasily looked down at the floor. "Come on!" he said. He was halfway to the narrow staircase when he skidded to a stop. "The painting!"

Esther hurried back and picked it up. She could smell smoke now.

Henson eased open the attic door. Massive flames were shooting up the stairwell from the first floor. Henson fought the intense heat as the fire shot toward him with a roar, its yellow

47

fingers clawing toward the attic stairs. He barely managed to slam the door shut again.

"Christ!" he shouted. "We're trapped. The stairs are gone."

They stared at each other for a split second. Fire goes up. It always goes up.

"The roof!" she said. "Is there a trapdoor to the roof?"

"The window!"

They scrambled across the plank floor. Esther saw wisps of smoke curling up between the floor seams.

Henson hurried into the area of open joists and tightroped across to the tiny window. "It's got a steel mesh! I don't see a ledge. It could drop straight to the street!"

"You'd rather burn?"

Henson whipped out his cell phone and dialed 911 as he examined the bolts that held the steel mesh in place. "Yes," he shouted into the phone, "there's a fire. We're trapped in the attic."

He looked around, eyes searching for something with which to tackle the bolts or mesh, and nearly stepped off his joist.

"I don't—" He turned desperately toward Esther. "The address!"

Esther looked at him blankly. She didn't remember. Her father had said to tell the cab driver what?

"I don't know," Henson shouted into his phone. "We're across from Wrigley Field. Yes! I don't know if it's Addison Street. A Samuel Meyer owned the house. Meyer! Yes. We're trapped in the attic!" He lost his balance again, and his foot touched the lathing between the joists.

"Careful!" Esther shouted. "You'll fall through."

"Hurry!" Henson yelled into his phone, then jammed it into his pocket with a look at her that meant "We're on our own."

Esther tried to recall the outside of the house. She had been so distracted she hadn't much noticed it. She thought there was a low, mansard-type roof. Would there be a way to climb up? Were there ornaments that might be used as handholds?

"Steel mesh! It's to keep people out!" she said. "There's got to be some way up to the roof!" She moved toward the staircase and saw that the paint on the door below was already peeling. What the hell kind of fire was this? They had heard the whoosh less than a minute ago.

Henson was trying to turn one of the nuts holding the mesh to the window with his bare hand, then clamped down on it with his teeth. "We need tools, any kind of tools!"

Esther jumped from one end of the floor to another, desperately searching the debris from the overturned boxes. Dresses? Tapes? The painting? Wasn't there anything solid up here? She fell on her knees at the edge of the planks and tried to pull one up. She could feel heat coming off the ceiling lathing below. The air was getting hazy. With a great effort she pulled and the plank broke loose.

It was a piece not three feet long.

Useless!

She looked at Henson, and a stray thought crossed her mind. *Who will visit my mother?*

When she focused again, Henson had smashed out the glass with his elbow and was shouting through the mesh. "Help us! Fire! We're trapped!"

"Kick it!" Esther shouted. "Kick!"

Henson grabbed the overhead beam and swung both feet into the mesh. He might have been hitting a brick wall. He grabbed the beam again and swung hard. Again he seemed to thud against it with no effect.

"The frame gave way!" he shouted. "I think the frame cracked!"

Esther briefly thought it was his ankle that had broken, not the wood, but the way Henson continued to kick meant he thought he was getting somewhere. Her eyes stung and filled with water. The old lathing beneath their feet was smoking. They didn't have long before it would burst into flame.

"Step back!" she shouted, waving her arms.

Henson kicked once more, but the steel sheet still held. He faced her, sweat and dust streaking his grim expression.

"Back, I said!"

He stepped across the joists and gripped a support pole.

Esther straightened herself at the edge of the plank flooring, gathered her strength and stared down at the joist running straight at the tiny window. There would be no second chance. She had to get into a mental groove immediately. She had to visualize it, believe it, and it just might work. The building was old, so the joist was slightly larger than new ones. *Huge*, she told herself. *A full two inches.*

*Confidence*, she purred to herself. *Confidence. Breathe deep. It's running a balance beam. Nothing to it.* She lowered her head. She shook the tension from her hands.

She launched herself forward.

One step, two steps, three steps. The bottom of her feet met the joist perfectly and her rubber soles gripped it. On the fourth step, her lead foot pushed and she launched herself sideways, turning her hip to get the full force of her leg and buttock muscles into the blow.

She was so full of adrenaline she did not feel the powerful blow of her foot against the mesh, but there was a crack like a gunshot as the window gave way. For a moment, there was a sensation of floating, and she thought she had broken her tibia. Both of her legs had shot out the window above the street, and she clawed for the frame, barely catching it.

The bottom of the window frame came up like a bat swung against her lower ribs, knocking the air from her lungs. Her legs slapped hard against the mansard roof and she felt nothing to stand on.

"Esther!" Henson shouted.

The frame she clung to was giving way.

He moved toward her. Somehow she pulled herself in far enough to cling to the joist, one hand on each side of it. Her shoes pushed against the nearly vertical shingles without getting purchase. The heat rising from the lathing as she pulled herself onto the joist made her think of a goat on a spit.

Henson planted his feet on adjacent joists and reached to help her up. As she gradually rose, he shouted, "You broke it! You broke it!"

"It's a long way down," she gasped.

She extended a hand to touch what she thought would be fractured ribs, but he jerked her upward under her armpit, and she saw that the lower part of the window frame had split through. The metal mesh was gone, having tumbled into the street below. The bolts that had held it hung loose. She felt a sharp pain and touched the warm blood oozing from the torn stitches of her chest wound.

"Out!" Henson shouted. "Out!" He lifted her toward the tiny opening.

"There's nothing to walk on!" she said. The air was cool in her face as she stuck her head and shoulders through the opening. Debris from the front of the house—glass from the front window, the tiny menorah, the magazines they had found in the living room—had been blown into the street. People were looking up and pointing. Sirens were closing in.

The roof curled outward, away from the eyebrow window. Only a yard or so down, below where her feet had dangled, was cast-iron gingerbread that ran the length of a six-inch ledge. Would it hold? It was their only hope.

Esther pulled her head back into the heat to go feet first out the tiny window. She slipped out, clinging to the broken frame, stretching with her toes for the ledge, getting ready to slide the short distance down to it. Henson, however, was headed in the opposite direction, tightroping across the joist into the increasingly dark smoke. "Martin! What the hell?"

She was about to pull herself back in when he emerged from the haze, holding his tie over his mouth and nose, wobbling across the joist, the painting pumping in his right hand like a bandmaster's baton.

*For God's sake*, she thought. "Drop the damned thing! Come on!"

He was moving fast. His foot missed the beam slightly and banged against the ceiling laths. He was moving forward quickly enough that he did not catch his foot as the lathing opened and a flame shot through.

"Go!" he shouted. She released the window frame and slowly dropped down the coarse shingles. She felt the ledge, took a deep breath, then began to slither sideways along the roof. She could feel the heat blasting against the other side of the shingles. There seemed to be no air, and she fought the sensation that she was going to faint.

Henson's face, streaked and greasy from smoke and sweat, emerged from the window. He chucked out the painting, which landed at Esther's feet on the ornamental railing. He grabbed the overhead beam and came out feet first, clinging like an insect.

"I see a way up! Over here!" he pointed.

The roof was getting too hot to cling to. The fire was racing toward them, but at least they were outside.

It all seemed simple now. Esther had to squat to pass under the belching window to where Martin had seen a handhold— an old television antenna bracket. They could use it to pull themselves to the top of the mansard roof. The painting was at her feet. She glanced at the street, then picked up the canvas and handed it to Henson. They shimmied frantically to where they could climb up, then ran across the roof away from the alley side of the house to an adjacent row house, scrambling over the low brick wall that separated the roofs. The siren of a police car searching for the fire closed in, then the roar of a fire truck. A burly firefighter pointed up at them from his perch behind the ladder. Nine one one had been fast, but not fast enough for such incredibly rapid combustion.

It was only after climbing down the stairs from a trapdoor on the roof two houses over that Esther staggered and fell to her bloody knees. Her legs went rubbery, and her shoes felt funny. Just before she fainted, she saw that as she had run across Meyer's roof the soles had begun to melt.

# FIVE

# A Happy Coincidence

"But do you think it's genuine?" Henson insisted, his hand shaking as he set down the teacup. In his office at the Art Institute of Chicago, Antoine Joliette, a visiting scholar, examined the painting with a magnifying glass. Joliette was a thin, light-skinned black man who wore a yellow suit and a blue bow tie. Henson had merely identified him to Esther as "someone he had worked with in the past," and Esther felt the implication that she shouldn't ask for further explanation. If the painting from Meyer's attic could be confirmed as a possible Van Gogh, Henson was to place it temporarily in the security of the Art Institute.

"Martin," said Antoine with a Gallic shrug, "if you were presenting me with a Delacroix or a Turner or a Constable I would be able to answer you immediately. But Van Gogh! Well, a bit too modern for my expertise." He glanced at Esther, who was sitting by the window, watching the traffic.

"You're the art expert. You can at least make an educated guess."

Antoine sipped his tea and stroked his mustache with the back of his delicate hand. "I must say, it looks like a Van Gogh to me. The style. The canvas and the paint seem old enough. It's not a reproduction—unless it's a very expensive one. There are such things, however. But there are also tests that can determine these things with more certainty. The chemical composition of the pigments, for example. The weave of the canvas. And then there is provenance. Is there any record of this painting's having existed *before* its discovery? How could it have gotten to Chicago? Umbrellas in attics near Wrigley Field do not usually contain Van Goghs."

"The Chicago police were quite blunt about that," said Henson. "It is material evidence in a murder, but their forensics expert found nothing in the way of fingerprints that were of any use. They took a few fiber samples. In fact, there were no fingerprints that they found in the entire house before it burned, other than Meyer's and Esther's. If the painting is not genuine, they have some other methods that might raise the fingerprints but damage the painting."

"But they allowed you to bring it here."

"After a little forceful hinting about federal jurisdiction and such."

"If they'd had rubber hoses, they would have used them," said Esther. "They as much as accused me of setting the firebomb. This while I'm having my wounds restitched!"

"The bomb accusation was a bluff to get you to provide an explanation more to their liking," said Henson.

"And I did," she said wearily. "My explanation is that there is no genuine explanation more to their liking."

"We were lucky we weren't in the kitchen when it went off," Henson said to Joliette. "We had searched the room, but it was well hidden. The device was placed behind the broiler tray in order to explode the gas pipe. Parts of the oven melted, if you can believe it. They are analyzing the debris blown into the street to uncover the chemical composition of the bomb."

"Perhaps he intended to kill anyone searching the house," said Esther.

"It could be. Maybe he just wanted to destroy the building. The lab will figure out how it was triggered. That might imply his intent."

Joliette pointed at the painting. "Why would anyone wish to destroy this?"

"We don't know that they wanted to," Henson said.

"Maybe they were after me," said Esther.

"Or something else in the house. It's all ash now," said Henson. "The arson investigator told me it was one of the hottest fires they've seen in years. Very professional."

Joliette continued to contemplate the painting. "If this is as it appears, a genuine Van Gogh, I can't think of a motive to burn it."

"*If* he knew it was there," said Henson.

"So you can't say one way or another if it is genuine?" said Esther, wrapped in her thoughts. *Why would my father have this painting? Is this what he wanted to give me?*

"If it isn't a Van Gogh," said Joliette, "it is an extraordinary facsimile. That is the best I can say at this time, Miss Goren." He set down his tea and stalked with long legs across the room to where the canvas had been unrolled on a broad drafting table. Each end was held down by a thick art book, one of which was by Joliette himself: *J. M. W. Turner et la poésie tempétuelle.*

"If it is a Van Gogh, it's value—whoof!" He flicked his hands like a magician tossing a white dove.

"Van Goghs are auctioned for tens of millions," said Henson.

"It is obscene," said Joliette. "It has nothing to do with art, this auctioning. But a previously undiscovered Van Gogh, whoof!"

"Tens of millions?" asked Esther. "*Dollars?*"

Both Henson and Joliette said, "Oh, yes."

"In 1998," said Joliette, "a Van Gogh self-portrait sold for 71.5 million dollars. A new record for the highest price ever paid for a painting at auction was in 1990. It was Vincent's portrait of Dr. Gachet: 82.5 million dollars. In May 1999, one of his paintings went for 19.8 million dollars and the bid was considered a disappointment."

Esther now remembered having seen something in the papers about records being set, but it hadn't stuck with her.

"If it's genuine," said Joliette, "thank God you saved it."

Esther looked at the painting and tried to see why it would be worth that kind of money. Van Gogh sunflowers and irises and self-portraits were on posters and bedspreads and kitsch everywhere, but it wasn't as if his paintings were that old or intrinsically valuable: they weren't made of gold and emeralds. "I don't understand. Even if this were the only Van Gogh painting in existence, why would *this* be worth so much? It's just a painting."

Joliette smiled but not in a condescending way. "It is inexplicable, isn't it? Great art is great art not because it goes for big prices at auction. Otherwise oil derricks and shopping malls would be our greatest artworks. Money does not create Van Gogh's greatness, nor does his greatness immediately translate into exorbitant prices. Actually, the money interferes with seeing the art for its true merits."

"But eighty-two million?" Esther asked.

"Exactly," said Joliette. "If you meet a man, and he's handsome and pleasant and mannered, a good prospect for marriage, that is one thing. But if you then discover the man owns a diamond mine, you can never quite see him for who he is. The money affects the passion. In one moment, he becomes more desirable; in another, there is the fear of being bought. The loss of a Van Gogh would be a terrible thing, a loss to our culture, quite apart from its price. Money is not the measure of worth, but it may take quite a while to get a decision about the painting's authenticity. Experts will hesitate when such prices are involved—lawsuits and all that. They may refuse to be definitive."

*"Money is not the measure of worth."* Esther was too ready to accept that, and wondered why. Wasn't it a bit of a cliché? "Look," she said, "I don't know much about fine art, but it is somewhat of a philosophical question, isn't it? What makes a Van Gogh more important than—I don't know—a painting by Martin's uncle?"

"Actually," said Henson, trying his best to hide a smile, "my uncle Lars took up painting before he died."

"Assuming," she said, "that Uncle Lars had skills approximately like Van Gogh's."

Joliette's lips pursed as he reflected. "You have a way of cutting to the bone, Miss Goren. There is no single answer. First, there is Van Gogh's historical importance. Every once in a while an artist comes along who changes the course of art history. Artists were liberated by Van Gogh. They suddenly saw the direction that the evolution of painting would take. They were no longer rehashing the same old themes, they were creating new themes."

"So Van Gogh is like Elvis or Bob Dylan or the Beatles."

"Well . . ." Joliette hesitated. "In a way, yes. No one could make art after Van Gogh without feeling his presence. They could work against his direction or with it, but they could not ignore it."

"Like science after Newton or Einstein," said Henson.

"I suppose there are many parallels," said Joliette. "But there is no doubt that this deeply disturbed and ultimately mad Dutchman changed painting. And in a very short time. He had failed at everything. He tried being an evangelist, did you know that? Then he started painting, and although the work was interesting, his style was a kind of dull realism that looked more like a lack of technique than a new vision."

"Like my uncle Lars's paintings."

"Maybe Van Gogh was a little better," Joliette said with a laugh. "But then Vincent moved to the south of France, and Paul Gauguin came to share a house with him. Suddenly there was an explosion of color in his paintings. Bright yellows had become available in tubes, and he was able to express what had been in his mind. His career lasted only ten years. He took up painting in 1880, but his greatest work is that done between 1888 and 1890, when he killed himself. No one else so drastically changed the course of art history in so short a time."

"I suppose all that business about cutting off his ear doesn't hurt the prices," said Henson.

"The romance of the meteor flaring brightly and burning out," said Joliette. "His mental illness was severe, but his letters reveal a man very conscious of his art, much more intellectual than the popular view of him as a wild man. He was very well-read, you know. He knew several languages and had studied Greek."

All this had gotten too deep for Esther. "Where would Samuel Meyer have gotten the painting?" she asked.

Joliette spread his hands helplessly. "Did he know he had it? Perhaps he had no sense of its value. Things like that happen all the time. You've seen those antiques shows on television—auntie's candy dish turns out to be from the Ming dynasty."

Henson looked at the painting. "I'll bet he knew exactly what it was. How could he not suspect it?" They thought for a few seconds. "Antoine, you said 'undiscovered.' Why 'undiscovered'?"

"Well, I am no expert on Van Gogh, but his oeuvre is quite small, and I think I would recognize any of the known self-portraits. Particularly anything reproduced. People love *Starry Night*, for example, and *Sunflowers*, so posters and copies of them abound. This self-portrait I don't believe I have ever seen."

"Which could lead to another problem," said Henson.

"Yes," said Joliette. "Like the Vermeers."

They nodded pensively until they were aware that Esther was eyeing them in exasperation. Martin explained. "There was a Dutch forger named Meegeren."

"Han van Meegeren," said Joliette.

"He did not make forgeries of existing Vermeers, but rather borrowed Vermeer's style and subject matters and then doctored his own paintings so that they looked as though they had been created in the seventeenth century."

"Voilà! A new Vermeer is 'discovered,'" said Joliette.

Henson leaned toward Esther. "Are you sure your mother never mentioned anything about your father painting?"

"This is a man who hung a baseball team and a motel

picture in his living room! No. My mother never said anything about the bastard, not a word other than that he left us, which you now say was not true!"

Henson raised his palms in surrender. "I'm sorry."

Joliette squinted quizzically. "A motel picture?"

"Ducks among the bulrushes."

Joliette winced. "I like that. 'Motel picture'! It's a definite genre, the motel picture." He made a note on his blotter. "Incredibly enough, there is a group of Dutch scientists and another in Brazil developing a computer program that can correlate many factors to identify a painting. It creates a pattern recognition of such things as brushstrokes and color usage from detailed digital images of the painting. The system has had some success, but we still rely upon experts. In a few years—" His pen hung in midair. "Wait! Why didn't I think of this? What a happy coincidence! Gerrit Willem Toorn may still be in Chicago!"

"Who?" asked Henson.

"Gerrit Willem Toorn! He is the person to whom I can refer you! He is one of the world's foremost authorities on Van Gogh! *The* foremost authority!"

"And he lives in Chicago?" asked Esther.

"No, but he was in town to appraise a set of Van Gogh pen-and-ink drawings for a private collector. He was—only ten days ago—in the main gallery. I recognized him from a conference in Austria three years ago. His appraisal is supposed to be confidential—perhaps a divorce or something is involved. I embarrassed him by making a fuss over him. We would have hired him to give a lecture if we had known he was to be here, but he said the appraisal would take at least a week."

"He could recognize if this is genuine?" asked Henson.

"If anyone can. He has such intense feelings for Van Gogh.

He believes Vincent to be the pinnacle of painting, which he argues died as an art in the twentieth century."

"But wouldn't he need to run the tests you mentioned?" asked Henson.

"As a backup, but he would know, I promise you. He would know." Antoine picked up his telephone. "Please, Miss Haymes," he said into the mouthpiece, "could you try to connect me with Mr. Toorn, Gerrit Willem Toorn? Find out if he has checked out of the Palmer House."

He glanced at Esther. "Keep your fingers crossed!"

"I am very grateful," said Joliette an hour later, "that you would see us on such short notice."

The bulky man who had answered the door grunted, broke off the handshake, and waddled back to the sofa with two silver-headed canes, one with the mask of comedy on its handle, the other with the mask of tragedy. He rotated slowly and sat. His splotched, bald head and flaring white eyebrows seemed to weigh down the lower parts of his face, squash them down on his shoulders until they spread. A black homburg and white gloves lay on the coffee table. "For you, Antoine," he growled. There was a strange hiss in his pronunciation of any *S* sounds. "I azzzhure you. My playzzzhur. Who are your friendzzz?"

"This is Mr. Martin Henson and Miss Esther Goren."

"Pleased to meet you, Mr. Henson. Miss Goren. Excuse my sitting, but— "

"No problem," said Henson. They shook hands.

"I must tell you that I am in Chicago on a most confidential matter, and only for Professor Joliette would I be available."

"Your courtesy is appreciated," said Joliette.

"But, please, I cannot be persuaded to lecture. The Art Institute is, as you know, one of the most preeminent collections in the world. It is flattering that you ask, but—"

"No, no," said Joliette. "This is far more important than a lecture, as I told you. For a lecture we make our request much more formally, and there would be publicity and so on."

"Well, then?"

"We are here, also on a confidential matter, and we desperately need your expertise."

Toorn's beady eyes scanned his guests. "Well, then, Antoine, speak up! What is the mystery?"

Antoine quickly summarized what Henson had told him: Miss Goren had come to visit her father and found him being attacked by an unknown assailant. Toorn raised an eyebrow.

Esther thought to say she barely knew her father, but simply nodded instead.

"Miss Goren was wounded, and her father was murdered," said Henson.

"The world can often be appalling," Toorn said with a shrug. "I am zzzorry for you."

"Among her father's possessions was a painting," said Joliette.

"I see. And what hazz this painting to do with me, do you think?" Toorn snarled.

"The painting appears to be a Van Gogh," Joliette said quietly. "I am no judge, of course, but . . . "

Toorn pointed at Joliette with his cane. "Antoine here is a better judge than he admits. You understand of course, Miss Goren, that normally I am very well paid to appraise Van Gogh, Gauguin, Cézanne, Bonnard, and several artists in that period."

"The post-Impressionists," acknowledged Henson.

"But Van Gogh is your specialty," said Antoine.

Toorn's eyes misted. "He changed the world. His vision was as ruthless and beautiful as God's."

Toorn seemed entranced, as if he had suddenly noticed the singing of a distant bird. A moment passed before Henson spoke. "We are not here to ask for a full appraisal or a definitive analysis, at this point."

"We simply want to know whether we should pursue this further," said Esther.

"If this is nothing, you will know instantly, eh?" said Antoine.

Toorn looked at them. "Normally, what you ask would cost you dearly, but I can afford to be generous because of the pen-and-ink drawings we spoke of earlier. These are Van Gogh as well. He sketched his entire life, even when he was a missionary."

"Earlier we had a brief discussion about why Van Gogh is considered such a great artist," Henson said. "Antoine was very helpful in explaining to us his historical importance."

"Though I suspect," said Esther, "only someone trained in art could fully appreciate that."

Toorn grunted. "Indeed, you are correct, my child. In order to place an artist in the historical context, one must not only be familiar with the history but have a feeling for the flow of it. However, you are wrong to say Van Gogh cannot be fully appreciated without that full historical knowledge."

Esther chafed at being addressed as "my child," but she held her tongue.

"He speaks more loudly than ever," said Toorn, "of the anxiety of man in the world. Everything is strange and wonderful, but only in moments of dazzling vision is God's creation fully revealed. Van Gogh is a prophet. He sees what has not been seen. He opens our eyes to God's creation that is all around us."

"Antoine was explaining that his technique—" Henson began.

"Technique! As if thick impasto and blue strokes are clues to reveal God! My friend Joliette will never understand the essence of Van Gogh, which is totally *feeling*." Toorn gestured with his sausagelike fingers. "Antoine is too French. The classicism of French painting, of the French *mind,* blinds him to race memory, the essence of identity."

Esther glanced at Joliette and then Henson. The mention of race might be an offensive subject to any and all of Toorn's small audience, but especially to a black man working in the very white world of European art. Joliette, however, merely looked amused. Henson lowered his eyebrows as if trying to better grasp what Toorn was saying, as if both Esther and he must have misunderstood the choice of terms.

"I will always argue that Cézanne's achievement was much greater than Van Gogh's, and, after all, how did Van Gogh achieve greatness? By traveling to France," said Antoine lightly. "By studying among painters like Monet and Seurat, so steeped in classicism that only they knew how to advance beyond it."

Toorn looked as though he had swallowed a live lizard and was about to spit it at Joliette.

"This is getting pretty high-brow," said Henson cheerfully. "Can we get your opinion if this is really a Van Gogh?"

"Dr. Toorn and I have had this argument more than once," explained Antoine pleasantly. "In Prague. And Rome." Toorn didn't seem as willing to agree to disagree.

With a grunt, Toorn raised himself and stood in the middle of the room. He raised his hand like a Roman emperor about to grant a gladiator life or death. "Unroll it by the window.

Carefully if you truly believe it is a Van Gogh! Van Gogh painted thickly. It cracks. If the paint isn't thick, you have been
bamboozled. That's what technique tells you, my child. Little
more." He smiled at Esther and rocked forward toward his
canes. "A small joke. Once, if you care to believe it, I was
asked to appraizzze a paper reproduction of a Tintoretto. Ha!"

He turned his back on the painting Henson and Joliette
were unrolling and wiped the moisture from his lower lip.
"But to know if it is a Van Gogh, I must see it all at once, in
a moment. Then it can flash. Then I can feel its power. It's not
unlike a wine taster detecting alcohol. Alcohol is tasteless,
but it flashes on the tongue. The power of that flash can whisper a precise percentage to a master vintner."

Esther attempted a smile in return. The man was among the
strangest and most pompous she had ever met. Joliette had
anchored the top of the painting with a cushion and the bottom with a heavy glass ashtray. The stiff curl of the canvas
nearly lifted the ashtray.

"We are prepared?" asked Toorn.

Joliette and Henson gingerly backed away from the canvas.
"Yes," said Henson, watching the ashtray's precarious balance.

"Well, then, gentlemen, please, move to this half of the
room." Toorn gestured in front of him. "And please be zzzi-
lent."

Henson gave Joliette a quizzical glance. Joliette waved him
away. As Henson passed Esther, he raised an eyebrow in
amusement. Esther looked down at the toe of her shoe.

"All right, then," said Toorn. "Silence, I beg you." He straightened his back as if about to salute, then closed his eyes. His
wide nostrils flared. He seemed like an opera singer listening
to the orchestra as it builds toward the first note of a difficult
aria, gathering his power, breathing deeply, calming himself for
the great test. Eyes still closed, he rotated on his canes in

twitchy steps until he faced the painting.

He opened his eyes, then opened them wider. He went pale and shuddered like a boxer staggered by a punch, but still managed to stay upright. Joliette, Henson, and Esther each shot to their feet and reached out to keep Toorn from falling. Esther grabbed his thick arm. He tore it away.

"No!" he said, gasping. "*Mijn God!* It can't be!"

Lurching forward, he landed heavily on his knees, resting the balls of his hands on the cushion edge, the painting between his outstretched arms.

"Dr. Toorn! Dr. Toorn!" said Henson. Esther moved toward him and pressed her fingers against Toorn's clammy neck, searching for a pulse.

Joliette reached for the phone as Toorn batted Esther's hands away and crumpled back into a sitting position.

"Come on!" said Joliette impatiently into the mouthpiece. "Front desk? This is—"

"Zzztop!" barked Toorn. "Zzztop." He panted. "I am not having a heart attack. Don't be an idiot."

Esther reached to help him. His withering glare cowed her.

"Hang up the damned telephone!" he shouted at Joliette.

Toorn twisted his body and raised himself to his knees. He was so close to the painting a drop of his sweat hit the canvas with a sharp *pat!* Joliette and Henson looked at each other. Toorn was almost nose to nose with the portrait. He sagged back to the floor.

"Aquavit," he said.

Joliette glanced around the room, then hurried to the long Queen Anne–style buffet. Next to the television was a tray with two glasses and a bottle. Joliette checked the label and poured two fingers into the short glass.

"Are you all right?" demanded Henson.

Toorn nodded and waved Henson back. He drank the

brandy in one gulp, then handed the glass back to Joliette, closed his eyes and pinched the bridge of his nose. Finally, he opened his eyes and glanced again at the painting before looking up and searching Esther's face.

"I don't believe it," he finally said. "Where did you find this?"

"It's genuine!" said Henson.

"It's been missing since 1945," said Toorn. "It's the De Groot! It was thought to have been dezztroyed. *Mijn God!*"

"De Groot?" asked Joliette.

Toorn caught his breath. "The De Groot was a small museum in Beekberg, Holland."

"I've never heard of it," said Joliette.

"It had an undistinguished collection, a hodgepodge of red-figure pottery, some arquebuses and other seventeenth-century Spanish and Dutch weapons, and only a few paintings. It's not in existence anymore. It was connected to a convent school that was closed in the late forties. Through shameful neglect, the roof beams rotted, and the bricks were sold to a movie star to build a summer home."

Joliette leaned forward. "That's why I've never heard of it. What happened to the collection?"

"The SS took most of it during the war. We had no choice. They took what they wanted."

Esther lowered her head. She had expected something like this, but still hoped that some odd twist would clear her father. Henson rested a hand on her shoulder.

"'We'?" asked Joliette. "You were there?"

"As it happens, Antoine, I worked there. I was very young, but there was a shortage of men. I was secretary to the curator. This was the finest thing in the collection, by far. The rest were merely antiquities, bric-a-brac. I stared at this painting for hours. It became my friend. It is the reason I made Van Gogh my specialty. I cannot believe it still exists!" Toorn grabbed Joliette's lapels. "I saw it burn, Antoine. The flames! The smoke!"

"I thought you said the collection was stolen," said Henson.

"It was," said Toorn. "The Germans removed it all to the De Groot family country house nearby. But as the Allies closed in, what was left was loaded into trucks. I myself supervised the packing. This painting was loaded into the back of one truck, an Opel Blitz, as I recall. Soon after it left, we saw a pillar of smoke. Only a few kilometers from the house, the truck was burning. It was strafed by a Spitfire and was consumed by fire."

Joliette pursed his lips deep in thought. "*Mijnheer* Toorn, could this be a copy of that original?"

Toorn thought for a moment, looking again at the painting, just to be certain. "No. Impossible. Somehow, someone removed it from the burning truck. Perhaps it was stolen in the packing and I loaded an empty crate. But I never took my eyes off it. Never. But I must have. *Incredible!*" He shook his head, utterly stunned.

"After the war, forgeries of it surfaced, of course. And they were sold to unsuspecting collectors who were not altogether moral about their collecting. But this is not one of the forgeries." He raised himself on his knees to look at the painting again. "This is it. I am certain this is it."

The only sound in the hotel room was of Toorn's heavy breathing.

Joliette finally spoke. "Did any of the rest of the De Groot collection surface after the war?"

"Only the Jewish things."

Esther raised her head.

"There was some medieval Judaica in the collection. A candle-stick. A sconce. A cantor's prayer book. Not much. Things from a synagogue the Spanish looted during the Dutch war of independence. Several of these artifacts reappeared in the Ukraine when the Soviet Union dissolved. A matchlock turned up as well."

"How did the Soviets get them?" asked Henson. "Is that known?"

"Looted, I suppose. First by the Germans, later by the Soviets. Who can know? Some records appeared in Berlin during the Cold War. There was a cache of so-called sales receipts for artwork. The De Groot Van Gogh was listed on one of the receipts. Some of the red-figure vases on another."

"Have the vases ever surfaced?" asked Joliette.

"Not as far as I know." Toorn peered at the portrait. "And neither did the Van Gogh. The receipts found in Berlin did not mean that it was ever there. We saw the pillar of smoke from the burning truck. The receipts were made either before the artifacts were to be shipped, or perhaps later, to conceal the fact that they were looted. Perhaps embezzlement was involved. There is no honor among thieves, you know."

"Someone working in the Third Reich," said Henson, "used a list of the items in the museum to fabricate purchase orders and the like, but whoever he was—or they were—he did not know several artifacts were destroyed or restolen. Investigations have run into that kind of thing in several other cases."

Toorn was not listening to Henson. Tears broke from his eyes and coursed down his cheeks. "This is unbelievable. It's like discovering a lost brother."

*Or father,* thought Esther.

She put it together. Stéphane Meyerbeer had looted art for the Nazis in southern France. Obviously he had escaped north into Holland and did the same there before escaping into Germany, assuming a false identity (Samuel Meyer), then immigrating to America by way of southern France. Henson was right: Meyerbeer's death in Switzerland had been faked. How else could a genuine Van Gogh appear in Samuel Meyer's attic in Chicago?

Esther's mother must have discovered this. Maybe she even saw the Van Gogh. That was why she left Samuel Meyer. Out of love for her daughter, she had guarded Meyer's horrible secret.

The dead lump in Esther's belly made her feel totally numb. Too numb to think. Too numb to cry.

# SIX

# The Rightful Owners

**T**wo days later, Esther woke to a pounding head and a steady rapping at her hotel door. Her mouth tasted as if she had chewed fiberglass insulation for half the night. The empty bottle of pepper vodka on the table lay on its side, its neck an accusing finger pointing straight at her.

She winced as she bent to look through the door's peephole. Martin Henson rapped again, seeming to slap the door against her forehead.

"It's me," he said.

"I can see that," she snapped.

She groaned and, with a great effort, undid the chain and deadbolt. "What the hell do you want?"

"Interesting things are happening," he said, barging in.

"Not to me," she said. She slipped into the bathroom and threw cold water on her face. It wasn't cold enough.

"You look like hell," he said.

"Flattery will get you nowhere. Jews are not good drinkers," she moaned.

"The better for them," said Henson.

"Not when they drink," said Esther. "Look, Henson, I'm going home to Israel. I know the truth about my father, and what happens from here on is no longer my business. I wish the painting had burned."

"It escaped two fires, one in 1945 and the one with us. Maybe it's destiny."

"Maybe it's a jinx. I just know I want to go home."

"Maybe you don't know as much as you should. I guess you haven't read the papers or turned on the tube."

Henson moved the vodka bottle and slapped down a copy of that day's *Chicago Tribune*. He flipped several pages, then noisily folded it back. "Take a gander at this!"

The light from the window drove twin icepicks into her eyes. She slumped into a chair. "You read it."

"Well, I wish it hadn't happened, I wish we could have kept the painting under wraps, but someone told the police beat reporter about it, so the Chicago police and the Art Institute admitted its existence. The long and the short of it is that the portrait has been international news for the last day or so."

"It should. It's a Van Gogh. It's worth a fortune."

"That's the general opinion, subject to further investigation, but if it was painted by our boy Vincent, who owns it?"

"Who cares? It isn't mine."

Henson leaned forward and peered into Esther's bloodshot eyes. "Maybe I'll order you about a gallon of espresso. Does coffee help?" He righted the vodka bottle. "You think this kind of thing will heal those bullet holes?"

"Please," she said, "don't lecture me. The doctors say they're no worse than bad cuts."

"Very bad cuts." He sat on the bed and smiled. "The question on the table is why you should care about our Van Gogh."

"It was never *our* Van Gogh. It was stolen."

"Yes," said Henson, "but from whom?" He stabbed at the paper with his index finger. When Esther lowered her head, he began to read. The day before, when CNN, CBS, and NBC had run stories on the painting's discovery and showed excerpts of the press conference at the Art Institute, several people rushed to claim ownership. First was the Dutch government. Its claim was based on the fact that the convent school fell into government hands when it went bankrupt in the early 1950s. Therefore, they argued, the painting was now a government possession. The ambassador from the Netherlands had made an official notification to that effect. Also claiming the painting were the Sisters of Divine Mercy who had absorbed the Sisters of St. Anthony of Padua, which had run the convent school that owned the De Groot Museum. *L'Osservatore Romano,* the Vatican newspaper, had stated the Sisters' intention to pursue the claim, though the Church itself took no official position in the dispute. Also filing a claim was a Dutch woman somehow related to the defunct museum's curator.

A German right-wing legislator made headlines by stating that the painting belonged to Germany because of the purchase receipts from 1945. It didn't matter whether the Third Reich had gone down in flames, he said. It had acted for the German people in buying the painting. It did not appear, however, that the current German government would pursue this case. "Buying" seemed a bit too euphemistic when there was no proof of any payments by the "buyer," and far too many people believed the receipts in the archives had been fabricated after the artworks had been looted.

"All right," said Esther, "so everybody wants it. Good luck to them. Maybe the United States can claim it somehow."

"It was found in Chicago, wasn't it?" Henson said. "Possession is nine- tenths of the law. "

Esther sneered.

"That was a joke," said Henson, "but listen, none of that is as interesting as this. Shortly after the picture was shown on the news, a man named Jacob Minsky stormed into the New York headquarters of NBC at Rockefeller Center. Minsky says that the painting used to hang in his uncle's billiard room in Marseille."

"This was before it was given to the De Groot?"

"He says it was *while* it was hanging in the De Groot."

Esther pressed the heels of her hands against her eyes. "Will you please make sense!"

"I am making sense. He says he would know that painting anywhere. It belonged to his uncle from sometime in the 1880s until the uncle died in 1932. Afterward, the widow owned it until she died in 1936, and then her son kept it until the Nazis in Vichy stole it in 1944."

"So the De Groot painting was burned, as Toorn said. And the one we found was Minsky's."

"But Toorn is absolutely certain that our painting is the De Groot."

"They are old men," said Esther wearily. "Either one of them could be mistaken."

"If that were all there was to it, Toorn would be the horse to bet. He knew the painting at first hand, and he has been a leading Van Gogh expert since the 1950s, when he first published a book on the subject."

" 'If'?"

"Well, Minsky's not entirely out of the picture, pardon the pun."

"Never," she said, "but go on."

Henson clasped his hands over his knee and leaned back. "Minsky says that his uncle was a commercial traveler who made many trips to Arles, where Van Gogh resided and did his greatest work. Minsky said his uncle Feodor was a kind-hearted man with direct experience of starvation who sometimes took the most hideous vagrants to dinner. Van Gogh qualified. Smelly enough. Hideous enough. Sometime in 1888 Feodor Minsky bought Van Gogh a meal. Vincent reciprocated by giving him a painting. Well, the uncle thought it was a terrible painting, just trash, and he kept it in a closet for many years. An amateur painter, he might have used the canvas himself except he thought it was too caked with paint. Then Uncle Feodor visits Paris just before the Great War. He is thunderstruck that the smelly and hideous Van Gogh had begun to be considered an important artist. He then hangs the painting in his billiard room."

Esther slumped back in her chair, accidentally knocking the empty vodka bottle to the carpet. They both looked at it for a moment.

"I don't know," said Martin. "Jews can't drink? I'm a Lutheran, and I've never been able to kill a whole one."

"I feel every dram of it. Listen, this Minsky story," Esther said impatiently, "it's very colorful, but there's nothing to prove it."

"But there is, circumstantially. Antoine did a little research. Van Gogh wrote lots of letters to his brother Theo. Theo sent him money and kept his brother from starving to death. In one of the letters, Vincent says that he feels as plump as a king because a 'son of Abraham from Marseille' has stuffed him with capon. What's more, there is a record of a pen-and-ink sketch of a 'Théodore Minsk, dans le café, 1888.' Antoine is trying to locate a copy of it."

"Neither of these things proves Minsky's story."

"No, but they're interesting, aren't they?"

"And what does Toorn say?" she asked.

"That it's all nonsense. A painting can't hang on two walls at the same time."

"Unless there's a mirror on the opposite wall."

Henson winked. "You read my mind."

She blankly stared at him. "Will you—?"

"Two paintings," he said. "Antoine told me that Van Gogh often repeated his paintings. He was known for making copies of his own work for friends. Also, part of the mental illness Van Gogh suffered exhibits symptoms like hypergraphia, in which a patient will write page upon page in a frenzy. Van Gogh could paint in a frenzy like that, canvas after canvas. Antoine said that on one occasion Van Gogh received word that Gauguin had finally decided to come live with him and he did an incredible number of canvases in a short period—a week or something—so that Gauguin would find the house full of art. Minsky had one portrait, and the De Groot Museum had the other. That would explain things, wouldn't it? Well, except that Toorn says that ours is the De Groot."

"Henson," Esther said, "you're giving me a headache. Or making it much worse. Or whatever. Leave me alone."

"Well, it's a thought. There's no real evidence for it. Antoine tells me there's no record of there being two of these, and nothing in Vincent's letters about it. But it's a thought. It's not just a remote possibility."

Esther crossed her legs. Minsky, Meyer, Meyerbeer: what

was the difference? The snuffbox Meyer had tried to pawn had once been part of Meyerbeer's loot. If the painting Henson and she had found was Feodor Minsky's, then it was more likely that Meyerbeer had been involved in the stealing of it. Meyerbeer had worked for the Nazis in Vichy, and, therefore, Samuel Meyer, who had hidden the painting in his attic, must have indeed been Meyerbeer. If the portrait, on the other hand, was not Minsky's but stolen from the De Groot Museum, then it was just as likely that Meyerbeer or his cronies had somehow arranged to steal it during their flight from the Allies. The point for Esther always came back to the fact that Samuel Meyer, her father, had kept the Van Gogh, and it was more than likely that he had it because he was actually Meyerbeer. It didn't matter whose Van Gogh it was. Her father was a murdering traitor.

"I'm flying out tonight. You figure it out," she said. "I don't need any more answers."

"Don't you? I want to persuade you to hang in," said Henson.

"And why would I do that, Martin? This is nothing but pain."

"A man murdered your father and almost murdered you. It may have been about this painting. If you join me, we can get to the bottom of this. You have skills that could go a long way toward righting many wrongs, if you'll let me explain."

"I am a witness, that's all. You expect me to play private eye?"

"What are you afraid of?"

She laughed. "I've been bounced down a flight of stairs and shot three times, that's all. But that wouldn't bother you, of course."

He stood and leaned over her. "That's not what you're

afraid of," he said with a smile, "and you know it. Your father was a witness. You just don't know *how* he was a witness."

Esther felt naked to his gaze, and he was seeing things that should have been secret within her. How dare he! Reflexively, her hand lashed out to slap him, but with a simple flick his own hand was up and caught hers by the wrist. She was astonished at his speed but even more infuriated that he had blocked her. She formed her free hand into "the knife" and thrust it toward his midsection. It clipped the flap of his jacket pocket as he adroitly stepped to one side. As he dodged the blow, she jerked her wrist free and attacked with both hands, cutting alternately, frantically—three, four, five times. But he matched each hack with a block of his own until she brought up her knee. Again he dodged the main force of the blow. It grazed his hip. His dress shoes slipped on the carpet, and he lurched into the table, crashing it against the wall. The heel of her hand then caught him good under the chin, but as he fell, he swung his leg under hers. She was mowed down like a scythed weed. Her rump struck the floor, and her head whiplashed back against the bed. That and the pain from her wounds stunned her, and she cried out.

They were both on the floor, knees raised. Henson coughed, trying to catch his breath. Esther panted with the exertion of her attack, then slowly sagged and began to sob. She was humiliated now. What had started as a slap had turned into a frustrated madness. She had wanted to kick him, to tear off his face with her fingernails, but Henson wasn't the cause of her pain. That came from inside. She could blame Henson's insistently boring in on her or her hangover or the throbbing physical ache from her healing wounds, but in the end, with her eyes locked on his, the simple fact was that she had lost control. Why hadn't her mother told her about

Meyer? Why should she have to bear all this alone? She knew Henson had been right. She was not afraid of danger, but she was terrified of what she might come to know about her own father. An image of French Jews staring from behind barbed wire rose in her mind.

Henson cleared his throat again. His hand gingerly dropped onto her shoulder. "Come with me," he said. "You need some coffee. It's okay. Let me explain. If you want to leave for Israel tonight, I won't try to stop you."

Tucked away from the winds off Lake Michigan, the coffee shop in the hotel's huge lobby was a foolish attempt to imitate a Parisian café safely removed from all the street bustle that makes Parisian cafés Parisian. It was also totally insulated from the Chicago sky, which even in June delivered its regular quota of wet misery above rings of balconies rising twenty floors to a glass dome. Ferns hung from trellis rails, a brass escalator glided up to expensive shops on the second and third levels, and a huge Steinway sat on a podium, waiting for a lounge singer to emasculate the greatest songs ever written.

"Latte. A double latte," Esther said to the waiter.

Momentarily lost in thought, Henson looked uncertain what to order. "Uh . . . Cappuccino, I guess. No, just make it regular coffee and a glass of water."

The waiter tilted his head and slipped away.

"You could get a drink," said Henson. "That's supposed to help. Hair of the dog."

"Does it?"

"I don't really know, but that's what they say."

"You don't know? You've never been hungover?"

"Not really. I've never drunk much."

"God," said Esther. "You're a lot stranger than you know, Mr. Henson."

"I'm not a prude," he protested. "I've just never liked that feeling. Sliding out of control."

"I rest my case," she muttered. "How anal!"

He shrugged as if to say, "I've been called worse," but he avoided her eyes by looking around the huge atrium and up toward the dome. "Only the truly rich," said Henson quietly, "can afford empty space."

It took a moment for his observation to sink in. When it did, Esther said, "That's truer in other countries than here. Israel, for instance."

"Truer in Manhattan," said Henson. "*That's* another country. Everybody knows New York isn't part of the U.S."

"What do you mean? It *is* the United States. Everything about it is the essence of the United States. The immigrants. The brashness. The energy."

"That's what they think there, anyway. We think differently in the Midwest. I'm just a flatbilly from Kansas."

"You've moved beyond your Boy Scout years to become a well-traveled sophisticate now, I suppose—a regular James Bond."

"I've been around," Henson said. "The weirdest place was Uzbekistan. Three months. Nothing to eat but mutton. Mutton stew, mutton on a stick. More mutton on a stick." He made a face.

Esther leaned forward. "You know, this is a very nice dance, Martin, but my head really hurts—even worse than the wounds, if you can imagine—so I wish you'd just get to the proposition so that I can turn you down."

"It was a nice dance you gave me upstairs. Not just anyone could do that."

"Please," she said. "It was unforgivable. I was not myself."

"I agree." He smiled wryly. "You've been under a strain lately."

"I apologize," she said through gritted teeth.

Henson raised his palms. "Actually, I was thinking that if you were yourself, you would have kicked my derriere."

She exhaled another sigh of embarrassment. "I don't know. You were pretty fast. You have training. And some talent."

"Not enough. It's never enough. I was better when I was younger," he said. "Sixth-degree black belt. I competed in Japan."

"Never mind that," Esther said. "I *should* have kicked your butt."

Henson eyed her for a moment. "Well, actually, that's what my proposition is about. An old man like me needs a little help defending himself, and I'd like to have you on my side."

She studied his face for a second and admitted to herself that she liked him. Because of, or despite, his aw-shucks Gary Cooper mannerisms, she wasn't sure. But she didn't like what he was proposing. "Don't waste your breath. I am totally loyal."

"I know you are. That's why I want you."

"You've got a lot of nerve, Mr. Henson."

He blushed. "Did you think— No, I'm not talking about, well, anything personal."

"Personal?" she squinted. "That— Well, that would be nothing. I'd say, 'No, I don't want to,' or maybe, 'Yes.'" He looked away from her dark eyes as if checking who might be listening. "I'm talking about information. Look, you're a very nice man, but even if I felt like sleeping with you, even if I were totally in love sex-mad for you, I wouldn't tell you a thing."

Henson's mouth moved, but no sound came out. He was rescued from his confusion by the waiter, who quickly put down napkins and a complimentary dish of macaroons. "Thank you," Henson said quickly, and watched until the waiter was out of earshot.

"Listen," he said. "Information?"

"Intelligence. Isn't that what you're all about? 'The Company'?"

Henson twisted his head to the side. "I'm not CIA," he said with a wry grin.

"Oh, really? You're a travel agent?"

"I don't have a cover." He fiddled with the cup handle with his index finger and thumb, grinning as he said, "Bond, James Bond." He leaned toward her. "Since when is the CIA interested in stolen art? *You* said I was a spook. I let you think it for the time being. After all, you *are* a spook, aren't you? You speak English like an American—that's two years as a grad student at Columbia. You speak Arabic like a Gazan, French like an Alsatian, then Hebrew, Yiddish, and German."

"My Yiddish and German are not so good. I can read and listen."

"You've done a number of dangerous missions, very dangerous. Oh, yes, you pretended to the Chicago police that you were so distressed by your father's crying out that you rushed in without thinking of the danger. In fact, a man with a gun is often no match for you."

"He nearly killed me."

"He was probably a pro, and he got lucky. Others were not so lucky, I understand."

"So you're not with the Company? That's why you know all these things. You wouldn't know any of this if you weren't with them."

"Yossi Lev briefed me."

She picked up a macaroon. "Yossi who?"

"I know—you don't know him. But he knows you and he

filled me in. Not with all the details. The boys in Langley probably know everything, but I'm not privy. I'm with Treasury, Esther. Customs, to be precise."

"And that's why you were in Uzbekistan?"`

"Counterfeit hundreds. The CIA is not interested in counterfeit greenbacks or stolen art."

"No? They seem interested in anything they seem interested in."

"And how would a travel agent know that?"

The waiter arrived with the latte and some kind of a cappuccino, not the regular coffee Henson had asked for. His eyebrows rose at the dollop of whipped cream floating on the coffee, but he didn't say anything as he shoved the topping aside with a spoon.

"Look, your government knows everything about me and about the special U.S. Customs task force," Henson said. "The German government, the French, and the Brits are also informed. Other nations are cooperating as well to a greater or lesser degree. Depending on whose ox gets gored."

"Go on."

"*Stolen* isn't quite the right word for the art we're seeking. *Looted* would be better. You know about all the art taken from Jews during the Holocaust. Göring wanted all the great art of Europe in his rumpus room. Himmler wanted to build a museum to an extinct race."

"They almost succeeded."

"The other great artworks were trophies. They would have emptied the Louvre if they could and moved it to Berlin. Just to make the point that they could."

Esther tasted her latte and dipped a macaroon in it.

"When the Third Reich began to collapse, everything was helter-skelter. People took what they could for themselves, spiriting it off to South America or to a vault in Switzerland or Lebanon. The Red Army took what they considered to be compensation for their losses and trucked them off to basements in Moscow. We're not talking just about items owned by Jews."

"So this is your job," said Esther, "running down these items. Why is that the business of Customs?"

"Most of the stuff is smuggled. Obviously the Van Gogh in your father's attic was smuggled into the U.S. We don't get into the law of it. We find out what happened, trace the provenance of suspicious artworks, then let the attorney general's office figure out how to go at it. Often all they can do is file an amicus curiae, 'friend of the court,' brief to help out whoever has the standing to sue or file charges or whatever is appropriate."

Esther raised her hands. "So? I am *not* a cop. Your team is your business. I know nothing about my father's life."

"This isn't just about your father. In fact, mostly it's not. Your intelligence background fills a need for my task force. You could be very handy in tight spots." He stared into the cappuccino as he stirred. "Major Lev could simply assign you, you know."

Why had Yossi Lev revealed so much about her? She might never be able to go safely undercover again. She remembered Yossi's theory that undercover missions have a large component of luck. Eventually the wrong number comes up. He had hinted he wanted to get Esther out of the field. That was it. He had gotten talky about her record in order to make it impossible for her to go undercover ever again. He was doing it for her sake. He was saving her life. *Well, damn him,* she thought.

Henson's eyes met hers. "But I don't want him to order you. I want you to volunteer. I need committed people. Finding you was kismet, destiny, whatever you want to call it. I'm in charge of putting together this team, and then, plop, Detective Thomas stumbles across the old Meyerbeer/Meyer business."

"And, plop, he finds you."

"Well, the *Sun-Times* found me, or I found it. They reported the detective's connecting his murder victim, Samuel Meyer, to the attempt to deport him back in the sixties. When I talked to Thomas, that's when I found you. And, of course, did what background I could. I have a full security clearance."

"Why should I do this?" Esther exclaimed. "All I want to do is forget about it all."

"Forget it?"

Her voice rose. "Forget about my father! Forget about Van Gogh! Forget about the Jews my father beat to death! I want to do what my mother wanted me to: pretend he never existed! End of story!"

Henson leaned back in his chair. She felt him watching her as she turned to her right and then her left. Finally, she looked directly at him. "What is that look?"

He leaned forward. "You want to know the truth about Samuel Meyer, that's what I think."

"Ha!"

"You want to know what really happened between your mother and father. What made her emigrate to Israel."

"You know me so well, why ask me anything?"

"What's more," Henson said quietly, "I think that if you don't find out, it will torment you the rest of your life."

"What a cliché!" Esther snapped, but her stomach flipped, and the coffee shop suddenly felt cold. She crossed her arms. Henson sat back poker-faced and twisted a spoon between his thumb and index finger.

"You don't know me," she protested. "If I so chose, this would never bother me again. There is an art to forgetting, and I am a master of it." She whispered, her voice intense. "You think there aren't things I have done that I have to forget? Lots." The phrasing was so awkward she lowered her head and started over. "I sleep very well, thank you. I can forget anything I want."

Henson lowered his spoon and let the silence weigh heavily for several seconds.

"You may be kidding me," he said. "But what's worse is, you're kidding yourself."

She could sit still no longer. "Believe what you like!" She bolted to her feet, felt one of her wounds spark from the sudden movement, but looked down at him almost contemptuously. "I'm going back to Israel, Mr. Henson. Don't think it has been a pleasure."

Henson suddenly tightened, as if he were about to explode in anger. His eyes narrowed. But he seemed to be looking through her, not at her.

He launched himself up from his chair and into her midsection. Esther doubled over his shoulder as she crashed backward over her chair. *What the hell?* Tumbling down, she reflexively brought up her hands to clap both of his ears hard under her cupped palms and burst his eardrums with agonizing pain. But the floor smacked her hard, and her hands harmlessly clapped together behind his neck. She felt a blinding pain in her chest wound and almost lost consciousness for a second. When the shock faded, splinters of wood and glass were scattering from the tables all around them, and the towering lobby reverberated with the familiar chatter of an Uzi.

There was a pause. She saw the gunman above them, changing clips. A woman screamed. Henson jerked Esther's arm, rolling her over. "Come on," he shouted, tugging and shimmying past tables toward the Steinway.

Again the Uzi opened up. Bullets shattered the hanging ferns, pinged off the poles, and spiked holes in the marble floor. Tugging and crawling, Henson had gotten them to the edge of the podium. The firing paused. Was the gunman changing clips again? Waiting for them to stick their heads out? Henson hesitated, but Esther gathered her strength and crawled under the piano. The Uzi ripped up the hard wood, slapped down the lid, scattered keys, and rang against the metal frame inside, but did not penetrate to where Esther had curled up in a fetal position.

The spray stopped abruptly. There was more screaming, an alarm, people running, pointing, shouting.

"Someone help!" a man shouted. "Charley's wounded!" Esther raised herself on one elbow and shook the splinters from her face and hair. She twisted back toward Henson. He lay motionless, face down on the floor, his brown hair greasy with blood.

As Esther gingerly crawled toward him, her only thought was, *My God! Martin is dead!* All the feeling in her went numb, as if this were a strange, horrible nightmare.

# SEVEN

# Persona Non Grata

I n the hotel conference room that the Chicago police had commandeered after the shooting, an FBI agent, Detective Aaron Thomas, and a newly arrived man from the State Department stood in a circle arguing. Sitting at the far end of the long table, Esther turned her head from watching a ship pass on Lake Michigan to see Henson gingerly touch the bandage on his scalp. He winced. A centimeter lower and the bullet would have entered his skull, rather than stripping off a thin layer of hair and skin.

"I don't think anybody gives a good goddamn *why* she's in Chicago," said Detective Thomas. "We just want her gone."

The bow-tied man from the State Department looked over the top of his reading glasses. "It is a serious matter if the Israeli government has misrepresented Miss Goren's activities in America." He turned to flash a brief smile at Esther. "Of course, we are certain that the amity between the United States and Israel would not allow such an eventuality to come to pass. Clearly that would be a serious misunderstanding."

"Gentlemen—" said Henson.

The FBI agent ignored him. "If there are terrorists operating in Chicago, we want their butts. We want to know who they are. We want to know everything she knows."

"Gentlemen!" said Henson more forcibly. "Have you put through that call?"

"They couldn't reach the attorney general," said the FBI agent, "but he's my boss, not yours."

"Will you listen to me?" Henson demanded. "I've explained what this is about: an international task force to trace looted artworks. You know that. Tell them, Detective!"

"Look, man," said Thomas, "one—I got a waiter who's dead. Two—I got an old woman who is critical because she was hit in the crossfire between your guy and the security guard."

"He isn't Martin's guy!" shouted Esther.

"So he's yours, then. That's even more important. Why is he after you, Miss Goren?"

"How the hell would she know?" said Henson. "This could have been a coincidence. He might not have been after either one of us."

"All the shots were directed at her," said Thomas. "He wasn't just spraying randomly. After she went under the piano, he shot only at the piano. He didn't fire directly at you."

"He may have thought he got me."

"So why would he waste time on the lady?"

Esther bristled.

"You're no lady?" said Thomas.

Henson stepped between them. "He's got to be the same guy who shot her father. Have you considered the Mafia? Did you check out Samuel Meyer on that?"

"You've got to be kidding," said Thomas, turning on the FBI man. "There's Cosa Nostra in this thing?"

"What the hell are you talking about? The guy spoke German," said the FBI man. "I don't know anything about—"

"It's a tong war! It's a jealous husband! *We don't know*," said Henson, holding his head. "I'm just throwing out possibilities."

Esther touched his shoulder.

Another FBI agent opened the door and handed still pictures to her partner. He turned and slapped them on the table in front of Esther.

"Well?" he asked.

She looked down at the smeary black and whites from the security cameras. There was the hefty man firing downward. His face in several pictures was obscured by the ferns or the flash of his muzzle. In the others, he was not recognizable, but his dark gloves and suit seemed the same, as well as his blond hair. "I can't be sure. It looks like the man my father called Stock." She had started to say "Colonel Stock" but thought that might restimulate the notion that some foreign government was behind all this.

"I hope the net is out," said the agent.

"You know damn well it is," said Thomas. "We APB'ed this bastard fifteen minutes after he stopped shooting."

The State Department man tilted his head to scrutinize Esther over his glasses. "And you can assure me we're not going to discover this Stock is with Hamas or al-Qaeda or some similar organization? We're not going to discover he is after you, are we?"

"Don't you try to blame this on me! I came to Chicago to visit my father!" shouted Esther. "You bring me someone from the Israeli consulate immediately. *Immediately!*" She struck the table with her fist and felt pain in her chest. Henson reached out and squeezed her forearm. She sank back to her seat.

"Rest assured," said the man from State, "my colleagues are in contact with your embassy. The ambassador himself is aware of the situation."

"Excuse me!" sneered Esther. "Did I hear something? Forgive me if I'd rather hear from him myself!"

In the silence that followed her outburst, a cell phone rang. The female FBI agent answered it, then pulled her colleague to the back of the room. He returned shaking his head, stopped, and glared at Henson and Esther

"Have a nice trip home," he said to her. He looked at his colleague. "Let's find this Stock." He snatched the photos off the table.

"Hey, we get some of those!" said Thomas. He jabbed a finger at Henson. "And I'm not through with you two yet. The attorney general is nothing to me."

The State Department man shifted his eyes warily. "I think I'd better check in with the undersecretary. We'll release your passport ASAP, Miss Goren."

"What?" said Thomas. "This woman is somehow the reason for this. We can't let her leave the country!"

"Wouldn't it be safer for the good citizens of Chicago?" asked Henson. "I'll bet your chief or the mayor himself is hearing that argument right now."

Thomas's eyebrows twitched as though they might fly off his face. "Maybe a dead waiter means nothing to you, but it sure means a helluva lot to me!"

Henson saw pain flit across Esther's eyes and reappear as

resolve. If she could find out who killed that waiter, he wouldn't have long to live.

"That, I didn't quite expect," said Henson, peering out of the taxi window at Lake Michigan. He wondered whether the driver really knew the way to O'Hare International, but he said nothing. By going out of the way to fatten his meter, the driver was giving Henson more time to talk to Esther. "Everyone seems to be in a hurry to get you out of Dodge before sundown."

"This is a new one. I've never been persona non grata before," said Esther.

Henson chuckled. "That's usually reserved for diplomats."

"I'll try not to let it make me vain."

"Enjoy the flattery. You've earned it."

Detective Thomas had argued ferociously to hold Esther as a material witness. The city administration took under advisement the attorney general's request that Esther be allowed to leave. The ambassador from Israel, after exchanging only a few pleasantries with Esther on a cell phone, advised her it was probably in everyone's best interests that she go home, and within twenty minutes the State Department had quickly declared Esther Goren's visa canceled.

"All I want to do is leave," she protested. "Why bother to kick me out?"

"Everybody wants to get Stock's collateral damage out of their jurisdiction. There's some reason he's after you."

"I saw him," said Esther. "I could identify him."

"I don't think it's that. He seems to have no trouble disappearing when he wants to. Manhunts are hit or miss, it's true, but they've had his description out since your father was murdered. The Uzi was found in a trash can on Jackson, near the Dirksen Building. It was like he was thumbing his nose at the feds who work there. There's no telling where he got it in the first place, but with the FBI and the Chicago police in a race with each other, something will turn up."

"He really wants me dead. Or you."

"Oh, it's you all right. And you're right, he *really* wants you. He can't wait. He's willing to try it in a risky place with security cameras. He must have followed us to the hotel. When you were in Cook County General, he took the risk of inquiring about you at the desk. We've enhanced the video-tape of Stock on the security camera outside the emergency room and have a pretty good image of him. He may have wanted another crack at you, but with the metal detectors and cops a-plenty, he may have decided to wait. As soon as the Chicago police made inquiries about you, we made you the queen in a game of three-card monte."

"Why wasn't I told?" Esther asked. "I kept wondering why I was shuttled from room to room. You think that was fun?"

"I'm sorry. What could we have done? You'd rather get up close and personal with him again?"

"You should have used me as bait. Then you would have him."

Henson smiled, shaking his head. "Man, you're too tough for your own good."

"Use me as bait now," she said firmly.

"I believe that's why they want you out of the States."

She crossed her arms. "He'd stick out like a baboon's ass in Israel. He won't come after me there."

"Hair can be dyed." Henson touched her elbow. "But, listen, the real thing is to figure out *why* he's after you. I don't real-ly believe it's because you can ID him, and it can't be to get the Van Gogh. You don't have it anymore, and there's no way he can get possession of it now. It must be something else. Did you take anything from your father's house?"

"No." Esther shrugged. "I stuck the two photographs in my pocket. The baby picture." She sighed. "The one of me."

"Is there anything special about it?"

She shook her head.

"And the other?"

"The one you gave me. My mother standing in a refugee camp in Trieste. She's as thin as a wire, but she is still beautiful, even after all they had done to her."

"Can I see it again?"

Esther took it from the pocket at the front of her purse, opening the folded cardboard in which she had protected it. Henson looked at the thin woman in the black dress. Behind her to the left were two men, to the right an Italian policeman holding a cigarette as if he'd just pulled it from his mouth. "Who are these people?" he asked.

"It doesn't say."

He flipped it over and saw the words "Trieste, 17 März 1946." "Is this your mother's handwriting?"

"It could be. She wrote that way, in the Italian hand, slashing her sevens. It's very similar."

"Why did you take this picture and none of the others?"

"It's my mother," said Esther, and Henson shrugged as if to say, "Of course."

He held it up to the window to see if there was a watermark or anything else. "Maybe it's those guys."

"Look at them," said Esther. "He's at least seventy. That one must be a victim of the Nazis. You can see every bone in his hands and face. If it's March 1946, he was liberated a good while before the picture was taken. He must be consumptive."

"You're jumping to conclusions. It could be that cop standing there."

"Why would that matter anymore?"

"Don't ask me," snorted Henson. "They're all probably dead, except for your mother."

"And she's not really alive," said Esther.

"I'm just looking for some reason this picture might reveal something someone doesn't want revealed."

"Heat it up and look for invisible ink," she said dryly. "You're running in a fog and getting nowhere. Whatever Stock wants is most likely to have been burned. He's just making sure with me."

Henson thought for a minute, then glanced up at the Sikh cab driver safely behind his Plexiglas partition. "So what's your plan?"

"What makes you think I have a plan?"

Henson chuckled. "You're not the kind of girl who forgives getting shot."

Esther said nothing.

"Look," he said, "I want this guy Stock as much as you do. I've got a permanent part in my hair that won't be very attractive, but you know what else I think? I think the trail to Stock lies through the Van Gogh."

"If it is a Van Gogh."

"Exactly. Why are you in such a hurry to get back to Israel?" The question was clearly rhetorical, as he answered it himself without waiting for Esther's response. "You plan to use the resources of the Mossad to see if you can get something on Stock. But if you work with me—if you join our team—you'll have more resources than just the Mossad's."

"You forget. I have been thrown out of the United States."

"True, but they didn't specify where you were to be thrown." Henson held up two plane tickets, KLM prominent on their folders. "After all, knowing whether or not the painting is genuine affects everyone, and not just the owners. The state of Illinois' murder case might hinge on it."

"The Netherlands?"

"Amsterdam, to be precise. We'll escort the painting."

Esther lowered her head and stared at Henson for a moment. "So you think we'll get this bastard?" She smiled, thought for a second, then pecked him on the forehead. "You wicked, wicked man! Snatching a girl away like this."

Henson glanced at the cab driver, who did not seem to have noticed. He quickly looked at her then out the window. His cheeks were cherry red. She found the way he blushed to be charming. Boy Scout!

# EIGHT

# Minsky's Picture

**M**artin and Esther arrived at O'Hare Airport three hours before their flight. After checking in and having their bags examined, they were escorted to the shipping area by a federal security officer and an airline representative. There, their documents were checked again, and they were directed to an even more secure area in which special shipments were kept.

"It doesn't look like much, does it?" asked Henson.

The wooden crate wasn't much taller than the box for a washing machine and no more deep than a microwave. Various numbers had been painted on the coarse wood and documents stapled to it. The latch was secured with a padlock and a lead seal. The words "Rijksmuseum Vincent Van Gogh" wound around the entire crate between two metallic straps.

"There's no getting into the box without leaving some sign," he said. "And it's never out of sight of human eyes."

"And cameras," said the beefy security officer. He squinted at the bandage on Henson's head. "You two are part of the group to watch the loading, right?"

Henson showed his Treasury Department badge. "Yes. This is Miss Esther Goren."

"Pleased," said the officer. "We'll load in about an hour. The plane leaves in ninety minutes. You're welcome to wait in the office over there. There might be some chocolate-chip cookies left."

"Thanks," said Henson.

The office was up a short flight of steps and had large glass windows overlooking the special shipments area. They could now see a Rolls-Royce parked at the far side of the floor. Henson pointed. "Can you ship those by plane?"

"Why not?" said Esther. "Maybe it's Hugh Hefner's. Doesn't he have a plane?"

"He had to sell it when everybody else got into the naked business," said Henson.

"Poor guy," said Esther. She slumped into an office chair and rotated it back and forth several times. She stopped and looked at Henson. "You knew I would come with you."

"I *had* to persuade you," he said.

"But you'd already put me on the list to be here. I barely know you, Mr. Henson. I shouldn't trust you. You might not be the boyish innocent you appear to be."

He was blushing again. "Am I that wholesome looking? Maybe I should get an eyebrow pierced, shave my head, get a tattoo. Perhaps I'd be more interesting."

"None of that would suit you. You're very American, that's all. Clark Kent. Alan Ladd. The strong and silent type."

He laughed. "Not as strong as I'd like to be, I'm afraid. Is there any aspirin in that desk drawer?"

She looked. A scattering of pencils, rubber bands, paper clips. "Sorry."

"My head feels like Stock bounced a cannonball off it. How do you feel?"

"Tired. Twenty-five percent of me is still patching."

"There'll be plenty of time to sleep on the plane." He turned with an empty cup, evidently to offer her one, but paused. "What does *that* look mean?"

"I mean to warn you."

"About what?"

"This is strictly a personal matter with me." She thought these weren't quite the right words. "Let me put it this way: I'm not really interested in this stolen art task force of yours. I want to know who killed my father and why. I want to know why they seem to be trying to kill me." She dropped her voice slightly. "I'd like to know who my father was. If he was Meyerbeer, all right, I can live with that." She took a deep breath. "Maybe. But then I'd like to know who Meyerbeer was and how he could have deceived my mother. I need to know how she could have loved such a man."

"That might be impossible to know even if they were alive, here with you instead of me."

"Well, that's not my point. I simply want you to know I don't see myself chasing after artworks. There are enough new evils in the world to deal with. Why make such an effort to revisit the old ones?"

"That seems an odd thing from you."

"Why?"

"We're talking about the events of the Holocaust."

"It may seem odd to say so, but I am more concerned about the survival of Israel now. Teenagers blow themselves up on the public buses. Who persuades the suicide bomber to do that? He kills his own people and many more of mine. What is the satisfaction in punishing decrepit old men? They can barely remember last week, let alone their crimes in the Third Reich. Besides, you're not even talking about that. You're talking about thieves. All sides had thieves. Americans looted, too, I'm sure."

His skepticism at her attitude showed in the way he shifted his head. "Just hear me out. During the Cold War, the important thing was keeping the world from falling under a tyranny as severe as the Axis would have imposed. The U.S. was cutting a lot of slack to anyone opposed to Communism, and I mean anyone. Oh, yeah, sure, it was wrong. The CIA had ex-Nazis working for us in Latin America and in the space program and so on. You know all this."

"It's what Toorn calls the historical context," she said sarcastically.

"Well, then you also know that with all the chaos of World War Two, a lot of looting went on. The Nazis systematically looted every country they conquered."

"They were nothing if not systematic."

"But the Russians looted, too. And American soldiers took medieval crucifixes home with them, and so on. Various claims have been around for years, but no one much bothered with them. Now a lot of smaller nations are trying to recover their history. Families are seeking the return of their relatives' possessions. The Swiss banks are having to account for looking the other way while doing business with the Third Reich. Large industrial companies are having to pay for having used slave labor."

"I read the papers."

"You're not listening," Henson said.

"Don't pout," said Esther. "Just get it over with."

Henson's face turned stony. "Maybe I thought getting shot at would clarify your thinking."

When he turned to leave, she stood. "Don't. You're right," Esther said. "You saved my life. I *will* hear you out. I owe you that. But that doesn't mean I'll do what you want."

"Fair enough," he said. He picked up a chair, spun it around, and sat on it backward. "What I am doing is forming an international task force to locate and identify looted artworks, as I said. Antoine Joliette has agreed to become part of it. I need him for his expertise in paintings. He knows everybody who knows what we need to know."

"As he knew of Toorn."

"Exactly. Antoine is a citizen of France, born in the department of Martinique. I'll represent the United States and use my background in Customs. There will be a German member of the task force, an Italian, a Brit, a Russian—if they ever get their act together—and a representative from Israel."

"Me. Or so you think."

"Yes, you, if I get my way. Representatives of these nations will form the core group, but I will be free to add other members as necessary. Eventually we might have to look at looting in Asia, for example. And Africa. And Latin America. I have hopes that someday we will grow into an organization that can protect people all around the world from misappropriation of their cultural property. Consider all the sacred objects and even the bones of people that are resting in some foreign museum."

"That's all very noble, but what has it got to do with me? Isn't most of the stuff in museums stolen? How can that painting we found be worth millions? The lawsuits aren't about cultural preservation, are they? Dutch culture is doing well, isn't it? It's a total mystery to me. I have no expertise in art. Toorn calls me 'my child,' and Joliette makes me feel like an idiot."

"I wasn't certain which nation would give me each of the particular talents I want, Miss Goren. I assumed Israel would give me the best Judaicist. But then this thing with Meyer happened. From the beginning I've known I need somebody who can go undercover, who can handle herself in tough spots. Who can break into a house without a trace and rappel down the side of an office building. When I checked on your background, it was perfect. You are all of those things and more. Your government is in support of the idea, if you're willing."

Esther shook her head. "This whole thing is just a bad turn in my life. Before all of you got together and decided I should become part of it, you should have come to me."

"That's what I'm doing, Esther," Henson pleaded. "I feel like I can trust you in a way I haven't felt with the other candidates. Besides, you're a woman. You're practically Superwoman from what Major Lev said. You're better than perfect for this."

His conviction was powerful, and Esther could see in him more intensity than she had recognized. But she shook her head. "Just accept that I like my current work. The Van Gogh is just a detour. I can't see myself chasing old paintings."

Henson rose from his chair and sat on the desk edge. "When I first saw you, I couldn't imagine you infiltrating terrorist camps. When you were a little girl, did you see yourself doing that?"

She blinked for a moment. "Yossi talks too much. And he exaggerates, too."

"I doubt that."

"He shouldn't have told you those things. It could compromise me."

"You *are* compromised. He says he's afraid any mission you next undertake will be your last. He wants to keep you out of danger. I don't think he could live with having created a circumstance in which you were killed. Maybe it's time for you to move on. Think about it. This group I'm charged with forming is high priority," Henson said. "We'll be concentrating on Holocaust victims at first. In a few years there won't be enough survivors left to know that much of this stuff was looted."

"What do you care? You're not a Jew. It's politicians playing up to the Jewish lobby. It's just a police thing to you."

"Hey, a minute ago you were asking why prosecute decrepit old men. Whatever the reasons for the impulse, it's the right thing, isn't it? It isn't often enough the politicos will sponsor the right thing. Criminals shouldn't profit from the sufferings of others."

"Most profit is from the sufferings of others, isn't it? Criminal and otherwise. What do you get from this? I notice you haven't answered that question."

"I don't know," he answered. "As I told you, I was raised Lutheran. Kansas."

"Of course, Kansas."

"It's not just a Jewish thing, you know. Call it my midwestern sense of justice."

"You aren't answering."

"That's the best answer I can give: because it's the right thing."

Esther tossed back her head. "The right thing! Do you often take advantage of women?"

"Excuse me?"

"You've been talking with Yossi behind my back, investigating me. It seems you know everything about me, and I know almost nothing about you. That's hardly right, is it?"

"No, but I can hardly run a want ad. No rudeness was intended." Henson shrugged. "There's not much to know about me."

"You've been to Uzbekistan. You grew up in the Midwest."

"Kansas, to be precise."

"How long have you been married?"

The question caught him off guard. She thought she saw a man struggling with his desire to lie about being married—at least for a night. It wouldn't have surprised her at all if he'd begun to lie about how lousy his marriage was, but his answer silenced her.

He curled his hand into his waist and touched his gold wedding band with his thumb. "I'm a widower," he said, avoiding her eyes, almost to himself. "It lasted five years."

Henson's usual mask of buttoned-down control dropped and he sagged. Esther saw he nursed the kind of pain she never thought he had experienced. "I'm sorry" seemed so weak and pointless she could not bring herself to say it. The silence hung heavy until there was motion outside the window. His professional mask returned, and she was able to breathe again.

"There's Joliette and the others," he said, moving toward the door and down the stairs.

Martin and Esther hurried to the group gathering around the crate. A pudgy bald man introduced himself as Hans Van-derhoek, an attaché from the Dutch consulate. Antoine Joli-ette then presented a sleek attorney with wire glasses: Clay Weston, an attorney for Jacob Minsky. There were also two people from the Art Institute and Vanderhoek's and Weston's assistants. After a general exchange of greetings, Weston offered a faxed letter from Minsky's New York firm.

"We must insist," said Weston, "that you wait for Mr. Minsky. He wants the crate opened."

"But why?" asked Joliette.

"To make certain that the painting being sent to Amsterdam is indeed the one purported to be the De Groot Museum painting, but which actually should be returned to Mr. Minsky."

"I sealed the painting myself," said one of the men from the Art Institute.

"Are you questioning the Art Institute's integrity?" demanded Joliette. "That is outrageous."

"We mean no offense and imply nothing," said Weston. "The stakes are, however, enormous. Mr. Minsky has a right to examine his property and, if it is his property, to make certain it does not leave the country."

"The purpose of the flight is to examine the painting," said Henson. "By the best Van Gogh experts in the world!"

Weston looked over the top of his glasses. "With all due respect, it was already examined by one of the alleged 'best Van Gogh experts in the world.' This expert, Dr. Toorn, was, in the opinion of Mr. Minsky, utterly wrong. Mr. Minsky would prefer that the painting not leave the jurisdiction of United States courts until he sees it himself. And probably not after that."

"This is mad," steamed Joliette. "Minsky could have come to Chicago anytime during the past two days to see the painting before it was crated. How can we establish its authenticity if it doesn't go? This is idiocy."

"A waste of time," said Henson.

Vanderhoek stepped toward Weston. "Sir, the Dutch government has a sincere interest in returning the painting to its rightful owner, whoever that is, and is quite definite in its desire to do so."

"Because the Dutch government believes it is theirs," said Weston, "that belief might well prejudice any group of Dutch experts."

"But the experts will not all be Dutch," said Joliette. "A Frenchman, an Englishman, and a German will also serve on the panel. The Netherlands will have two panelists."

"Toorn?"

"Yes," said Joliette. "And Dr. Erik Luits."

"No American?" asked Weston.

"This is mad," repeated Joliette. "You've known about these arrangements for days! Minsky agreed to an authentication, as did all the parties with a claim!"

"Yes," said Weston in a cold tone, "but first we demand that the crate be opened, so that Mr. Minsky can identify his painting. If it is his painting, we will decide whether to release it for travel."

"But Minsky isn't even here!" said Henson.

"His plane was delayed," said Weston. "Fog at LaGuardia."

"That is his problem," said Joliette. "Surely the painting must leave on time. I've made all the arrangements for the panel to convene. A Treasury Department representative is accompanying the painting, for pity's sake!"

"And you trust the government?" said Weston. He glanced at Henson. "No offense intended."

"That's a stupid thing for a lawyer to say," Henson shot back. "No offense intended."

"There is nothing to prevent the painting's leaving on time," said Vanderhoek, "and my government will be very distressed if it does not."

"You forget the court order," said Weston.

"What court order?" said Henson incredulously. "Have you got a court order?"

Weston opened his briefcase and held out an envelope. "Mr. Minsky has a right to inspect his property, regardless of the inconvenience this might cause other claimants."

Henson snatched the document and began to scan it.

"But it has not been established that it is his property!" said Joliette.

"If you delay its shipping," protested Henson, "you are delaying the disposition."

"This is an insult," said Vanderhoek, turning red. "My government protests. In the interest of resolving this issue, the United States, French, and German governments have all agreed with *my* government's suggestion that the painting go to Amsterdam for evaluation."

Weston shrugged. "I am assured Mr. Minsky will arrive at any minute. His plane was to land five minutes ago."

Esther checked her watch. There was still a slight possibility she could catch the El Al flight leaving in an hour, if they waived the usual security precautions. Who was she kidding? El Al wouldn't waive security for the prime minister of Israel.

"Perhaps Mr. Minsky would like to reimburse the people of the Netherlands for the shipping!" shouted Vanderhoek.

Weston crossed his arms. "He may be delighted to."

"Opening the crate takes time!" said Joliette.

"Then I suggest you get started." Weston spun on his heels and crossed the wide room in order to make a cell phone call at the other end.

"Can you open it enough so that Minsky can get a good look at it without entirely unpacking it?" Henson asked Joliette. Joliette looked at the man from the Art Institute, who shrugged in disgust.

"Mr. Vanderhoek," said Henson, "as the representative of the

Dutch government, would you mind observing?"

"I will not let it out of my sight, of that you can be certain!"

"We don't have the Art Institute's seal," said Joliette. "It may be a violation of our insurance policy if the crate is opened and then sent without the seal."

"Lawyers! Insurance companies! They are the true government of America," snorted Vanderhoek.

"Well, we can't change that before the plane leaves," said Joliette.

"Break the seal, open it up," said Henson. "I will write a receipt. It is no longer in the Art Institute's care."

"Can the Treasury Department be responsible in a situation like this?" asked Vanderhoek.

"Oh, for God's sake," said Esther. "Open the damn thing! I should have taken my flight home to Tel Aviv."

The men all looked at her for a moment.

"Do you have a pry bar and a hammer?" Joliette asked the security chief.

The lead seal was snapped, and the iron bands that had been so carefully tacked around the crate were pulled loose, curling back with noises like a twisted saw. Joliette had just begun to insert the pry bar between the lid and the crate when a golf cart raced toward them, driven by a security officer. Two elderly men sat in it. The one in the front was white-haired with pink cheeks. The one in the rear sported a silvery Vandyke beard. The golf cart skidded to a stop.

"Where is my lawyer?" shouted the pink-cheeked man. "Is this my picture?"

Henson stepped forward. "And you are Mr. Minsky?"

"Yes! Who else? What's it to you?"

"I'm with the Treasury Department. We've taken responsibility to look after the painting."

"I have Professor Emeritus Dr. Allman here, all the way

from SUNY Binghamton! How do I know my picture's in there?"

"Sir," said Joliette, "I assure you that the painting found in Samuel Meyer's attic is in that crate. We were about to open it for you."

"Antoine Joliette!" exclaimed Dr. Allman, rushing past Minsky. "What a pleasure! I recognize you from your dust jacket!"

"You know this guy?" asked Minsky.

"He is one of the most remarkable young scholars in the art world, sir. Absolutely!"

Minsky tilted his head back to get a better view. Esther had the impression of a bulldog of a man, who, despite his age, would never let go. "Is that so?" He gestured toward the pry bar. "Well, let the remarkable scholar open up my picture, then."

Embarrassed, Allman lowered his face slightly. Joliette, however, gave a quick laugh and struck the pry bar with the side of the hammer. The boards separated about a centimeter. He forced the bar farther into the seam and struck again.

Minsky eyed each member of the group one by one. "And who are you, young lady?" he asked.

"Esther Goren, sir."

"Hello, Esther Goren with the almond eyes. Don't use that 'sir' with me. Ah, to be seventy again! Are you a cop? Don't tell me you're a cop."

"I'm not a cop," she said a little too sharply. Minsky blinked, so she added, "I'm with him." She tossed her head toward Henson, who smiled in a way guaranteed to infuriate her.

"Ah, now there is a lucky man. A lucky man. What do you think of all this, eh?" said Minsky. "Nearly sixty years since I saw my uncle Feodor's painting, and then there it is on the television. If it is Uncle Feodor's painting."

"I thought you were sure," said Esther.

"From the television and the newspaper, I am. I'll never forget that picture. Never! I just want to make double sure. In person. They say it could be worth millions. I don't want to be a million-dollar fool. I'm a TV star, you know that? I was on CNN last night."

"I missed it," said Esther.

"I was a regular Ramon Novarro."

"And soon you'll be rich, if it's yours," said Esther.

"Don't tempt me," said Minsky. "What'll an old man like me do with all that money? Nah. I'm going to give the picture to the Holocaust Museum in Washington. I'll get a brass plaque. 'Feodor Minsky's Van Gogh,' it'll say. 'The bastards murdered everybody but his nephew.' That's all it needs to say. No plaque is big enough to list them all."

Esther nodded.

"Are you ready, Mr. Minsky?" asked Joliette. He held one side of the lid while Henson held the other.

Minsky shuffled in front of the crate and took a deep breath. "Okay," he said. "Shoot."

Henson and Joliette lowered the lid like a drawbridge. Van Gogh's self-portrait was just visible under a layer of packing material. Joliette peeled it down. The smell of the years it had hung in Samuel Meyer's attic rolled out.

Vincent stared out at them, vortexes of blue and green swirling around his red hair. His coat seemed to pulse, as if alive, his hands to quiver.

"My God," said Professor Allman, breathlessly.

Minsky paled. His lip quivered as if he might weep. "Unbelievable," he muttered. "Unbelievable."

He took another deep breath and exhaled.

"It's the eyes," Minsky said. "The eyes. I used to stare into those eyes. I didn't know what it was at first. It scared me. Then later, after I was a bar mitzvah—you know, more of a man—I knew that I felt what he felt. He felt what I felt when my grandfather died. He felt what I felt when I read the news out of Germany. The man spoke to me from his picture. He said, 'God help us. God help us.'"

There was the rumble of a jet taking off, then the huge room was silent. Minsky turned to Esther. "Do you see it? In his eyes. He knew what it was to be a Jew. He wasn't a Jew, but he knew what it was to be a Jew."

She looked at the painting. "I think I do," she said. She stared into Vincent's eyes for several seconds, then saw Minsky was staring at her.

"You see it," he said quietly. "I can see you do. I know you and your man will take good care of it."

"But, Mr. Minsky," said Weston, "if the painting is indeed yours . . ." He began to open his briefcase to bring out another court order.

"I trust this young lady!"

"But—"

Abruptly, Minsky raised an arm. "Gentlemen, you pack my uncle Feodor's picture good or I'll personally kick your butts!"

"He'll do it, too!" said Esther. "Believe me!"

Minsky winked at her as if he had shed thirty years.

# NINE

# Flight Delays

Henson and Esther scurried toward their business-class seats, breathless from rushing to the gate. When they flopped into them, they sat quietly, catching their breath.

"Excuse me," said a florid man at the window across the aisle, "but don't you think it's particularly rude to keep an entire jumbo jet waiting?"

"Excuse me," said Esther, "but have we been introduced? I don't think so. How rude!" Henson suppressed his laughter as the man ruffled his *Financial Times*.

"Well," Henson said, "we're on our way to Amsterdam!" He asked a flight attendant for a glass of orange juice and then turned to Esther, who had leaned back and closed her eyes. "What did you make of that business?"

"Minsky? He wanted to see the painting himself and to have someone of his own choosing verify that it was worth all the legal trouble. After all, suppose the painting were a copy of the one that had hung on his uncle's wall? It could have been embarrassing for him. Old people don't like to look foolish."

"Toorn said it was definitely not a copy."

"He also said it wasn't Minsky's."

"Toorn is the expert."

"Did you see Minsky's reaction?" she said. "He was seeing a ghost."

Henson stretched out his legs and leaned curiously toward the window to see why they weren't moving. Only the jetway and an abandoned luggage train were visible. "Think of it this way," he said. "Jacob Minsky was a young man once. He lost his youth as all people do."

"Speak for yourself."

"But Minsky lost his world as well as his youth. His mother, his father, his cousins, his brothers, all the people he grew up with, argued with, shared holidays with. They were mowed down, their bodies reduced to ash. How much would you beg, cry, anguish to get any of that world back? A man who's lost everything he cherishes—" Henson paused, as if something suddenly distracted him.

"So you're saying he only *wants* the painting to be his uncle's?"

Henson gathered his thoughts. "I'm saying he believes it to be his painting, the way a child believes in Santa Claus. On Christmas Eve, a child can hear him, see him. Minsky saw a ghost all right."

Esther thought for a moment. "Well, I like him. I don't think he's deluded."

"No. Perhaps 'deluded' is not the right word." Martin lowered his head slightly. "I'll tell you what I think. I don't think he cares whether he gets the painting."

"No, the money means nothing to him."

"Exactly. He just wanted to see it one more time. If it flew off to Amsterdam and got tied up in the legal system, he could die before ever seeing it again."

Esther studied Henson.

"What?" he asked.

"That's very"—she thought a moment—"perceptive of you. Very sensitive for a spy from Kansas."

Henson looked up to see a flight attendant offering them glasses of champagne from a tray. They each took one.

"You know, Martin Henson," said Esther, "a more cynical man would have said Minsky was in it for the money."

"He may be, who knows?" Henson said, grateful to be flippant. He sipped the champagne, made a face, then set it down. "I was supposed to get orange juice, you know. It'd be nice if I got what I asked for once in a while."

"Live a little," said Esther. "Who is this Dr. Allman from SUNY Binghamton? Why did Minsky bring him?"

Henson shook his head. "Joliette told me the guy taught art history. Maybe he's Minsky's drinking buddy. He isn't really an expert on Van Gogh and never pretended to be. Maybe Minsky just wanted some kind of expert on his side."

Esther drummed her fingers on her armrest and took a deep breath. "Look, I want it to be clear, just as I told you: my coming along does not mean I am willing to sign on to your task force."

"I am grateful for your help, nonetheless."

Esther smiled. "I don't know why. You seem perfectly capable of taking care of yourself, Mr. Boy Scout. You saved my life back in the hotel."

"And you saved me from a burning building when you

kicked out the window. Call it even." He raised his glass in an informal toast. "So, now tell me again why you are traveling to Amsterdam with a man you barely know?"

"I must find out about my father."

"May I presume to offer an additional theory?"

"Oh, how elegant!" she said quietly. "Presume away."

"I think you're very much like me," he said.

She leaned her head forward and rolled up her eyes. "Come on!"

"No, I mean it. You're right. I *was* a Boy Scout. I reached Eagle Scout. At the bad end of the Vietnam War I was on shore patrol in Saigon. Later I was a small-town cop until I got my degree and went to work for Treasury, where I had a pretty good record working smuggling. A big one involving pre-Columbian art was what got me this gig."

"You were in Vietnam? You don't look old enough."

"At the very end of the war. I was just a kid. I feel pretty old sometimes. Fifty's a few years up the track."

"So far, you haven't said a thing that makes me 'like you.' "

"You're not reading between the lines." He leaned closer to whisper. She could feel his breath on her ear. "You joined the Mossad, why?"

"You know I can't talk about the Mossad. I don't even know what it is."

"Of course not." Henson grinned, then grew serious. "But let me offer a theory. A simple explanation. You wanted to seek justice. To do a good thing."

Esther shook her head. "Assuming such a thing were true, intelligence work is hardly the place to find moral clarity."

"Nor law enforcement, strangely enough. After a while, you do the job. You don't worry about what's right as much as nailing guys. When Celeste—my wife—passed away, I threw myself into my work as an escape. I didn't care so much about why I was doing it. I just wanted something to do. I misplaced myself for a while."

Esther nodded.

"But when the undersecretary of the treasury approached me with this task force idea, something clicked. I saw it as a chance to do something good, something a little less gray. Oh, I know, many of these cases may be ambiguous—who owns what and so on—but the basic thrust is to restore artworks to their rightful owners. That's a good thing. I sleep better when I'm sure I'm doing something positive. Not just locking up bad guys for a few years, but getting things back to their rightful owners."

"You're so American," said Esther. "A naive optimist."

"Naive optimists can do great things. They created the state of Israel, didn't they?"

Esther shifted in her seat. "They were hardly naive."

"To build a nation surrounded by enemies?" He touched her arm. "Join us. We will do good things in this task force."

"You don't give up, do you?"

"Not until the fat lady sings and the curtain comes down."

"Look," she said, "you're very persistent, but I am not fat. I am just here because of my mother and I'm flattered you ask, but, well . . . I'll promise to give it some thought if it will make you feel better. That's all I'll promise."

"That's all I'll ask for now. We'll consider it a test drive."

"Who knows? Maybe I'll end up with the Van Gogh, sell it for a billion dollars, and retire," Esther said sarcastically. "Why haven't we taken off yet?"

"Airports! We'll soon be on our way," said Henson. "They can usually make up the time on these overseas trips."

Esther toasted a smooth flight and their glasses clinked, a

dribble spilling over the lip. She took a deep swallow, then decided to apologize. "Listen," she said, "about back there—about your wife. I didn't mean to pry. It wasn't any of my—"

"Forget it," he said, avoiding her eyes.

"I pictured you as a guy with three kids. The kind who teaches his boys to play baseball. I didn't expect—"

Again, she could see she was causing him pain. She felt stupid but didn't know why she kept stumbling forward. "I'm sorry," she said. He didn't answer. She finished her champagne and was digging for her seat belt when the captain made his announcement.

"Ladies and gentlemen, we regret to inform you that we must ask you to deplane and return to the gate area."

A collective groan went up. "What now?" Esther said.

"Please exit orderly and quickly," said the captain, "and leave your carry-on bags on the plane. We will care for them."

People were already thronging the aisles.

"When they ask people to leave their carry-on luggage they intend to reboard the passengers," Henson said.

"I hope you're right."

"Please step lively," said a flight attendant. "Don't rush. Just move quickly."

Esther scanned the flight attendants' taut faces and instantly knew. *This is a safety matter.*

They hurried into the jetway, briefly separated by the crush of the crowd. Esther rejoined Henson as he stopped by a porthole to look out at men with batons. They were getting ready to guide the plane as it backed up.

"What is it?" asked Esther.

"Please keep moving," shouted a Chicago police officer.

"Come on," said Henson. He took her wrist and pulled her into the gate area.

"What is it?" Esther repeated.

He pulled her aside and whispered, "FBI. I recognized an agent in the lower doorway. And they're going to move the plane."

"To get it away from the building," said Esther, nearly choking.

Henson nodded subtly as his jaw muscles flexed.

The passengers, disgruntled but weary-looking, continued to emerge from the jetway. They assumed it was the usual air travel folderol: mechanical problems, overcrowded runways.

"What about the painting?" asked Esther.

Henson paled. He approached an airline employee. He stood close to her and showed her his Customs badge. "I'm with Treasury. Can you direct me to the agent in charge?"

The woman eyed him suspiciously. "The ticket agents are—"

"No," he said. "FBI. You know what I mean, ma'am."

She hesitated a moment, then led him to an officer. The policeman scrutinized him, studied Martin's ID, then turned his back to use his radio. They waited. The last passengers emerged, as well as the flight attendants. The engines whined as the plane began backing away.

"What did I tell you?" Henson said.

A secure door opened in the corner, and two FBI agents peered out. Esther recognized them. They had been among the men who had interrogated Esther about the shooting at the hotel.

*Here we go,* she thought.

The men grimly waved them in and followed behind them down a long staircase. They hurried through a narrow corridor used by incoming international passengers, then through another secure door with a push-button lock and into a stark room. Several men were gathered around a weeping Hispanic man wearing an airline jumpsuit. Chicago Police Detective Thomas spun on Esther as soon as he saw her.

"I should have known!" he said, his breath slapping her face. "Can't you just get the hell out of my town? And if you can't, will you tell me why this Manfred Stock is so intent on killing you?"

"*Manfred* Stock?" said Esther. "Is that his full name?"

"You sit right there and don't you even blink."

"Hey!" said Henson. "What is this?"

"You shut up and be a good boy, or you'll be sorry," said Thomas. Henson glanced at the FBI men, and it was clear they were all too willing to help the Chicago detective make him sorry. Henson sank to the metal chair.

"Okay, son," Thomas said to the weeping Hispanic man, "explain it all to Special Agent Marsden here, just like you explained it to me."

# TEN

# Vincent's Gym Bag

Hector Arce-Bartol had worked hard as a baggage handler since 1985. Landing on his feet, he had survived two airline bankruptcies to become a group supervisor at Northwest, which serviced KLM flights in Chicago. The previous evening had begun much like any other. He had dozed through an uninspiring ball game—Kansas City 11, Chicago 6—then was roused by his wife, Miranda, to climb the stairs and kiss his four girls good night. He thought perhaps Serena, eight years old, had a bit of a temperature, but the twins, three, fell asleep quickly, and Teresa, six, made her usual protest about going to bed before ten.

Now was Hector and Miranda's time. Sometimes that

meant a videotape and a beer, sometimes one of Miranda's Univision *telenovelas,* and sometimes a shower together and quiet lovemaking. This night it meant sharing a cream puff. Hector and Miranda had made it a secret tradition between them. On their first date exactly eleven years before, they had shared a cream puff, and she had laughed when a gob of it flopped and hung from his chin like an old man's goatee.

They were licking each other's fingers when their dog, Cesar, yelped. They listened but heard no more. Cesar often got nipped by an insect or scratched by the neighbor's cat, but they did not hear the cat's usual squall. Miranda reached for the last piece of pastry to shove it into Hector's mouth. She froze, however, the pastry hovering in the air. Hector initially thought it was some sort of game, but her face told him otherwise.

He spun from his chair to see a large blond man aiming a black handgun at them.

"Don't scream," said the man. "I wouldn't want to hurt your babies, enh?"

"No," said Hector, swallowing. "Take what you like. The stereo is new."

"No one will be hurt," said the man, "unless you force me. No one wants that." He pointed toward the front windows with a blue gym bag in his left hand. Hector noticed the bag had the KLM logo on it. "Close the curtains. We are going to explore possibilities. Lights out. Just as if you have gone to bed."

"If you hurt Miranda . . ." said Hector.

"Don't force me to, then. In here!"

They went into the kitchen. He ordered them to sit at the opposite end of the dinette table. He placed the gym bag in front of him.

"Now, then, keep your hands on the table and don't get foolish. I will explain."

Miranda noticed the man's gloved fingers were glistening with drying blood. She remembered the dog's yelp and bit down on her knuckles to keep quiet.

Hector wept, sucking air through the fingers covering his mouth. Detective Thomas sat next to him and rested his hand on his shoulder. No one spoke until Hector had pulled himself together.

"He told me I was to go to work as usual," said Hector. "I was to place the gym bag on the flight to Amsterdam. An hour after the flight took off, he would release Miranda and my babies."

Thomas gave Esther a withering stare. *My God!* she thought.

"Miranda said no, I must not do this, hundreds of people will die. 'If he does not do it,' said the man, 'he will have no children or wife to come home to.' Still, Miranda says I must not, God will protect us. The man, he is surprised by this, but his eyes grow cold as a snake's and he says—" Hector gasped and wiped the sweat from his face.

"Go on," said Special Agent Marsden.

"He says he will give us three minutes to choose which baby will die. He must prove he is serious to us. Maybe one of the twins, he said. 'You have one extra. You'll hardly miss it.' "

A cold draft seemed to move like a ghost through the sealed-off room.

" 'You will not kill a baby,' I said to him. 'Listen to your heart.' But he just looks at the kitchen clock. I beg him. A minute passes and then Miranda drops to the floor on her knees and begs and takes hold of the man's legs and says she will do anything, we will do anything, and I think I must die if I see him hurt Miranda or my babies, I must jump at him like a tiger and tear at him until he kills me because I cannot look upon my babies dying."

Hector broke down again, weeping.

"That's all right," said Detective Thomas. "We understand."

"Then the man says, 'Good.' He didn't want to hurt anyone. He just wants me to put the gym bag on the flight to Amsterdam." Hector spread his hands. "I told him that would be nearly impossible now: video surveillance, dogs, luggage tracking. He told me he knew I could find a way. I must have thought about it a hundred times. Well, of course, if you work there you think of it, mostly because you don't want someone else to do it. But it doesn't mean you *can* do it. And then I thought, it is just drugs. He doesn't want to hurt anyone, just get the drugs through. But then I think it can't be. If Miranda and my babies are free an hour after the plane takes off, I could still call and tell, and the police would meet the plane. So I know then what it must be—he wants me to put a bomb on the plane.

"I explain to him that it is not easy to get another bag into the baggage area, not easy at all. I will be caught. I explain it is even harder for me to get it on the plane. It isn't like the past. He says I am a supervisor. He is sure I will know how. I said I don't. He says I will think of a way, that I must think of a way."

"So," said an FBI agent taking notes, "he knew details about your work?"

"He came to my house!" said Hector. "He killed my dog!"

Marsden interrupted. "Did the man ever say anything about

why he wanted to bring down the plane? Did he say anything political or religious?"

Hector thought, then shook his head. "He said nothing like that."

"You're sure?"

Hector thought hard and shrugged.

"Just tell us what happened," said Thomas.

"We sat in the kitchen for hours, then he moved us to the living room and told us to rest on the sofas until the sunrise. I close my eyes, not to sleep—how could I sleep?—but praying he will go away because he is a nightmare and not real. Whenever I open them he is sitting straight in the dinette chair, straight like a tin soldier, staring, grinning, like I am a foolish child. He is never tired. I think he will kill Miranda and all my babies no matter what I do. Then he looks at the clock and says, 'It is time,' and he hands me the bag. I look at Miranda as I go out the door. She is crying. She says, 'I forgive you. I forgive you everything.'"

"What did she mean by that?" asked Thomas.

Hector almost leaped from his chair. "That I would never see her alive again!"

Thomas nodded.

"And then I think she must mean I must not do this thing, but I think that I must. My babies! The only chance they will have is if I do this thing, and then I think no one must ever find out who did this because my babies will have to live with knowing their lives have been purchased with two or three hundred lives. And they are worth that much to me. I am sorry, but that is true. But then I get to the airport and I see the passengers in cars and taxis, and I see them kissing good-bye, and I think they have babies, too, and mothers and brothers and fathers, but still, I tell myself I will do this thing because I am not strong enough to let Miranda or my babies die."

"No one can blame you," said Thomas. "I have kids and I would go to hell for them."

Hector spoke without blinking. "I *was* in hell. I *was!* I would either kill my own family or dozens of families. How would I choose?"

Henson met Esther's eyes. A ball of molten lead flopped to the bottom of her stomach. She suddenly knew that, for whatever reason, this Manfred Stock was willing to bring down an entire 747 in order to get her.

Thomas placed his hand on Hector's shoulder again. "It wasn't a choice. The man knew it wasn't a choice. To even think it was a choice shows you're more of a man than most of us."

Hector looked up as if he were being condescended to.

"So you never got it into the baggage area?" asked Special Agent Marsden.

"No," said Hector. "I left it in the trunk of my car. I went inside to see if it really was possible. It was like he said. I am a supervisor. I knew the one at the door. I thought I might distract him when others were going through."

"If you know any cracks in the system, you need to tell those things to security," said the second FBI agent.

"I thought maybe I could put the gym bag in someone else's suitcase, then there would not be an extra bag to count. But I had to do that after the random screening, and then I was worried if I did it too soon that the dogs might come through."

"And sniff out the plastique?"

"The what?"

"The explosive."

"Of course."

*A dirty trick,* thought Esther. The question was posed to find out if he knew the nature of the bomb.

"And then," Hector continued, "I must find a way to take things from a bag. Most of the bags for Europe are so stuffed I would not be able to get the gym bag into them without taking out clothes and extra shoes or something. It would look like I was stealing from the luggage."

"So you left the gym bag in the car until you could figure it out?"

"In the trunk. I think to drown it in the toilet, but what about the babies?" Hector took a sip of water.

"The car's been isolated," said Marsden. "They will be extracting the bag in a few hours."

"I waited, not knowing what I was going to do. I thought I was going to have to do it, to take a bag from the cart, and let others think I had a reason."

"But you didn't?"

"I was in hell." Hector crossed himself. "But the Lord saved me." Hector pointed upward. "I am told there is a phone call for me. I think it is the man calling to make certain, but I hear Miranda and what she says I don't believe." Tears came to his eyes again.

"The man had gone," stated Marsden.

"He used his cell phone to call someone. Then he locked Miranda and my babies in the closet and left. It did not take too long for her to get out."

"We're searching the plane just in case there was more than one," said Marsden to Henson.

"We've got to get that painting off it," said Henson. "It could be the key."

"We can't rush this." Marsden glanced at Esther.

"I know," said Henson. "Just get them to be aware of its importance."

A uniformed Chicago cop opened the door to the cramped room. "They're here" was all he said. A woman rushed in and flung herself around Hector's neck. Two little girls squirted by each side of the cop, and the four Arce-Bartols kissed and wept and muttered wetly to one another. The cop then stepped aside to reveal a double stroller. Soon all six of them formed an indivisible ball.

"You can't automatically blame her!" said Henson. "You are leaping to a conclusion. Maybe this Manfred Stock is after me."

Detective Thomas balled up his fist and brought it down hard on the metal desk. It boomed like a distant explosion. He and Special Agent Marsden had pulled Henson and Esther into an adjacent room, and then Thomas had lit into them.

"Calm down," said Marsden.

"Yeah, right," said Thomas. "There's a hostage incident and then I'm notified that this Stock is involved. And then I get here and who's the target? Our little friend from Israel!"

"I'm no friend of yours," said Esther weakly.

Henson leaned into Thomas's face. "She was supposed to fly out on El Al, *sir,* not KLM. How could the man have known she would be on the flight to Amsterdam? I only convinced her to come with me this afternoon. Stock had been holding Hector's family hostage for more than fifteen hours by then."

"But you bought the damned ticket *yesterday,*" said Thomas. "In the name of Esther Goren."

Esther looked at Henson.

"It was a refundable ticket," said Henson.

"That's hardly the point," said Marsden.

"He couldn't be sure which flight I'd be on," said Esther. "KLM or El Al."

"Now, if I were a damned assassin," said Thomas, "I'd bet on the most recent ticket. Wouldn't you?"

"Would you bet an entire 747?" asked Henson.

"It depends how much I wanted to kill Esther Goren," said Thomas. "Maybe he thought a planeload of people was a fair enough price."

Once again the ball of lead thudded at the bottom of Esther's stomach. She thought of the grumpy man with the newspaper who'd been seated next to her on the plane. The rows of children and old women and lovers eagerly waiting to take off for Amsterdam.

"Or it's an act of terrorism," said Marsden.

"He didn't go through with it," Henson said. "He talked on the phone and then abandoned his hostages. Why?"

"The bomb was on its way," said Marsden.

"But he must have known Mrs. Arce-Bartol would call her husband. Could it have been meant as a warning? He never intended to carry it out?"

Marsden almost snarled. "It wasn't a big bomb, my people tell me. But it would probably have brought down a 747. In flames. Pop a hole in the fuselage, tear out the hydraulics— that's all it needed to do. The bomb was a core of plastique attached to a magnesium powder incendiary device."

"Magnesium?" Henson was thinking of Samuel Meyer's house.

"It burns at an incredibly high temperature," Esther said, "if you'll remember from your high school chemistry. Ironically, it is also used in alloys to strengthen the aluminum in a plane's fuselage."

"Well, isn't that informative," snarled Thomas, turning on Esther. "Don't you think it's about time you explained who

Manfred Stock is?"

"He's the man who killed Samuel Meyer," Esther said with a shrug. "It's all I know."

"You seem real awful incurious about the son of a bitch," said Thomas.

"The man killed your father," nudged Marsden.

"What do you know about my father?" said Esther. "He was no father to me! He ran away when I was a baby!" She felt heat flushing her neck and ears.

"Your mother left him," Marsden corrected, his superior smirk begging to be slapped away.

The muscles in Esther's forearms tightened, but she gripped the arm of the chair to keep herself from flying into his face, as she had with Henson. "She had a reason. Whatever it was, he was never part of my life! What do I care about him?"

Henson reached out to calm her with a touch, but she slapped him away.

"You came thousands of miles to see him," said Thomas. "And he just happens to have a Vincent van Gogh in his attic, and he just happens to be in the process of being murdered by this Manfred Stock, who is then going to extraordinary measures to blow up the plane you're riding on. You know what? I just happen to be a cop, if you hadn't noticed. Cops don't believe in coincidences. They're just not part of our world."

Esther sagged back in her chair, boiling. There was a long silence.

Henson quickly stood up, wedging himself between Esther and her interrogators. "Look, I hate to break up such a fun party, but I think it's been made clear to you both that this is a matter which supersedes either one of your jurisdictions."

"Don't give me that," said Thomas. "I've got a murder and a hostage incident and a damned dead dog to boot."

"An act of terrorism is a bit more pressing than who stole

some old painting," said Marsden.

"Stolen from the homes of six million dead Jews," said Esther.

There was a silent standoff.

"Look," said Henson, "the solution to one thing is the solution to all of it. Tell me who Manfred Stock is, all you know about him. Where did you get his first name?" He addressed this to Marsden, even though Thomas had used Stock's full name. It was the kind of information more likely to come out of the FBI's sources, rather than the Chicago Police Department's. Besides, Henson had more leverage with feds.

When Marsden set his jaw and stared defiantly wordless back at him, Henson added, "I'll get the attorney general of the United States on that phone and you'll be one sorry-ass special agent."

Marsden gave Henson the evil eye, but he answered. "Manfred Stock is a Chilean national. His name is tied to several corporations down there. Uniforms for the Pinochet regime. Ranching. Mining. According to the records they gave us, he is over eighty."

"This man was middle-aged," protested Esther. "Fifty-five, I'd guess. Didn't you hear the baggage man?"

Henson threw up his hands. "Miranda Arce-Bartol wasn't held hostage by an eighty-year-old!"

"No, but the Chilean national who flew into LAX two days before the murder of Samuel Meyer was named Manfred Stock. He fit the description of the man who went through passport control."

"And his passport said he was over eighty?"

"No, that was what the Chileans returned to us when we inquired about Manfred Stock."

"So, there are two Manfred Stocks!" said Esther.

"No," said Marsden. "The man must have forged a passport

using Stock's name. Or else the Chilean government got the wrong Manfred Stock. Chile had a lot of German immigrants in the 1800s. German names are common. We do know this: our boy rented a Buick yesterday at Midway Airport."

"We'll find him if he's in the area," said Thomas.

"Did the Chileans say whether the real Manfred Stock was a colonel?" asked Esther.

"Not in their armed forces. Not honorary or anything," said Marsden.

"Meyer called him SS-Standartenführer Stock," said Esther. "I'm certain of it. Then the killer said he was *not* the colonel. Could Meyer have mistaken this fifty-five-year-old Manfred Stock for an older Manfred Stock he once knew?"

"The killer's father or uncle, maybe," said Henson. "Or perhaps the killer was neither and Meyer flashed back to some memory from the war."

"You're forgetting that someone named Manfred Stock entered the United States," said Esther. "It's too much of a stretch to think that's a coincidence with Meyer having a flashback."

"I don't believe in coincidences," repeated Thomas.

Marsden crossed his arms. "I want to know what this has to do with the Mossad," he said firmly.

"Nothing," said Esther. "I don't know anything about the Mossad."

"Right. We get two, no, three attempts on the life of a Mossad agent and it's not connected? Pardon my Hebrew, lady, but that isn't kosher. That's bullshit."

The phone rang. Marsden waited for Esther's response as it rang three more times. She seemed to be trying to X-ray his brain with her eyes.

"Aren't you going to pick that up?" said Henson.

Marsden snapped the receiver out of its cradle and turned

his back to mutter into it.

Thomas twiddled a pencil. "You've got no right bringing your people's war into my Chicago," he said.

"It's got nothing to do with the Mossad," she repeated.

Marsden slammed down the phone. "A NATO military plane is to fly you three to Amsterdam."

"A military plane?" said Esther.

"You *three?*" said Henson.

"Courtesy of the Dutch government," said Marsden. "You two and the Van Gogh." He looked at Thomas. "So, that's all she wrote for us."

"You've got to be kidding!"

"From the AG himself."

Thomas shook his head, then leaned forward and spread his hands. "Come on. Off the record. Meyer's dead. A waiter's dead. A planeload of people was a target because you were on it. Are you going to sit there and say there's no Mossad relationship to this?"

"If Miss Goren did happen to work for the Mossad, it still wouldn't necessarily mean that there's any relationship," said Henson. "But she's a travel agent."

"Come on," Thomas begged. "We're all after the same thing, aren't we?"

"It's a coincidence," said Esther.

Thomas hmmphed. "Well, you know how I feel about those, don't you? But who the hell am I? I can't even keep you in Chicago!"

# ELEVEN

# Across the Pond

The NATO transport was far less military than they had expected. Normally used by high-ranking officers and diplomats, it had a well-stocked kitchen, four sleeping berths, and a washroom with a narrow shower. Esther, overcome by the strain of the past two weeks' events, quickly retired to one of the berths. She had learned to snatch any rest she could, even in the most dangerous circumstances, but she kept waking from strange nightmares. Manfred Stock was her father's real name. Vincent van Gogh's suicide in 1890 was faked, and he lived in Chicago as Samuel Meyer. And, of course, there were dreams of fires. Hot fires. Manfred Stock threw portraits of Jews into a blinding white magnesium fire.

All the Jews left on Earth were loaded onto a 747 and blown out of the sky with a rocket while the Gentiles watched from bleachers. This was all her fault somehow. She begged to be on the plane, but a rabbi said that her father was a Nazi and she would spoil the beautiful white light of the explosion.

When the Dutch soldier who served as the attendant gently tapped on her berth wall and offered coffee and breakfast, she felt as if she had not slept at all. Worse, maybe. When she took her seat at a small table in the forward cabin, Henson cheerfully said, "It's a beautiful day in Amsterdam, I'm told. Seventy degrees and hardly a cloud."

"How nice," she said vaguely. She thought how stupid that sounded but hadn't the energy to do better.

As their limousine glided down the highway from Schiphol Airport to the city, she contemplated the rich green countryside carved with canals and flat farmland. The landscape was so different from the cities she had usually found herself in, human outposts in the middle of deserts, with any trees or vegetation sustaining themselves on the stubborn insistence of the inhabitants that they should have at least some greenery. Ultramodern buildings appeared at intervals along the highway, prosperous and clean, seeming to have sprouted from the rich soil. The radically modern ING bank building, a steel and glass structure shaped like the hull of an old trading ship, looked as if it were docked beside the highway, ready to sail across the portions of the Zuider Zee that had long been filled in. As they rode toward their hotel in the center of Amsterdam, the picturesque houses and canals seemed unreal, like the model towns built around toy railroads.

Esther dozed and thought of the brief and terrible moments in which she had seen her father alive. She glimpsed a couple holding hands as they stopped at a street vendor for Italian ices, and she imagined her mother and Samuel Meyer kissing. She heard the shattering of the glass at the end of their wedding ceremony. She imagined them in bed entwined together, their forearms marked with the tattoos of the concentration camps.

"Martin?"

Except for a slight sag beneath his eyes, Henson looked as if he suffered no jet lag. He pointed out the window at an ornate building. "Isn't that beautiful?"

She leaned forward, catching only a blur of red brickwork. "Martin, did Samuel Meyer have a tattoo?"

"A tattoo? What kind of tattoo?"

"On his arm."

"Oh," he said, looking away. "That kind of tattoo. There was a scar where it should have been. He said he had cauterized it away."

"Why didn't you tell me this?"

"Does it mean something?"

"Everything means something!"

Martin was suddenly interested. "What, then? Do you have any idea why he would have burned it away?"

"My mother wore hers proudly," said Esther. "She said that no one should ever forget."

"Maybe Meyer wanted to forget."

"Was Meyerbeer ever in a camp?"

Henson suddenly looked more tired. "He was not. The investigators in 1966 assumed your father faked the burn. We have people in Germany looking into the records again. In `66 it was thought many of the records might be locked behind the Iron Curtain in East Germany or the Soviet Union. So far, nothing has turned up."

"Why haven't you told me these things, Martin?"

"You're not really part of the task force, are you?"

"Oh, please! He was my father!"

"Yes, but was your father Stéphane Meyerbeer?"

Esther sagged. How else would an old man get a Van Gogh?

"I'm sorry. I would open the entire file to you, but—"

"You're just blackmailing me into joining your group."

Henson looked at a group of long-haired, bearded men wearing tie-dyed shirts and sandals. "Now, there's a blast from the past," he said.

"You play such an innocent tourist very well," she snapped.

He smiled. "I'm just a boy from the Midwest. At heart, I'm still looking for excitement in the winter wheat."

She crossed her legs and pressed her cheek against the door. It smelled of a citrus cleaning fluid.

"Listen," Henson said, "there is something I should tell you. I got a message on the plane."

"Well?"

"Manfred Stock got away."

"Did you think he wouldn't?" said Esther. "He seems to be quite skilled in what he does."

"He's not that good," said Henson. "He hasn't gotten what he wants."

"Yet," said Esther.

"You're still alive. The Van Gogh's on its way to the museum. The car he rented at Midway Airport turned up in Windsor, Ontario."

"In Canada?"

"He must have driven to Detroit and crossed over. We've got the RCMP looking for him, but Canada's a big country."

"There's no passport control between the United States and Canada?"

"Well, yes, but it's not too hard to get back and forth. I don't know how you could get from Detroit to Windsor without passing through the booths on the bridges, but who knows? There are ferries on the St. Clair River as well, and another bridge up the road at Port Huron. He must have gone a long way on interstates without being spotted by any state police."

"This would never have happened in Israel," she snorted.

"Maybe. You guys aren't invincible."

"So he's still after me, then?"

"We can't know that. He may have finished and gone back to Chile. Whatever he couldn't find in Samuel Meyer's house is ash."

It had been a very hot fire, she recalled. Begun with magnesium, fed with gas. Too hot to fight in the normal ways. The firefighters managed to save the building across the alley, but the next row house burned and the fire threatened to take down the block. The old woman who lived next door had barely escaped. Her son had played hookey from work to drink beer and cheer the Cubs. If he hadn't stopped in . . .

Henson sighed. "The house is a shell of overdone brick filled with hot ash. The question now is, why did he burn your father's house?"

Esther's head suddenly cleared, and she realized immediately what Henson meant. How Stock had gotten inside, or even when he did, did not much matter. According to the preliminary FBI analysis, Stock had set an altimeter fuse on the bomb for the plane. When it reached 25,000 feet the bomb would have gone off. Since they had recovered the bomb intact from the trunk of Hector Arce-Bartol's Camry, the FBI would be trying to trace the parts, the wires, the chemical signature of the explosive, the gym bag, even the tape used on the wiring. But Stock could have set a timed device in the house weeks ago, on the day he shot Samuel Meyer. When she and Henson had searched the house, they had missed it. The fire had exploded from behind the broiler pan at the bottom of the kitchen stove, right where the gas pipe hooked up.

Stock was a brazen operative, a professional. There was no question about that. He was so physically noticeable with his thick body and short, blond hair, and yet so elusive. No amateur could be this lucky.

"There was something in the house he wanted to destroy," said Henson. "That's the way I see it. Maybe something that he was afraid of was in the house."

"And it couldn't have been the Van Gogh."

"Who knows? But he also seems to be afraid, or to have been afraid, that you removed something. Or that you know something that is somehow dangerous to him or to the people he works for. The painting was already gone when he shot at us."

"I told you, I only took the photograph of my mother and the baby picture."

"Something about the other men in the photograph?"

"We've been over that. How could he know I had that? Why didn't he take it himself when he searched the place?"

"It'll bear checking, nonetheless." Henson took a notepad from his jacket pocket and opened his Montblanc fountain pen. "Who would have data on the refugee camp in Trieste?" he asked himself, scribbling a note.

"Tito tried to take the peninsula at Trieste, as I remember," said Esther. "Truman and Churchill had it occupied to keep it in Italy."

"Did your mother say anything about who ran the camp?"

"She complained about British food, I think, but maybe the

Brits just supplied it. She mentioned Italian guards who smuggled her shoes and a decent dress. It must be the dress in the picture."

"Do you remember any names?"

Esther closed her eyes but nothing surfaced. "They were just 'the Italian guards.' It took her a lot of effort to speak of those years. It was these small acts of kindness she wanted to tell me about. Maybe it was a way of allowing that human beings have a shred of decency in them. After all she went through, that would be hard to believe."

"Maybe we can get the Italian in the photograph identified." Henson snapped his fingers. "Say, what about the baby picture? Are you sure it's you?"

"Yes. The '1966' on the back seems to be in my mother's handwriting."

"You're not sure?"

"It's her hand. And before you grasp at another straw, there's absolutely nothing in the photograph other than a chubby baby in a bonnet and booties."

Henson sighed. "You're right. I am grasping at straws. I'm just afraid that our chance to sort all this out went up in smoke in Chicago."

"There's still the Van Gogh," Esther said. "Stolen or forged, a lot of people seem very interested in it. If we can trace it—"

Henson looked out the window. "This is it. I think it's our hotel." He reached for his wallet and froze. "Oh, damn! I forgot to convert any money!"

"You're not exactly inspiring confidence, Mr. Henson." Esther sighed.

# TWELVE

# Convening the Experts

O n the next afternoon, still a bit groggy from jet lag, Esther and Martin took a taxi to the Rijksmuseum Vincent van Gogh. The guard at the door of the basement auditorium had almost no accent in his English. "Pardon me, sir, but this is the press entrance."

Henson opened his credentials and leaned close so that he couldn't be overheard. "The other door is much less crowded," said the guard, but Henson simply thanked him, gripped Esther's elbow and plunged into the jostling sea of press. Photographers from several international news organizations were elbowing into position, while cameramen flung a babel of insults at those who blocked their view of the disputed painting. A pair of bright lights came on almost simultaneously along the far wall as a Japanese correspondent and one from CNN prepared to speak. Henson and Esther reached a barrier defended by museum guards and were barred from crossing until Antoine Joliette stepped down from the podium to wave them across.

Joliette extended his hand. "Very pleased to see you again, Miss Goren."

"I'll wait in the back," she said.

"I have seats for you over there in the second row. I insist."

"Thanks," said Henson.

"I believe there will be controversy," Joliette said, rubbing his hands with delight.

"Really?" said Henson.

Joliette smirked. "Where there are two art experts, there are seven opinions. *C'est toujours ça!*"

"In Israel we say, 'Two Jews, three political parties,'" said Esther.

"Trust me, my dear, art experts are worse!"

"Maybe Jewish art experts?"

"Ha!" Joliette snapped his fingers at the quip and recognized a professorial man with wild gray hair and a bow tie entering through a side door. "Excuse me, that's Lord Hazelton." He rushed toward him.

"That's all we need if they disagree on its genuineness," said Henson. "We'd never be able to trace it then."

"I'll go to the back," said Esther.

He leaned close to her. "The cameras aren't on you, and in any case, you're a travel agent. Remember?"

She looked at him, surprised at the serious snap in his voice. It was easy to underestimate him as the ever-optimistic, boyish American.

Henson softened and smiled a bit sheepishly. "You're my date," he whispered. "Hey, it'll enhance my reputation. Think of it as charity on your part."

"I try to be charitable," she said.

"Anyway, you'd draw more attention in the back."

They took their seats as the panel of experts assembled on the podium, shaking hands. Two of them embraced as if they hadn't seen each other for quite a while, while another seemed to be studiously avoiding any contact with his peers by carefully examining the agenda through slit-like reading glasses. In the audience Esther noticed Jacob Minsky's lawyer talking to an elegantly dressed man with a hawk nose, presumably a European attorney. She also counted six plainclothes security men scattered along the rough divide between the audience and the podium. These were in addition to the uniformed guards at the doorways and at the podium edge.

"This is security worthy of a head of state," she said to Henson.

"It's a Van Gogh," said Henson. "It's more important than a head of state. As the song says, we're still trying to understand what Vincent said to us."

"Song?"

"You don't know 'Starry Starry Night'? Don McLean?"

She felt from the way he said it that she should know it. Maybe it was the jet lag, but she was drawing a blank. "I just hope it's enough security to keep Colonel Stock away."

"Everyone's alerted," said Henson. "The RCMP, Interpol. Nobody's spotted him." He gestured around the room. "And nobody here resembles him."

"My enemies worry me more when I cannot see them," said Esther.

"An old saying?"

There was a short burst of applause from among the invited dignitaries and docents. Gerrit Willem Toorn was lurching his way slowly across the podium to the expert table. One of the experts rushed to escort him, but Toorn waved off his help. The expert who had been studying the agenda looked over the rim of his reading glasses as if motivated by mere curiosity, not respect. Toorn's chair was not at the long table, but rather off by itself at the end. He dropped into his chair and rested his hands on the cane in front of him. He pursed his lips and tilted back his head. The movement was either one of utter disdain for the excited spectators, Esther thought, or a pose of disdain, an attempt to serve up the image expected from the "world's greatest expert." She did not know why she had the impression that he might be deliberately striking a pose. When they had gone to the Palmer House to show him the painting, he'd had more than enough arrogance and contempt. He was old, however. He might be afraid of the younger experts and modern techniques supplanting him, even if he were certain he was right. If this motivated his arrogance, she felt a little sorry for him. The fear of vulnerability, of the certainty that your fate is not in your control, could be more chilling than the actual vulnerabilities of age.

Antoine Joliette went to a modernistic glass lectern to the right of the panelists. He tapped the microphone with a silver pen. "Ladies and gentlemen, *mesdames et messieurs, dames en heren*, allow me to introduce myself. I am Antoine Joliette of the Art Institute of Chicago, and my delightful task at this press conference is to introduce this panel of extraordinary experts who have assembled to determine the authenticity of the newly rediscovered self-portrait of Vincent van Gogh. We have decided to conduct the press conference in English, as all panel members are comfortable—"

A white-haired man whose name card said "Baleara" interrupted. *"Somewhat* comfortable!"

Much of the audience and the experts, other than Toorn, laughed.

"—as the panel members are at least sufficiently comfortable in English that we shall use it as our lingua franca," finished Joliette. "If your English is not fluent, the press release is available in French, German, and Dutch, I believe, and among the docents, as was explained earlier, there are a number of people willing to translate into several other languages, including Russian, Japanese, and Arabic."

"The world is watching," whispered Henson to Esther.

Joliette turned toward the uniformed guards at the doors behind to his left. "And now I believe it is time to introduce the guest of honor." He nodded and they opened the doors. Two additional guards carried in an easel draped with a white satin cloth. The audience stirred. The press jostled for position like horses just out of the gate. Some members of the audience rose to their feet in anticipation. The guards set the easel down in the circle of a spotlight and took up positions flanking it.

"You may remove the drape," said Joliette.

"Let's hope it's still there," whispered Henson wryly.

Esther scanned the audience as the guards delicately raised back the covering. There were gasps and applause and the flashing of camera lights. One of the docents had covered her mouth and was weeping.

Toorn twisted in his chair and raised his arm, nodding. "You see!" he growled. "The De Groot portrait! Of all the self-portraits, the greatest!"

Vincent stared out from the canvas in three-quarter profile, his eyes bleary, his jaw tight. A universe of pale blue, aqua, and white swirled around his tousled red hair.

The photographers were as animated but reverent as if they were in the presence of a legendary movie star: Marilyn Monroe, Katharine Hepburn, John Wayne. Many of the audience members were in a state of veneration, transfixed by the painting.

Joliette allowed several moments for the full impact of its presence to be absorbed, then he stepped back to the lectern. "It is an incredible piece, n'est-ce pas?"

"But is it the genuine article?" shouted one of the British reporters.

"Of course it is genuine!" snapped Toorn, banging the tip of his cane against the floor.

"That's what we're here to determine," said Professor Baleara.

"To verify," said Toorn. "This is the painting that hung in the De Groot. If you prove it to be a forgery, then it has always been a forgery." He raised his cane. "Ever zzince Van Gogh painted it!"

The audience laughed.

"As may be apparent, Dr. Toorn has already made his decision," said Joliette. "Let me introduce him to you, and then each of our panel members will successively explain the methods they will employ to verify or dispute the painting's authenticity."

Joliette began listing Toorn's credentials, saying that the panel and anyone else well informed in art history considered him a household name. Seventeen books, innumerable articles and show catalogs, and consulting for almost every major museum had been part of his career. Toorn rose to the applause, and though Joliette urged him to speak from his chair, Toorn walked slowly to the lectern, a great rhinoceros enjoying the eyes upon him. He placed his hands on both sides of the lectern, cleared his throat and began.

"Azz far azz I am concerned," hissed Toorn, "this examination of the painting is merely a formality. Science is not the only font of truth." He stretched out one arm and swung it to point at the painting. "This is exactly what it appears to be. It is the portrait of Vincent that hung in the De Groot collection in 1943. I was a very young man then, but this painting was my friend. I spent many hours sitting with it, communing with it, listening to what it had to say. It became my brother."

He stared at it, his chest heaving, the air whistling on each exhale.

"And then the Germans came. They seized my brother. As the Allies moved closer, the local SS colonel and his slave workers loaded my brother and all the other artwork into an Opel Blitz truck, and the SS colonel, a soldier and the slave worker left. The truck was still in sight of the museum when it struck a mine. The resistance, the Communists, whatever their intentions—it is only they who could have placed the mine—have always to me borne a heavy responsibility for that mine. The politics of any day is nothing compared to a work of art such as this. People come and go: you, me, SS colonels. But great art? When I saw the column of smoke and the burning truck, I truly felt I had lost a brother, which is perhaps why I later particularly specialized in Holland's greatest painter."

He breathed slowly and closed his eyes. "I know I must be among the last few still alive who saw that painting hang on the De Groot wall. I am also a person who cannot be deceived by the shoddy work of counterfeiters. This was the painting that hung in the De Groot. My colleagues here will demonstrate the obvious. *Mijn broer is thuis!* My brother is home!"

The rhinoceros began to lumber toward the painting, then stood staring at it and wiping his eyes. The audience applauded with a roar, even more people were now weeping, and at least two of them had cameras thrust at them to record their emotion.

"This is quite a show," said Esther.

"This means a great deal," said Henson. "This is what I'm saying we can do together, restore stolen objects to the nations that rightfully own them."

"My sympathies lie with Minsky," she said.

Joliette was at the lectern again. "Now I'd like to introduce the other six experts who so graciously and quickly flew here to Amsterdam to comprise our panel, and I will ask each to explain exactly what his or her role shall be. First, our kind host for today, Dr. Erik Luits of the Rijksmuseum Vincent van Gogh. He will be searching the archival records both here and from the De Groot estate and elsewhere for any information that might be relevant in tracing the provenance and establishing the authenticity of the painting. Dr. Luits?"

Luits leaned forward to his microphone and said, "What Antoine says is true. It is often the case that we cannot find any independent record of the creation or existence of a painting during the lifetime of the painter. Certainly one item of interest that I intend to pursue is the letter to Theo van Gogh which is argued by Mr. Minsky, Jacob Minsky of America, to support the idea that the painting was a gift to his uncle. This may prove nothing or may prove a great deal, but there are many avenues to explore the whole question. Accounts by neighbors, sales records, and so on." He waved his hand as if bored by his own occupation, the ultimate dispassionate scholar.

The next expert was Paolo Crespi from the University of Bologna. "My area of expertise," said Crespi, "is the chemistry of paint and varnish. Different paints have been used at different times, of course. In the Renaissance, artists had the additional problem to create their pigments or buy rare materials of color from sailors or something like that. In Van Gogh's day, of course, paints could be purchased as they are now. We have relatively good records on what sorts of paints were manufactured when and by whom and whether they were likely to be available to a particular artist, such as Van Gogh."

He got up from his chair and approached the painting. "In the case of Van Gogh, there may be something especially helpful to us. As almost everyone knows, from the sunflower paintings especially, Van Gogh was a great user of the pigment chromium yellow. You will notice here in the jacket the artist is wearing, especially here on the buttons, that there are yellow highlights. It is also possible chromium yellow or another yellow was mixed into the swirls around his head to create this bluish-greenish effect. In any case I am intending to concentrate on these yellows initially. You see, what is interesting about chromium yellow is that it undergoes a slight color change as it ages. Yes, it begins yellow and remains yellow, but becomes—how do you say it?—a different shade through chemical change. If this painting originated in the 1880s and this is indeed chromium yellow, it will have changed more than it would have if it were painted in a more recent time. If it were painted more recently, in order to make it look like Van Gogh's chromium yellow, a forger would be forced to use a substitute or somehow alter the paint. Also, I cannot tell immediately, but if anyone applied a varnish to the painting, I will be able to tell much from that."

"Surely," barked Toorn, "we will not allow damage to the painting with these chemical tests!"

"Of course not," said Crespi. "You know that. I am not a

monster! The instruments we have now are so sensitive we may test a sample the size of a pinpoint."

"Any damage to the painting is unacceptable!" said Toorn.

"Of course," said Joliette. "I can attest to Professor Crespi's past work."

"There will be no damage," said Crespi, sitting back in his chair and crossing his arms.

Henson leaned close to Esther. "Academic Ping-Pong," he whispered.

"I suppose all police experts always agree," she said.

Henson smiled. "Touché, but they aren't usually quite as histrionic."

Joliette had already introduced Juan-Fernandez Baleara, who studied paintings with X-rays and ultraviolet and infrared light. Baleara had aged well. His white hair set off his dark eyes, and his accent gave him a mature sexiness. In the past year, Joliette said, Baleara had also made a significant advance in magnetic resonance analysis. He began by apologizing for his English, but it was better than he gave himself credit for. He explained that other wavelengths of light normally invisible to the human eye revealed a whole different image of a painting. It was possible using X-rays, for example, to reveal any underpainting that lay beneath the visible layers. Several types of information could be gained through the technology. For example, older paintings had been covered by more recent artists who were saving money on canvas. Artists often didn't like what they initially painted and covered it up. This had been useful in determining what the artist had originally intended. Sometimes a later artist had modified a painting to please a patron, by adding a significant object on the table, such as a medal or some other honorific. Baleara mentioned an early nineteenth-century Spanish painting in which a noble infant who had died was covered, perhaps because the image was disturbing to the mother. Also, unusual spectra of light were useful for revealing the brush technique of the artists. "The brushstroke," concluded Baleara, "is for some artists as unique as the fingerprint."

Esther noted how intently Martin Henson listened, often taking out his fountain pen to scribble notes on a flip-top pad. She was feeling a little light-headed from jet lag and longed for a nice bed with cool, smooth sheets.

There were two other experts. Professor Laura Iarrera of the Università Mediterranea di Reggio Calabria would use an electron microscope to examine spores, pollen, and other tiny biological materials that might have adhered to the canvas or fallen into the tiny cracks in the paint. These cracks were vast canyons on the microscopic scale, and the motes that fell into them could reveal the whole history of a painting's travels, depending on the species of pollens and spores. She would also be looking for any unusual dirt on the painting. In order to simulate age on a faked painting, she explained, forgers often heated a canvas to create the network of fine cracks, or craquelure, that normally appear in old paint. However, the cracks could not appear to be new, so to simulate years of random dust and fireplace, candle, and lamp smoke, the forgers would rub lampblack over the surface and into the craquelure. Unfortunately for the forgers, the lampblack, having been applied all at once, would be more consistent in texture and particle size than many seasons of random dirt, dust, and smoke.

The final expert was Joost Bergen, who was introduced as one of the world's great experts on fibers. His job would be to examine the canvas. Different manufacturing processes were used in the making of cloth at different times, and these could be revealed sometimes by microscopic examination of the canvas. Bergen could often predict the age of a cloth or the country it was manufactured in by the nature of the weaving or the composition of the threads. Obviously, if the canvas were made after Van Gogh's death, he could not have painted on it. If the canvas were of a manufactured type that was the proper age, but from a source not likely to have been available in southern France in the late 1800s, the painting's authenticity would also be brought into question.

"What about simply doing a carbon-14 test?" asked a reporter from the British press.

Joliette turned to the panel. "I don't believe that such a test would be helpful. Am I wrong? Should we perhaps consider such a test?"

"This is not the Shroud of Turin," said Baleara, "a thing of much antiquity." He slid his hand from side to side. "Radiocarbon can only give a range of dates. For example, in a modern sample, before nuclear testing took place there is a standard deviation. They calculate a laboratory error multiplier as well. Plus or minus five years can be quite problematical for an artist whose whole career lasted a decade, less actually."

"Yes," said Joost Bergen. "This is my understanding as well. The range would not be helpful, you see. Plus or minus twenty years would tell us very little, though I suppose it could be significant in some respects."

"This is certainly *not* the Shroud of Turin," growled Toorn. "The shroud is a medieval fraud."

There were some "oohs" from the audience, a whistle, and a little laughter. The panelists all looked uncomfortable.

"Well," said Joliette, "we are fortunately not convened to settle that question."

"It *was* zzettled," sniffed Toorn.

"Perhaps there are more questions?" said Joliette cheerfully.

A woman from French television stood, and ignoring the

general agreement that the news conference would be in English, fired a long question at Joliette.

"*Ah, oui,*" he said. "*Peut-être, madame.*"

"I should think," said Baleara, picking up the question, "that we could come to some preliminary conclusions in only a few days." He looked at his fellow panelists for assent.

Crespi seesawed his right hand. Bergen shrugged. "If it is a forgery, it usually does not take long," said Luits.

"And as it is authentic," said Toorn, "it will take a long time?"

"My own research is time consuming, since it is archival," said Luits, "but the science may immediately produce a contradiction."

"Of course," said Baleara. "The absence of contradictions is not proof of an affirmative."

"If you contradict me, you will be wrong," said Toorn. "There is no doubt whatever, it *is* the De Groot self-portrait."

The British reporter jumped to his feet again. "Assuming Dr. Toorn is correct and this is a genuine Van Gogh, how much would it fetch at auction?"

The panelists looked at each other with quizzical expressions.

"A tidy sum," said Bergen finally, and everyone laughed, other than Toorn.

"But how much?" persisted the reporter. "A million euros? Ten million euros? Twenty?"

"You must understand," said Joliette. "We have no expertise in the marketplace. If it is genuine, it remains to be determined who the owner is. It will be up to that person or organization to determine whether they will sell it or not. That has nothing to do with our role."

"But don't tell me it isn't on your mind. There are some

people very interested in the outcome of your research." The reporter pointed at Jacob Minsky's attorneys. "You might very well make someone rich."

"Van Gogh's *Sunflowers* sold in 1987 for over 39 million dollars," said Joliette. "There has, by the way, been a controversy about whether that painting was authentic. Later that year, however, one of Vincent's paintings of irises sold for nearly 54 million dollars, and then in 1990, a portrait of Dr. Gachet sold for 82 and a half million."

Toorn leaped to his feet. "Art is not commerce!" he hissed. "Art is more important than money! It is idiotic to pretend it could be priced! What motivation have I to prove what I know? Like the back of my hand I know! This is the De Groot portrait! It is beyond value!"

The fierceness of his words, the slashing of his cane, set the camera flashes ablaze. The press had gotten what it was looking for, thought Esther.

Henson rolled his eyes at her as Toorn spun to leave, but the audience shot to a standing ovation at Toorn's outburst. The session quickly adjourned afterward.

Henson and Esther crossed the Paulus Potterstraat and continued up the Van der Veldestraat toward the Acca International hotel. "Well," said Henson dryly, "I guess we get a day or two for sightseeing."

"Have you ever seen an expert come to an opinion in two days?"

Henson shifted his head to one side, as if jerking a crick out of his neck. "Toorn," he said.

"That may be the unreliable voice of ego," she said.

"The mother of all egos. Or certainty. Ego doesn't mean he's wrong. I think we should proceed on the assumption that he is right. He ought to know." Henson stepped away from her side to avoid a fat tourist sweating in a safari vest. "We should trace the painting as much as possible. If the panel concludes it is a fake, they say it shouldn't take long. It wouldn't be too much wasted effort."

"Maybe you should just go sightseeing at the government's expense."

"I hate wasting time. Have you ever been in Amsterdam before?"

"I'm a travel agent, remember?"

"The concierge told me the shopping district is just across the canal."

"I have everything I need."

He chuckled. "Imagine that. Okay, then. Why don't we have dinner and decide how to go about this? The concierge also said the nightlife is nearby."

"I'm thinking about going home."

"Your mother?"

Esther paused at the fountain in front of the hotel. The stub end of a cigar was disintegrating in the still, greenish water. "What if she hears about Samuel Meyer? They have televisions in the home. She doesn't seem to have any contact with the world, but what if the shock— I should go home."

Henson stood quietly, his hands in his pockets, looking at the blue awning at the hotel entrance, listening to the horns of automobiles in the nearby streets. "You'd never have the answer then," he finally said, looking at her to see if he had gone too far.

She crossed her arms. That was the point, wasn't it? She was afraid that her father had been one of *them*, one of the men who had been part of the Final Solution.

"I was thinking we might drive out to Beekberg tomorrow, where the De Groot Museum used to be."

"I don't know," she said.

"The hotel has a little bar. Why don't we have a drink? I don't drink often, but, hey, it's Europe and—well—what the hey, you know? A wine? A beer? Something like that? This is a capital of the beer world."

She watched him talk, thinking he might actually be blushing, and she didn't think it was about wine. Boy Scout. "Listen," she said, "I'm going to take a walk in the Vondelpark, then go upstairs, take a long bath, make a few telephone calls, and have a good night's sleep."

"It's only four in the afternoon," said Henson.

"And then tomorrow I'll go with you to Beekberg. No promises after that."

"Good," he said. "Good."

"So don't stay out too long in the *wallen*."

"In the—?"

"Red-light district."

"God, no," he said.

"It's an old area. The architecture is very interesting there."

"And I only buy *Playboy* for the cartoons."

"You buy *Playboy*?"

"Well, no, not really. It's an expression."

"Boy Scout!" She laughed, then set out for the park.

"Hey!" She didn't look back. He wanted to protest, but had no idea what to say.

# THIRTEEN

# A Trip to the Country

"How is your mother?" Henson asked, finally able to relax as the traffic lightened. They had finally cleared the outskirts of Amsterdam and were following the A2 highway toward Utrecht. Later he would be looking for the Ede-Wageningen exit on the A12, but it was too early for that.

"Not much changed. They assured me several times she was healthy. I don't want her to die alone, even if she doesn't know I am there."

"I understand."

She started to say, "Do you?" but remembered that he was a widower and would understand perhaps even better than she did. "Maybe it doesn't matter," she said.

"You've got to live with yourself."

"Not always an easy thing to do," she said, looking out the window. "I talked to Yossi Lev, as well. He is pushing me very hard to work with you."

"Good."

"I don't like to be pushed."

"Neither do I," said Henson, "but don't let it keep you from making a sensible move." He swerved past a truck loaded with beer barrels, then glanced out at the horizon. "This is one beautiful country," he said.

"Too green," she said. "Too wet."

"Really?"

"Like paradise," she said. "Speaking of such, how was the red-light district?"

"I ate at an Indonesian restaurant, De Kantijl en de Tijger. Stuffed me. Sorry, but it was nowhere near the red-light district. I was in my hotel room by ten. I watched the NBC Nightly News."

She slapped his thigh. "And that's your story and you're sticking to it, eh? All those details, maybe that's pressing it."

"Do I look like a guy who's been partying all night?" he said.

"That's just good Kansas genes," she said.

Beekberg was a small town with picture-postcard houses and narrow streets. Henson and Esther went to the town hall and introduced themselves to the only council member who was in his office that afternoon. When they explained what they were interested in, he led them to an archive on the second floor, where a plump woman supervised a rearranging of the file cabinets. The De Groot Museum had been in a Roman Catholic school for girls. That was all she knew. Her grandmother had gone there. Much of the town was hit by shelling during the war and was never rebuilt. She pointed to a photograph from 1945. The town hall was recognizable—barely.

The buildings around it had been reduced to rubble. "Mine father said there were many Jewish townspeople before. This is why boom, boom, boom, as the British came."

Henson nodded.

"If it was a sizable Jewish community, there may be records at Yad Vashem," said Esther.

"Ma'am," Henson asked the Dutch woman, "is there anyone alive in Beekberg who might remember more about the De Groot Museum?"

She squinted, trying to remember. "Anton?" She shrugged. "Anton who?"

"Houdelijk. He is a book merchant."

The bookshop was only a dozen yards from where they had parked the rental car. It had no sign and the building it was in was one of those postwar concrete slap-ups designed to relieve the housing shortage. The front window, however, was quite old-fashioned, with a checkerboard of small panes. The door tinkled as Henson opened it: a bell on a spring. Esther edged inside. Old magazines and books were piled helter-skelter on the floor, on bent shelves, as if the owner had just moved in, but the thick layers of dust and musty smell spoke of years of stagnation.

An old man in a yellowed T-shirt and papery slippers came through a low door in the back. He was holding a black pipe in his gnarled right hand, though it did not seem to be lit. He seemed to be uncertain he was actually seeing someone in his shop.

"*Dag*," he said.

"Do you speak English?" said Henson.

"*Ja*," he said. "My mother was an Englisher."

"My name is Martin Henson, and this is Esther Goren, my colleague."

"*Ja?*"

"And you are Anton Houdelijk?"

"I am."

"I'm wondering if you could help us. We're interested in learning as much as we can about the De Groot Museum."

The man nodded. "The painting, *ja?* The Van Gogh."

"Why, yes, our interest is related to it."

"You are someone who is claiming it?"

"No," said Henson, "we are trying to restore it to its rightful owner."

Houdelijk's sour expression distorted itself into a smile. He was missing a tooth. "Maybe that should be me."

"Believe me, if you can prove you are the rightful owner, we would make certain you got it."

The expression turned sour again. "I am joking, young man. What would I do with a house full of guilders? Buy a gold casket? A young man like you couldn't spend them before he died. Me? Ha!" He padded toward a desk half hidden by books and sat in a creaky chair.

"Do you remember the De Groot Museum?" asked Esther.

"Of course, of course. It was nothing special. There was a Greek vase I rather liked. Achilles and Hector."

"The Van Gogh? Do you remember it?"

"Oh, *ja,* a messy thing. This was a mad man in Holland, then he goes to France, where madness is a religion and he is an *arrrtist.* There hasn't been a great painter since Rembrandt. He was the end of painting. He made everyone think they should be *original,* be *arrrtists.* And that is the end of art."

"You may have something there," said Henson.

"I am correct," said Houdelijk. "The museum had nothing in it to show after the Germans looted it, so it never reopened. The school had never done well, and farmers left the land and it did not have enough students. It closed in 1949, and the nuns went to the East Indies."

Esther moved closer to the desk. "We have so little information about those days. Is there anything you can recall about the museum, particularly the Van Gogh?"

Houdelijk thought for a moment and chewed on his cold pipe. "There was a foyer with a guard in it, then the main room with different things that Mijnheer and Mevrouw De Groot and their children had collected. Things like the vase. Some things from a synagogue the Spanish burned in the Orange wars. Then there was a corridor. It had landscapes on the wall. Mostly local artists from the end of the last century. No one anyone cares about anymore, I don't think. Cows and cowherds and milkmaids and mist, that sort of thing. Some were good."

"Motel pictures," said Henson.

Houdelijk looked confused by the remark but went on. "The corridor led back into the old chapel for the De Groot family. It was round with high windows. Sitting on the old stone altar was the lunatic's painting. It was all arranged like his art was the apotheosis of all art. On the old altar!" He shook his head. "But it was easier to guard it that way. Only one way in and out. Piet Duik sat just inside the chapel to guard it. We joked he never left there."

"What happened to Duik?"

"Bergen-Belsen."

"He was a Jew?" asked Esther.

"No, he was Catholic. But he hid a Jew in his closet. He loved her, I think. That's what my father told me. We didn't like the curator much, but he ended the same way."

"Gerrit Willem Toorn wasn't the curator?"

"Later. Hoogen was the curator. His daughter-in-law was a Communist."

"So the Nazis arrested him and Toorn became the curator?"

"*Ja,* he was very young, but there was no one else. He was

161

Hoogen's secretary. It was said that he wrote the letters because Hoogen wasn't very good at that. Hoogen wanted to give away some of the art."

Esther and Martin exchanged a glance. "Give away?" asked Martin.

"They say he sent a few pieces to Field Marshal Göring, which was how the Germans got interested in the collection, such as it was. Beekberg is not Rotterdam, after all."

"He was trying to buy his safety, is that right?"

"His daughter's. Maybe he wanted a bigger post," said Houdelijk. "There was that, too. It didn't work. They shot the wife on the street, and Hoogen and his son disappeared in Bergen-Belsen."

"You were lucky to survive."

"I was not a Jew," said Houdelijk. "I was very Aryan. They did not know what was in my heart." He stared as if looking into the past. "I was encouraged to join the Dutch National Socialists. My father talked me into it. He had a radio. I heard things here and there. He radioed these to the Englanders. Queen Wilhelmina presented him a medal. The queen herself." He pointed at a dusty display case. "We were excellent spies, no?" Dimly they could make out his father's award.

"That was very courageous."

"I am no hero. It was hard to know what to do. Sometimes I wasn't sure I was doing the right thing." He seemed to read Esther's mind. "That sounds terrible now, I know, but that was a different time."

"You said Toorn wrote Hoogen's letters to Göring?" Henson made a note. It might lead somewhere. Surely lots of letters to Göring had survived the war.

"Oh, yes. Gerrit was a most enthusiastic member of the party."

"The Nazi party?"

"*Ja, ja.* This was why he remained curator."

"Why do you say 'enthusiastic'?"

Houdelijk smiled. "He strutted. He put on the uniform and stuck out his chin like Mussolini."

"Did he participate in violence against Jews?" asked Esther. "A little."

"What do you mean 'a little'?" she demanded.

"He egged bullies on. He made speeches. After someone was already on the ground, he might put in a kick, but it was all show. He was a weakling."

"And he was never called to account for this?" asked Henson.

"My young friends, you are beautiful and strong, or so you think. You do not know what it was like then. Some weakened a little. Some weakened a lot. The government could not punish every weakness. We could not shoot half the Dutchmen who had survived. We shot enough to make a point. There had been enough killing."

"So your friend Toorn walked away free?"

"Young lady, I do not have to talk to you, do I? I am an old man." He sat back in his chair. Henson touched Esther's elbow, and she pulled away, staring down at the floor.

"Anything you can tell us would be helpful," said Henson.

"First of all," said Houdelijk, "Gerrit was no friend of mine. I testified against him."

"So he was tried?"

"But acquitted. He said he had only been pretending. He said he had to after what had happened to Hoogen and Duik. He also claimed to have made a number of fakes, which he sold to the Germans at a very high price."

"Fakes?" Esther's head rose and her eyes locked with Henson's.

"He produced receipts that supposedly originated in

Berlin. They were for paintings and a bronze that were still in the collection."

"Who made the fakes?" said Henson. "Toorn himself?"

"Before he was Hoogen's secretary, he was an art student in Rotterdam. He taught painting in the school as well." The old man squinted. "Yes. That's correct. He said he made them himself and concealed the originals."

"And this was his patriotic duty to Queen Wilhelmina, I suppose," said Esther.

"He told the judges that it showed the stupidity of the Germans and that it was draining their resources."

"Right into his own pocket," said Henson.

Houdelijk pursed his lips like he'd tasted something sour. "Oh, he gave the money back. That was why he was acquitted, really. He bought his way out. Why the Reich would pay for what it could steal was never clear."

"I hope it cost him a fortune," said Esther.

"*Ach*"—Houdelijk waved his hand—"it was the widow's money. He put on his uniform during the occupation and courted the widow De Groot. Why she married him—" He shrugged.

"Perhaps she was afraid of the Nazis."

"That's so," said Houdelijk. "Anyone with decency was."

Henson looked at Esther. "Mijnheer Houdelijk, do you remember anyone named Stéphane Meyerbeer?"

"A French poet?"

"No," said Esther, "back during the war."

Houdelijk shook his head.

"He might have come north late in the war. From Vichy France."

"It was chaos. The attack at Arnhem, all of that. There were refugees all along the roads. I don't remember anyone named Meyerbeer."

Henson reached into his coat pocket and produced a four-by-five blowup of Samuel Meyer's driver's license. "He would have been younger." Houdelijk squinted, then shook his head. "How about this man?" He showed the sketch artist's picture of "Manfred Stock." Houdelijk scratched at his neck but didn't recognize him either.

"A drawing," he said. "I remember something. Young lady, on the bookcase there, on the second shelf at the top. The red cloth."

The book cover was so faded that Esther pointed. "This one?"

"Next to it."

She strained to reach it and gradually clawed the dusty volume out. Houdelijk seemed to savor her figure as she stretched up. The book was in bad shape. The binding barely held as Esther brought it down. Two pages fell out.

"It is a commemorative publication. It celebrates the school and the museum."

Esther picked up the fallen pages. One had a group photograph of twenty or thirty students, flanked by sturdy nuns. The second page had a meticulous line drawing of an antique gun, something like a harquebus or a matchlock. Esther brought it gingerly to Henson. The pages were so brittle that many of them had cracked and the dog-eared corners had fallen away.

"When was this done?" said Henson.

"I don't know. Before the war."

Esther was staring closely at a second group photograph. "The teachers," she said. "Toorn is third from the left. The one with a baby face."

"Not very clear, is it? He looks younger than the students."

They turned very carefully through several pages of text. About a third of the way through, the book shifted attention from the school to the museum. There were etchings of the buildings from the De Groot estate, then sketches of the museum artifacts. "This could be very useful," said Henson. "It's a record of the collection, more or less."

"Why didn't they just photograph the artifacts?" said Esther.

"Ah, young lady, that would have involved a great expense back then. Plates had to be made. Better paper would have been necessary. The De Groots were generous, but they were frugal."

At the end of the book was the Van Gogh, reproduced in a line drawing. It lost a lot in translation. The yellows in the jacket, the blue ether swirling around the artist's red hair, had been rendered in precise but awkward lines. There was nothing of the fluidity of an accomplished sketch artist. Vincent's hand at the bottom of the drawing between the two buttons on his coat looked more like a claw than a hand.

"That's it," said Henson.

"And the sketch is by Toorn," said Esther. She pointed at his signature beneath the drawing.

"I don't believe he shows a lot of talent," said Henson.

"I don't believe he could fool Marshal Göring," she said.

"Exactly."

The old man raised his cold pipe. "We never believed him, but the judges were tired of everything. We all were."

"Well, I'm not tired," said Esther.

"You will be," said Houdelijk. "The world is relentless. It wears everyone down. Oh, *ja*, everyone."

# FOURTEEN

# The Homey Apartment

Esther took over the driving on the outskirts of Amsterdam and wound through the streets and over the bridges of the city to Antoine Joliette's hotel, the InterContinental Amstel, a five-star establishment overlooking the Amstel canal. In the crush of late afternoon traffic, she was a little too daring a driver for Henson's taste, but he tried not to leave his fingernails embedded in the dashboard. To die was one thing; to let a woman know her driving terrified you was another.

The InterContinental Amstel was another of those hotels designed to remind most ordinary mortals just how far down the food chain they really were. The desk clerk was very polite, but Monsieur Joliette was not in. They thought about leaving a message, but Henson realized he had pocketed his American cell phone by mistake and left his European one at his hotel.

"If he comes in," said Henson, "please tell him that Mr. Henson and Miss Goren are dining in the restaurant."

"Certainly, sir."

Esther leaned in close to Henson as he took her elbow. "We don't want to eat here," she said. "It's La Rive, one of the most expensive restaurants in a very expensive town."

"So what? I'm in the mood for their chili dog. Failing that, pheasant under glass. What do you think?"

"I think Americans have more money than they ought to."

"You might be right, but we deserve a reward, don't you think? And it's on the secretary of the treasury's tab. He signs the currency, you know."

Esther knew Henson would never fleece his employer, that he was going to take it all on himself, but, well, she was hungry, and it was ungracious to refuse a gift.

They ate almost to bursting and quietly discussed what they knew so far. Was the painting a fake? Toorn had specialized in making fakes, or so he had claimed after the war. Only the experts could tell them that. If it was a fake, then the search for the rightful owner would be ended. Neither of their governments would be interested in a worthless fake passing for Holocaust loot. And if that happened, there might never be an answer to the two questions both of them wanted answered: How did the painting get to an attic in Chicago? Was Samuel Meyer really the Nazi Stéphane Meyerbeer?

They were leaving the restaurant when Joliette arrived. "Where have you been?" he asked. "I've been leaving messages all day."

"I picked up the wrong cell."

"Toorn has walked out."

"What do you mean?"

"Puff! Up in smoke! Vanished." Joliette reached into his jacket pocket and produced a note on monogrammed paper. "This waited for the committee when it assembled this morning."

Henson opened it. *"Madame et messieurs, rien que vous ferez ne changera mon jugement. Adieu."* He showed it to Esther. "'Nothing you can do will change my opinion. Goodbye.' What do you make of that?"

"It looks like it was written with a quill," she said, taking the note and rubbing the fine paper between her finger and thumb.

"Not just his 'opinion,'" said Joliette, "but 'judgment.' What an insult to the panel! As if they were all idiots! They spent an hour sputtering their anger. They will prove him wrong if they can, I tell you."

"Are you saying he may have tainted the process?"

"Baleara was so angry he was ready to declare it a fake without examining it!" said Joliette. "But, no, these are all good people with reputations to protect. I don't believe they will act out of spite."

"Where did Toorn go?" asked Esther.

"All we have is his address in Amsterdam. I drove there, but no one answers."

"Take us there," said Esther.

"It's some distance. Some members of the committee said they might call me later," said Joliette. "They are still working."

"Take us there," said Henson. "Or give us the address. But neither of us speaks Dutch."

"I'll notify the desk to take messages," said Joliette. "Do you think something has happened to him?"

"If it hasn't, it should," said Esther.

"Oh, dear," said Joliette.

Joliette drove almost as madly as Esther, but Henson's mind was churning possibilities. Both he and Esther were alarmed by Toorn's flight, but why? Couldn't this just be another arrogant gesture? Was there something in his Nazi past that he was afraid they'd discovered? How would he know that? Someone in Beekberg called him? Or was it simply that he knew that the portrait of Van Gogh was a fake because he had made it? But why would he declare it genuine to begin with? No one would have known that *he* had made it.

The building where Toorn lived turned out to be a modest brick structure with a watchmaker's shop on the ground floor. Joliette pointed to the dark windows above. "His place is on the second."

"He climbs stairs?" said Henson.

"This is just a pied-à-terre," said Joliette. "He has another house in the country, maybe more than one."

Beside the shop windows, sealed tight with metal shutters, was a black door. A small brass frame held a plastic card with the name "Toorn." Henson leaned on the ringer for many seconds. It was loud enough to be heard in the closed apartment even from the street.

"What kind of lock is it?" said Esther.

Henson glanced both ways up the narrow street. "You aren't serious?"

She bent and looked at the lock. She winked.

"Oh, no," said Henson, "this isn't really—"

"Wait in the car, if you like," said Esther.

"There's a bar at the corner," said Joliette.

"You, too?" said Henson.

"Someone needs to be lookout. Isn't that right?"

"You look like you need a drink, Martin," said Esther, unzipping a side pocket on her purse. Henson hadn't left. "Well?"

Henson checked the street in both directions. "I'm not hanging out in some bar."

"This is exciting," said Joliette. "I've never seen a lock picked!"

Esther lifted out a set of keys on a ring. Nothing about it really distinguished it from millions of key rings. It would go through an airport X-ray and not even a trained eye looking at it closely would see that several of the keys separated into a variety of picks. She set about her work while Henson checked the street again.

"Try not to look so furtive," said Joliette.

"Amazing," said Henson as the heavy door swung back.

"An easy one," she said. "And no alarm."

"Oh, God," said Joliette, his eyes wide.

"Didn't you know?" Esther winked.

"Okay, then, let's see if the fat man is home," said Henson.

"I thought you were the lookout," said Joliette.

"Can we hurry?" said Henson.

Joliette paused. "Perhaps I shouldn't violate the great man's apartment."

"Then *you're* the lookout," said Henson. "Sheesh. And if anyone asks, the door was already open, right?"

Esther felt along the wall until she found a rotary switch. The narrow entryway was only a couple of yards deep. A flight of stairs led up to a similarly small landing with a tiny lightbulb. They climbed up, thinking about Toorn and his canes mounting the stairs with only a few inches on either side of him. The door at the top was painted in a red lacquer and had a lock that Esther popped open in fifteen seconds, at most.

"You'd be a helluva burglar," said Henson.

"If necessary," she said.

"Dr. Toorn? Hello?" The open room had a vinyl floor, visible even in the dim light, in dramatic black and white concentric squares. When she switched the lamp on, the walls were white and the furniture black. An Eames chair sat in the corner. The table next to the chair was Chinese style, gold dragons on black lacquer, like the armoire. An old-fashioned gas heater was the only thing in the room that did not seem to have been chosen with great care. There was no carpet, no random items like magazines or an ashtray on the table next to the chair. It was as stark, thought Henson, as a museum exhibit.

"Isn't this homey?" he said.

Esther studied the single painting, a wide landscape with shepherds and shepherdesses drinking wine under a thick tree. A small brass tag identified it as "Jaap Donkers." "What does this mean?" said Esther. "Is it a name?"

"The artist?" Henson crossed the floor and tugged the tasseled knobs of the armoire. "Locked."

Esther had moved to the back of the apartment. The kitchen was as clean and empty as the living room. In the upper cabinets were fine porcelain plates with red and black Japanese designs on them. In the lower cabinets were various sizes of enameled pans. The small refrigerator held only a dish of butter.

While Henson checked the bedroom, Esther picked the simple skeleton lock of the armoire. A banjo-shaped bottle of armagnac was flanked by a kirschwasser, an anisette, a single-malt scotch, and a variety of wines.

"Nothing back there," said Henson.

"With the exception of the liquor cabinet, I've seen better supplied hotel rooms."

"Why even keep the place?" said Henson. "When he comes to Amsterdam, why doesn't he just rent a room? It doesn't really look like he's spent any time here."

"Do you think he's been here at all?" asked Esther. "This looks like a safe house."

"On the bedroom wall, there's a portrait of a young man. I think it's him. It's signed 'G. W. Toorn.'"

"Maybe he painted it."

"It looks like him," said Henson. "But the style is like Van Gogh."

"You want a drink before I lock it back up?"

Henson had gone to peek out the window. "Uh-oh," he said. "Antoine's talking to someone."

Quickly, she relocked the cabinet and started for the door.

"Take a quick look at the portrait. Tell me if it's Toorn."

She went into the bedroom and was surprised at the size and round shape of the bed. It certainly hadn't come up the stairs. They must have hoisted the furniture in through the windows.

Oh, yes, there was no question about the portrait. It was Toorn—an emaciated version, but nonetheless Toorn. He had the same arrogance about him, the jutting chin, the condescending eyes. The attitude was there forty, fifty, maybe even sixty years ago. World's leading experts weren't made, they were born.

The painting itself was a very conscious attempt to simulate Van Gogh. It was done in thick impasto. Areas of it looked like a relief map of a mountain chain and though the colors swirling about Toorn's head were much less bright, the pose was exactly as it was in the sketch in the commemorative book printed by the De Groot Museum and school. The head was turned three-quarters, like Vincent's. The hand curled upward, as if it were cupping a tennis ball as it hovered between the top two buttons of the coat. He had tried to imitate the De Groot Van Gogh. Was this the first step toward creating a forgery of it?

Esther considered taking the painting but thought that would be too obvious. She stepped into the immaculate bathroom, folded over several sheets of toilet tissue, then used her fingernail to flake off a tiny piece of the yellow impasto near the portrait's hand. She enclosed it carefully in the tissue and zipped it into her purse. By the time she stood on the landing, relocking the apartment door, Henson and Joliette were waiting at the bottom of the stairs.

"Hurry," said Henson.

"Police?"

"Just hurry."

"Shouldn't Antoine see the portrait?"

"What portrait?" said Joliette.

"Later," said Henson.

Esther climbed into the backseat of the car. Joliette put it in gear, and they pulled away. "What happened?" she asked.

"The old woman from across the street," said Joliette. "She came back from the market and saw Toorn leaving. She said it looked like a chauffeured car picking him up. The driver was wearing a black suit and black gloves."

"Yes?"

"But the driver dropped this as he got into the car. She didn't know what it was but thought he might need it."

"She thought we might know him," said Joliette, turning west toward the center of town.

Esther looked down at an airline luggage tag. "Gerhart Brewer" was the passenger, traveling Toronto to Amsterdam on the previous day. "So we find this Brewer?" she asked.

"The old woman described this driver as about six feet. His hair was blond."

"Manfred Stock!" said Esther. "Now he's got Toorn!"

# FIFTEEN

# Buttons

"That's it," said Henson, tossing his cell phone on his hotel bed. "A Manfred Stock flew out of Milwaukee just hours after releasing the baggage handler's wife. He was carrying a Chilean passport, just as he did when entering the U.S. They traced him to Ottawa. Later, Gerhart Brewer, carrying an Austrian passport, flies from Toronto to Amsterdam."

"So, Brewer is Stock?"

"The timing is right. He must have flown from Ottawa to Toronto, but he must have used a third name for that."

The long night was disappearing as the sun rose. Henson yawned. Esther held onto the armoire and slipped out of her pumps.

"Do you think he is still after me?" she said, raising her foot to massage it between her fingers.

"Or us," said Henson. "Or God knows."

"What about Toorn? Do we need to call the Dutch police again?"

"I was maybe too insistent with the inspector. He told me that a man getting into an automobile, even if the driver might be a suspect in a shooting incident in Chicago, is not proof that he is being abducted. It didn't look forcible to the old woman, he said, so what exactly did I expect them to do? They promised to send a man to Toorn's house in the country again, but they say he comes and goes and no one knows when he is supposed to come back."

"Face it," said Esther. "Stock and Toorn are working together."

"Don't be so sure," said Henson. "If they're not, I doubt we'll ever see Toorn alive again."

"Toorn holds the secret, don't you think?"

"I don't know what to think. I *can't* think." He flopped back on the bed and squeezed the bridge of his nose.

She bit her lower lip, then crossed to sit on the edge of Henson's bed.

He looked at her. "What is it?"

"I'm tired, too," she said, lying down beside him.

He sat up. "I could call you if anything comes up."

She hesitated, as if trying to understand an obscure joke, then closed her eyes and turned on her side, resting her cheek on her flattened hands. "Umm."

"I could call you in your room."

She opened her eyes and closed them again. "Don't worry. I'm too tired to take advantage of you, Martin." She sighed.

"It wouldn't be the professional thing to do," he said.

"That is not my profession," she said.

"You'd be more comfortable in your room, wouldn't you?"

he said, but she did not respond. She was asleep? He leaned closer and listened to the whisper of her breath. It reminded him of his wife's breathing when she was filled with painkillers and finally receiving a few hours of peace. He lay beside Esther, crossing his arms on his chest and staring at the ceiling.

When the phone rang, he was dreaming they were traveling to Provence to question Vincent van Gogh, but as it was 1888, the roads weren't really made for a Thunderbird convertible, and they were having difficulty finding gas.

He grabbed the receiver, nearly knocking the phone off the end table.

"Martin?"

"Antoine?"

"The panel has some preliminary findings."

"Is it real?"

"The canvas is a common type from the period. Crespi is still in the process of analyzing the paint, but it seems to be authentic so far. Dr. Iarrera has found nothing unusual in the microscopic particles in the craquelure, but of course it could be expected to have pollen from southern France, Holland, Chicago, and everywhere en route. It does not, she says, appear to have been artificially dirtied to simulate age. She is identifying the pollen to discover further clues."

"So far, so good," said Henson. "What about the X-rays?"

"Baleara hasn't gotten back to us yet."

Henson was immediately alert. Toorn had evaporated. Please not the Spanish scientist, as well!

"Baleara works late and sleeps late," Joliette continued.

"Just don't tell me he's missing."

"Well, no." Joliette's tone darkened. "I don't think so. The hotel said he left word at the desk that he was not to be awakened until two. That isn't unusual for him. Why do you ask? You suspect something?"

"No," said Henson, rubbing his eyes. "No."

"What is it?" said Esther, sitting up. "What time is it?"

"Is that Miss Goren with you?" asked Joliette.

"Uh, yes," said Henson. "We were meeting for breakfast."

"Ah," said Joliette. "Room service?"

"Well, no—"

"*Rien voir, rien dire,*" said Joliette. "The reason I called is that Jacob Minsky and his attorneys are coming down to the museum at two to check on the painting and to discuss it with our panel. I expected you wanted to be here?"

"Yes," said Henson. He covered the mouthpiece and quickly explained it to Esther.

"So Minsky traveled all the way here?"

Henson shrugged.

"They are trying to decide what their next step is," said Esther.

"Give us thirty minutes," said Henson.

"There is no rush," said Joliette naughtily. "We might have more information at two."

"We'll be there," said Henson.

Esther glanced at the mirror and ran her fingers through her hair. "I look horrible. How long did we sleep?"

"It's just after noon."

"You didn't take advantage of me, did you?"

"God, no!" he said. "How can you ask—"

She smiled and put her index finger across his lips. "Sssh. I'm joking, Eagle Scout. I think I'd remember it. You don't have to act like it's the worst thing that could happen to you."

"I didn't mean that."

She smiled again. "I know."

"It's just that this is a professional situation, for one, and I—"

"You don't have to explain, Martin. Really." She leaned toward him. "Don't you know when you're being teased?" He looked up at her, his mouth open. His unshaven cheeks were dark. A lock of hair was sticking out comically from the side of his head. "I'll meet you in the lobby in an hour. I need a nice warm soak."

"It's not that you're not attractive to me," he said.

"I'd better be at least that!" she said, pausing in the door to wink. "I'd worry about you if I wasn't."

He blinked, unable to react until she was gone. "*I* worry about me," he said to himself. It was easy for others to say that it was time to move on, to get back in the stream of life. But he wanted his work to be enough for the moment. Get the task force up and running. He thought of the soft way Esther breathed when she was asleep. How was he supposed to keep his mind on this case?

It wasn't easy for a man as elderly as Jacob Minsky to deal with traveling across time zones, but he had dressed in his best and smiled broadly when he saw Esther walk into the conference room with Henson on her elbow. "It's been a long time," he said to her.

"Not that long, Mr. Minsky," said Esther. "Just a few days."

"Then it seems a long time!" he said.

"How are you, Mr. Minsky?" asked Henson.

Minsky ignored him, never taking his eyes off Esther. "The clock doesn't matter at my age. It feels long; it is long."

Esther noticed Minsky's American attorney hovering, as if afraid Minsky might say something that would compromise a potential lawsuit. "How are you, Mr. Weston?"

"A little jet-lagged, but holding up, Miss Gorman."

"Goren," she said.

"Oh."

Minsky looked up at Weston as if irritated at the interruption.

"So," he said, "you think they're going to steal my picture?"

"No one wants to steal anything from you," said Esther.

"Ha!" said Minsky. "If they want it, they take it. It won't matter if it is a real Van Gogh or not. If they want it, they'll take it."

"We're here to make certain that doesn't happen, Jacob," said Weston.

"Live my life and tell me that!"

"Might we all take our seats?" said Joliette. "The experts would like to get back to their research." Crespi and Iarrera were speaking to each other in Italian and moved to their chairs without slowing their argument. Joost Bergen was poorly shaven and sagged into his chair as if he might never get up. Joliette took the head of the table. Minsky was flanked by two Dutch lawyers on one side and Clay Weston on the other. "Would anyone like some coffee? Tea?"

"Coffee," said Bergen with a bilious roll of the head.

"Let's get to business," said Minsky. "I need my afternoon nap."

"The entire panel isn't here," said Weston.

"Dr. Luits insists he has little to comment and thinks it would be far too preliminary for him to comment. He has obtained a copy of Vincent van Gogh's letter to Theo which mentions a 'son of Abraham' who has fed him on some occasions. The letter appears to be authentic. However, it does not specifically mention Mr. Minsky's uncle, and Dr. Luits is searching the archives for other possible references to this charitable man."

"This was my uncle Feodor," said Minsky. "Kind as any man who lived."

"So far, Dr. Luits has not found any indication that Van Gogh gave a painting to this 'son of Abraham,' who may indeed be your uncle."

"We will want to see this letter," said one of the Dutch attorneys.

"It will be available, of course. Dr. Luits"—Joliette glanced at his watch—"has just caught the train to Paris. He believes he may have located Van Gogh's drawing of one Théodore Minsk, which is referred to in two books published between the wars."

"And where is Gerrit Toorn?" asked Weston.

Joliette kept a poker face. "We were unable to contact him about this meeting."

"Unable to contact him?"

"In time," said Joliette. "Dr. Baleara will be along shortly."

"Fine, fine," said Minsky. "What about my painting?"

"Pardon me," said Crespi, "but I must say that the purpose of our research is not to prove who owns the painting, but whether it is genuine."

"Yes," said Joost Bergen, pouring more sugar into his coffee. "I do not understand why we are having this meeting at all."

"Because Mr. Minsky is entitled to know the facts concerning his property," said Weston.

"Then let him wait for the results," said Bergen.

Henson interrupted. "The United States Treasury has joined with representatives of several nations to form a task force to deal with art which has been misappropriated through military force or theft. It is our job to investigate ownership and return the works to their rightful owners."

"And Miss Goren is with you on this?" asked Minsky.

Henson looked at her.

"Yes," she said. "At least until this case is resolved."

"Then I will trust this young man because I trust you," said Minsky.

"If necessary, Jacob," said Weston, "we may have to turn to

the courts to assert your rights." The Dutch attorneys nodded.

"Mr. Weston," said Minsky, "I want proof that the painting was stolen from my uncle Feodor. What good will it do me otherwise?"

"If it is a forgery," said Esther, leaning toward him, "there may be no way to continue the investigation, no matter how much you and I want to know."

"Then prove Uncle Feodor was not a liar. He said he got it from Van Gogh. Personally. Feodor was not a liar! The Minskys are not liars."

"Can we move on?" said Bergen. "I examined the canvas and removed two sample threads for carbon dating. This may not be informative if those threads were contaminated by handling or getting wet or insects or something of the sort. The fibers and the weave are consistent with canvas manufactured 1885 to 1901, which brackets the time period of Van Gogh's activity. It also shows the aging, in my judgment, that would be expected. I found nothing to contradict the hypothesis that Van Gogh painted on this fabric."

One of the Dutch attorneys said, "Most excellent."

"None of this is proof that he did, of course. There will be a complete report when I am finished. Is that sufficient for this morning?"

"Dr. Paolo Crespi is engaged in the analysis of the paint," said Joliette.

"Yes," said Crespi, "but I have very far to go. At this point, however, like Professor Bergen, I can say I have found nothing inconsistent. For example, there is the characteristic chromium yellow that Van Gogh so often used and it seems to have aged—shifted color—as it would have."

Weston wanted a further explanation of this, which Crespi provided. Crespi also commented on the blues that Van Gogh had available to him. While Crespi was going through the chemistry with Weston, Esther thought of the flake of yellow she had removed from the self-portrait in Toorn's apartment. If Crespi could match their composition to that of the Van Gogh, it should prove the Van Gogh was forged by Toorn.

"This is looking very good, indeed," said Weston.

"Let me reiterate that this is only a preliminary report," said Joliette.

"But the wind seems to be blowing in only one direction," said Henson.

"I can tell you this," said Laura Iarrera. "I believe the painting to have spent some time in southern Europe."

"Arles!" said Minsky.

"Well, I cannot be that specific," she said. "Are you aware that the European Pollen Database is located in Arles? It is a strange coincidence, is it not?"

She glanced around the table. No one reacted.

"In any case," she said, "the pollen of *Olea europaea* was plentiful in most of the cracks I sampled. This is the olive tree, which is a native of Asia Minor but which is so often depicted in Van Gogh's paintings. There is also pollen from species of the *Cupressaceae*, or true cypresses, which prefer benign climates."

"How many times Van Gogh painted cypresses!" said Joliette.

"Well, the cypress is widespread, but it is an indicator. There is also *Lolium perenne*, ryegrass, which is the most common species in Europe but is also grown in the United States. Some of the pollens are American, and I am not as instantly familiar with them; however, since the painting was found in Chicago, one would expect that, and I shall make a detailed list after I consult with my American colleagues to be certain. One would also expect the pollens of the Low Countries, if the painting were taken from Holland, and this has proven true. What is significant to us are the pollens characteristic of southern Europe. Furthermore, I believe I have discovered some pollen that was imbedded in the paint, as it dried."

"This is very compelling evidence," said Weston. Henson thought he could see the dollar signs in his eyes.

"But recall," said Joliette, "oil does not dry completely for some time."

"Soon enough," said Crespi.

"Ah," said Joliette, standing, "Professor Baleara! Join us!"

Everyone turned to see the white-haired Spaniard coming in the door with large manila envelopes and a couple of rolled papers bristling from under his arms in odd directions. "Good afternoon," he said with a slight bow. He dropped one of his envelopes, and Henson picked it up for him.

"I have brought prints," said Baleara.

"That wasn't necessary," said Joliette. "We are merely providing an update—"

"But yes it is," said Baleara. "I have found something interesting." He began removing one of the prints from its envelope. "This is the infrared." He set it aside. "But here, the latest technology, the digital radiograph developed"—he nodded in Crespi's direction—"at the University of Bologna."

"You discovered something in the X-rays?" asked Joliette.

"Yes," said Baleara. "Very interesting." He found the one he wanted and laid it on the table. It began to curl itself up so he anchored one end with Bergen's coffee cup. Everyone craned toward it, most of them except Minsky rising from their chairs. "At first I thought the equipment was defective, but the photograph will confirm the digital image, I am certain."

"Underpainting?" asked Crespi.

"Now, then, correct me if I am wrong," said Baleara, "but Van Gogh suffered from a kind of mania at times. He would work frantically in periods, producing canvas after canvas."

"It was akin to hypergraphia," said Joliette.

"He once," said Iarrera, "filled the yellow house at Arles with paintings for when Gauguin would arrive."

"Exactly. So that one does not expect the kind or amount of underpainting which is characteristic of the old masters. We expect spontaneous alterations, over paint that is still wet, so that the underpainting doesn't properly set up. It isn't truly underpainting at all. Now," said Baleara, "look at this area."

"It looks like a sonogram to me," said Weston. "Where's the baby?"

"This is a print from a digital X-ray," said Baleara, not getting the joke. "Do you see there? And there?"

"It's a hand," said Henson.

"You see how it is different?" asked Baleara.

"Yes!" said Joliette. "He overpainted the original hand."

Baleara looked at the confused faces of Esther, Henson, and the attorneys. He unrolled a large photograph of the portrait in natural light. It had been gridded in centimeter squares. "Down here," he said. "This area." He circled the upturned hand with his finger.

"I see," said Esther. "Originally, the hand was flat against his belly."

"Exactly," said Baleara.

"Then he painted it over," said Henson, "turned up."

"I don't get it," said Weston. "What does it mean?"

"Nowhere else in the painting is there any substantial difference between what is beneath and what we see, almost as if it were painted without a single correction," said Baleara. "Why?"

"A hand signal?" said Weston. "He was a member of the Dutch Crips. What are you saying?"

"The usual reason is that the painter is not satisfied with the original result."

"Perhaps it was a question of additional meaning for him,"

said Joliette. "The overpainting might have a special symbolism, related to his interest in Buddhism."

"So this is a Buddhist hand gesture?" said Weston. "You're saying Van Gogh was interested in that?"

"Hand, schmand," said Minsky.

"But this," said Weston, "would be further proof it is genuine, then."

Baleara shrugged. "I don't know. But it is very interesting. You see, with his use of impasto, he would have had to scrape the painted surface to change it. Otherwise the underimage would interfere with the overpainting. But for us to recover the image, it would have had to have been scraped off when the paint had dried for some time."

"Did he go back to his paintings?" Crespi asked Joliette.

"I don't think so," said Joliette. "We'll have to ask Luits to research that point, but I'm reasonably certain he didn't. He painted when he was moved and stopped when he was finished. That is my understanding. Like Mozart, he didn't have much time for introspection."

"But what does this mean?" demanded Weston in exasperation. The experts looked at him and shrugged.

"It means the painting was changed," said Joliette. "It is an intriguing detail the scholars will have to assess."

All at once, the detail of the hand hit Esther like a slap. "It's not the De Groot," she said.

"What?" asked Weston.

"But this has no bearing—" Baleara began.

"Yes, it does," she insisted. "Look at the photograph." She pointed to the area of the hand.

"So?" asked Minsky.

"Now look at the X-ray."

"It was painted over, *señora*," said Baleara, "as I pointed out."

Esther looked at Henson. "Do you see?"

"It was changed?" He could not grasp her point.

"But when?"

Weston spread his hands. "I think an explanation is in order, Miss Goren."

"Martin," she said, "do you have the commemorative book from the De Groot?"

"It's in the hotel," he said. He squinted at the painting and back at her. He did it again.

"Two buttons," she explained.

"Buttons?" said Henson. He looked at the puzzled faces around the table. "There was a yearbook done for the De Groot school and museum. Miss Goren is referring to a drawing of the Van Gogh that was in the book."

"Drawing?" said Weston.

"Yes," said Henson. "They did not photograph the painting, maybe because of the expense."

"Perhaps they were afraid of the flash light," said Baleara, "on the camera."

"The flashbulbs," said Joliette.

"Or powder," said Baleara.

"The point is," said Esther, "that the drawing shows two buttons. The hand is positioned between the buttons in the drawing. In this painting, there is only the button beneath the hand."

"But the X-ray of the underpainting," said Crespi, "has two buttons."

"Exactly," said Esther. "The painting in the De Groot museum had two buttons, or Toorn wouldn't have drawn it that way."

"It was kind of sketchy," said Henson doubtfully. "It could just have been a mistake."

"What kind of mistake?" said Joliette.

"It was intended to represent the painting," said Henson,

"to get people to come see it. It might not have been intended to be accurate. It was a sketch."

"Do you really believe Toorn would have been that casual?" asked Esther.

"I'm just saying," said Henson.

Weston said, "We'll ask him."

"When we find him," said Joliette.

"I would say, however," said Weston, "that this is a clear indicator that the painting found in Chicago could not be the painting which hung in the De Groot. This 'one-button' painting must be my client's."

"I don't know if a sketch really proves that," said Joliette, "merely because it differs in a detail that might have been inadvertent."

"Toorn," said Esther, "also did a self-portrait of himself. It imitated the Van Gogh. The hand is positioned as it is in the underpainting. Two buttons."

"That might be suggestive as well," said Crespi, his eyes twinkling, "but it is not proof. Paint is proof. Suppose I test that area? Suppose that area is much more recently done?"

"So the overpainting was an attempt to disguise the painting?" asked Baleara. "I do not think you will discover this. I looked at the area very closely."

"But it could still be," said Crespi. "Say the 'disguise' was put on in the nineteen forties. It would appear old now."

"But more inconsistent, don't you think?"

"Do the tests," said Henson.

"And while you're at it," said Esther, "test this as well." She handed Crespi the tissue with the paint flake she had scratched from Toorn's self-portrait.

He unfolded the tissue. "What is this?" asked Crespi. "It looks like chromium yellow."

"Just check if it matches up to the yellow on the Van Gogh. I'll explain later."

Henson looked at her curiously but didn't ask. Crespi shrugged. "As you ask," he said.

Weston had leaned close to his client and whispered.

"Button, schmutton!" shouted Minsky. "Who's got the button? The painting is the one that hung on my uncle's wall, I don't care what was painted on top of what. This is what I saw."

"So the painting must be yours," said Weston, patting the old man's forearm. "It cannot be the De Groot portrait. It burned, just as was originally supposed."

"I must say," said Dr. Iarrera, "that based on the pollen, this painting clearly spent some time in northern Europe."

"Perhaps in transit to America," said Bergen.

"Perhaps," she said, "but the pollen was not difficult to find."

"You should see specifically if there are any pollens imbedded in the overpaint," said Baleara. "That might tell you where the paint was wet, eh?"

"*Bene,*" said Iarrera. "Might we not get back to work?"

"By all means!" said Joliette.

"This was what hung on my uncle Feodor's wall," said Minsky. "Work all you want!"

"We shall want those drawings secured," said one of Minsky's Dutch attorneys.

"Immediately!" said Weston.

Henson assured them the commemorative book would be under lock and key within the hour. "It should be easy to make reliable photocopies," he added, "so everyone concerned can take a look."

Henson cocked his head to draw Esther into the corner.

"I think we've proved it is Minsky's," said Esther, "and I'm glad for the man."

"Maybe," said Henson. "It depends when the hand was redone. We'll see what the tests prove." He watched the others to avoid being overheard. "Are you thinking what I'm thinking?"

"That Meyerbeer must have taken it?"

"No," he said. "Toorn. Think about it."

Suddenly she knew what he meant and they nodded at each other. "If Toorn was so familiar with the De Groot portrait," she said, "why did he identify this one as the De Groot?"

"You got it," said Henson. "He is not some guy who glanced at it in passing through the museum. When he saw this painting in the Palmer House, he nearly passed out."

"As if he didn't know it still existed. As if he thought it had been destroyed."

"That could have been a genuine reaction, but why identify it when there is a risk, a very strong chance that he will be proven wrong?"

"Could he have done the overpainting? Why? In order to disguise it? What can he get from doing that? Poor Mr. Minsky! If the paint in that self-portrait of Toorn is a match for Meyer's Van Gogh, it should prove Toorn is a master forger."

"Whatever," said Henson. "I think we need to find the son of a bitch and ask him some tough questions, don't you?"

"My, Martin Henson is getting testy!"

"I guarantee you," he said, "you ain't seen nothin' yet. Come on!"

# SIXTEEN

# Mevrouw Toorn

Esther and Henson swung by Toorn's pied-à-terre in the off chance he might have returned to it. No one appeared to have entered Toorn's Amsterdam apartment since she had first seen the painting, but it was further evidence that Toorn had known he was misidentifying the Chicago Van Gogh as the De Groot Van Gogh, so they took Toorn's self-portrait from the wall of his bedroom and secured it in the trunk. Firebombs and disappearances had been a little too frequent in the last month. She and Henson then set out to visit Toorn's country home, the former De Groot estate near Beekberg. Esther drove while Henson used his cell phone to check with the Dutch police and Interpol.

The man known as Manfred Stock or Gerhart Brewer had not been located despite an international APB. So far as the authorities could tell, he had not left the European Union under those names, but who would believe he didn't have a dozen other names and the passports to go with them? A convenient bottle of hair dye could be plucked off the shelves of shops anywhere. The local police had gone by Toorn's country home the previous afternoon, but they reported that the housekeeper living there said she had no idea where he was. Henson asked his contact with Interpol to look up the legal records concerning Toorn's collaboration trial back in 1947 and get copies. After hanging up, he mused that maybe the old man Anton Houdelijk or someone else could identify Stock or shed more light on the button controversy.

As Esther drove, her mind was on her mother. It made her sick to think that Samuel Meyer might have been Stéphane Meyerbeer, but the shock would have been ten times worse for a woman who had been through the camps, tortured by her jailers, then violated repeatedly by the troops that were sup-posed to be her rescuers. Perhaps the Alzheimer's was the result of all that evil, trapped in her memory, a poison that weakened you so that oblivion was the only antidote. Esther had told herself she was going along with this investigation for her mother's sake, but she knew that her mother could never know or appreciate whatever justice might be exacted, whatever truth might be revealed. No, she could finally admit that she was doing this for herself, but that she might have to go back to living without an answer. Her mother could have told her the answer, but would never speak again. The Van Gogh self-portrait could tell her the answer, but, even with all those experts, it wasn't easy to make it speak. In the end, she had to admit, she might have more questions than when she had begun.

After getting directions from the town hall, she and Henson wound down a country lane flanked by deep ditches. It was narrow enough that two Fiats would have trouble passing each other. They had just passed a cluster of trees when the road swung left and Esther said, "There!"

The land dropped down to a small river and a stone bridge. On the rise on the other side stood a sturdy three-story stone mansion. It was squat and solid in the manner of a nineteenth-century post office or library. The grounds were grassy and pretty much untamed, except for a small area surrounding the building. Esther pulled over at some distance so they could study the place.

"What do you think?" said Henson. He rolled down the window. The fecund smell of the damp grasses filled the car.

"The House of Usher," said Esther. "That's it, though. It has the same arches over the windows that the convent school had in the commemorative photograph."

"The school site is farther down the road," said Henson. "I don't hear a dog. Do you see one?"

"It's worse. There are geese." She pointed to the gaggle. It was scattered over the lawn, searching the grass for anything edible.

"Darn," said Henson. Geese were much harder to deal with than dogs. Sneaking by a watchdog was often easy compared to geese. The honking racket they started would wake a frozen mammoth.

"Someone just passed the first-floor window over there."

"I saw it."

"The housekeeper the police mentioned: does she live there with Mrs. Toorm?"

"I assume so from what they said. Mrs. Toorm is pretty old."

"I can still handle it," said Esther. "I just won't be able to search as thoroughly."

"Nah," said Henson. "We've broken enough Dutch laws. All I need—"

"I thought that's why you want me on your team. Trust me, I can get in there and take the old woman's hearing aid out of her ear, if she's got one, and she won't know until morning."

"Sometimes it's better to go straight at them."

"How American," she said.

"Drive up to the front door."

"How naive."

He grinned. "Just follow my lead, Miss Goren."

As soon as the car crossed the bridge, the geese came running and honking. An elderly woman appeared in the first-floor window, then stepped through the front door. She was wearing an apron stained with something orange. The geese honked and watched suspiciously, raising their beaks, sniffing the air as if they expected someone to throw bread. Henson was surprised by their size. The bigger ones could have pecked at his tie knot.

"Hello, ma'am," he said, "I'm Martin Henson, and this is Esther and—excuse me, do you speak English?"

"Yes," said the woman.

"We have an appointment with Dr. Toorn and Mrs. Toorn."

"Professor Doctor Toorn is not here," said the woman curtly.

Henson looked at Esther as if confused. "But I don't understand. He was supposed to meet us here, with Mrs. Toorn."

"Mevrouw Toorn does not receive guests."

"We've come so far! I don't know what the mix-up could be. Would it be possible to speak to Mrs. Toorn?"

The housekeeper emphasized each syllable. "*Mevrouw Toorn does not receive guests.*"

"Is there some way to reach Dr. Toorn then?" The woman

began to shake her head, but Henson continued pressing. "You see, I am Mr. Henson from the United States, and we entered into discussion with Dr. Toorn about our foundation leasing the building and grounds to establish a European campus for the University of the Higher Arts. Dr. Toorn was going to give us a tour of the buildings before we had to return to the airport—"

"I know nothing of this," said the woman.

"But surely someone must know how to contact Dr. Toorn? Suppose his wife were to take ill?"

"She *is* ill," said the woman. "She is very old."

"Exactly."

"I'm sorry," said the woman. "I cannot help you."

Esther stepped forward before she closed the door. "Would it be too much trouble if we looked around? If the building is not suitable to our needs, then we won't have to waste Dr. Toorn's time, and we really must be getting back to the United States."

"I'm sure Dr. Toorn would be very grateful," said Henson. "We would certainly be grateful."

The woman eyed them. "When Mevrouw Toorn was healthy, she used to open the gardens to tourists sometimes. She asked for about"—she pursed her lips—"five euros?"

Henson held out a twenty. "Will this do?" The housekeeper glanced behind them and took the money.

"There is nothing to steal," she said, walking away. "See for yourself. But do not disturb Mevrouw Toorn."

They entered a huge open foyer, dimly lit by false-candle sconces. The woodwork was dark, and the furniture looked as if it had been old when the house was built. The moist, oppressive air in the building showed even more unfamiliarity with fresh air than most Dutch buildings.

"Thank—" said Esther, but the woman was already gone.

"Okay," whispered Henson, pointing to a staircase. "I'll go up and you check down. Look for anything that might tell us where Toorn is."

"Hurry," said Esther.

Henson climbed the stairs, while Esther stepped into a parlor that reeked of old smoke. The chair by the fireplace looked Spanish and very old and might have been worth something, but otherwise the room was rather spartan. There were decanters in a cagelike cabinet. A bookcase of leather-bound editions. The painting over the fireplace was Rembrandt—dark from being just above the fireplace and never having been cleaned. The cheerful day scene had aged into what looked like an obscure night scene: two country gentlemen walked down a lane, talking and gesturing with long clay pipes. A reaper watched them.

Esther glanced in a hazy mirror to see if the housekeeper might still be behind her, then opened a few drawers. Odds and ends. Paper clips. Boarding passes from a dozen flights, most of them a year old or more. A receipt for a case of Sauternes. A notebook with sloppy handwriting. Was it Toorn's? There were dates and times. She thought she read the name "Samuel Meyer," but when she tilted the notebook to better catch the light, it said "Schiphol," the name of the Amsterdam airport. Several telephone numbers filled the next page, but they meant nothing to her.

She moved into the next room, which was larger, as if it had been a ballroom, but it hadn't been used for years. The chairs along the walls were covered with sheets: a neat cadre of ghosts. At the far end was a set of French doors. They didn't look as if they belonged in the building, but the glass was very clean. As Esther strolled closer, her heels clacking on the tiled floor, she saw roses outside, a wrought-iron filigreed table, and a turbaned woman in a wheelchair.

As quietly as possible, she went outside.

The woman's turban was silk, and the sunlight played on the folds as her head swayed barely, as if catching an invisible breeze. Her gaunt hands moved over the ironwork in front of her, feeling the intricate swirls.

"Gretchen?" she said in a reedy voice. When she turned her head her eyes were moist and blank and white. "Gretchen?"

"Mevrouw Toorm?" asked Esther.

"*Oui,*" said the woman. "*Qui est là?*"

Esther momentarily thought to ask her if she spoke English, but decided to continue in French. She was relieved that the woman hadn't begun in Dutch. "Pardon," she said in French, "I did not intend to disturb you. I saw your lovely garden and was drawn to it."

The woman listened and did not answer.

Esther thought of her mother, but there was, despite the blindness, more life in this woman's eyes than in her mother's. "I am an acquaintance of Dr. Toorn's," she said.

The old woman dropped her chin slightly and made a noise like "boof." "*Le Professeur Docteur Gerrit Willem Toorn! Ha!*"

"Yes," said Esther.

"Airs! Such airs!"

"Dr. Toorn?"

"He's no more a doctor than a cabbage."

"No?"

"He married me for my money. He was no lover and I am no fool. There weren't many men who could keep the Germans from sniffing around."

"Your husband could keep the Germans away?"

"I knew what they wanted. You couldn't refuse. They took this house, Papa's house."

"Was Dr. Toorn an important Nazi?" asked Esther.

"You can hear the screams at night. The blood cannot be washed away."

"Are you saying that Dr. Toorn was involved in torture?"

The woman's head froze. "Torture? Doctor? Who is that? We cheated them. The fat pig Göring himself!"

Esther bit her lip and knelt beside the woman, fighting to keep a clear head as memories of her mother flooded back. She swallowed hard and said hoarsely, "Gerrit, your husband, he sold paintings to the Germans?"

"The roses," said the woman, "do they smell of the dead?" She inhaled. "We return to the soil. The dead rise through the roots and stalks and emerge in the scent of the blossoms."

"That is very poetic, Mevrouw Toorn. Do you remember the De Groot Van Gogh?" asked Esther patiently.

Mrs. Toorn sat silent, her head gently swaying.

"The Van Gogh that hung in the Beekberg museum."

The gravel on the walkway by the house crunched. The housekeeper angrily strode toward them, but Esther raised a finger to her lips.

"She's asleep," said Esther.

The housekeeper looked at Mrs. Toorn, then at Esther. "You should not have disturbed her."

"I came out to the garden. I complimented her on it."

"I think you and your husband should leave," said the housekeeper. "What if she should tell Dr. Toorn?"

"I'm certain he pays a great deal of attention to what she says." Esther walked past the housekeeper, back through the French doors, and into the ballroom.

She looked through several small rooms in the back of the

house, finding nothing interesting except a painting studio in which the brushes and tubes of paint were all dry. Rolls of old canvas stood in the corner in a wooden box in which mice had nibbled a hole. The only stretched canvas in the room was on a dusty easel. It had been in the process of being undercoated with white when the room was abandoned to spiders and mice. The large gothic windows hadn't been washed for years. By contrast, in the old-fashioned kitchen every shiny surface sparkled, and the pans, knives, and ceramic canisters were all neatly arranged.

"You could operate in here," said a voice.

Esther spun around to face Martin. "Don't sneak up on me!" she said firmly.

"I'm sorry," he said.

"I could . . . I could overreact."

"That could be unhealthy," said Henson. "For me."

"I talked to Mrs. Toorn," Esther whispered.

Henson glanced to see if the housekeeper was near. "Did you see the Great Toorn's study?"

"I didn't go upstairs."

"It's under the staircase."

"Under?"

"Come on." He took her elbow and led her to the foyer. At the back, under the landing of the stairs was a heavy door with an ornate knob. He quickly stepped in, pulled Esther, and closed the door behind them. A large table, slanted like an architect's, held several oversize books.

"How could I have missed the door?" said Esther. "Is there anything in here that helps?" She moved toward the bookcase covering the wall to the ceiling. Art books as tall as a meter and more filled it. Several were leather-bound. Some had Cyrillic or Greek lettering. "Quite a collection," she said.

"There is a volume of Van Gogh's letters next to a set of notes," said Henson, "as if Toorn's writing another book. But that isn't what I wanted to show you."

He moved around the desk to another door and reached to the woodwork above, bringing down a skeleton key. "The wine cellar."

"I could use a drink," she said.

"That isn't what's interesting." Henson opened the door to the top of a cast-iron stair. The air was cool but clean smelling, not as it was in the stuffy rooms Esther had explored. She was surprised at how deep the cellar was; in the Netherlands you would expect it to have flooding problems, though the house was on a rise and well inland. The room itself was small, dominated by two giant casks two-and-a-half meters high and as wide as two armwidths. By comparison the wine rack looked tiny. There were only about a hundred to a hundred and fifty bottles.

"They must have built these down here," said Henson. "They couldn't have brought them in." He rapped a stave.

"It sounds empty."

"Toorn probably drank it with lunch one day."

"It's big enough for him to bathe in," Esther said, crossing to the wines. Some of them were very old, but there were several from the 1970s, 1980s, and 1990s.

"This is what I wanted you to see," said Henson. He pointed up at one of the iron balusters. It bulged at the center as it dropped from the rail to the stair. In the center of each bulge was a circle with a swastika. Every baluster had the same decoration.

"The Germans must have put that in when they seized the house," said Henson. "What kind of storage would they need? Ammunition. This was a regional policing center."

"Interrogation," said Esther, staring up and thinking how screams would echo in this tall, tight space. "The wine should turn sour. This was a torture chamber."

The cellar suddenly darkened as the housekeeper filled the door at the top of the stairs. It was the only way out.

# SEVENTEEN

# Road Trouble

"This looks like an excellent place for storage," Henson said happily.

"How did you get in?" said the housekeeper.

"The key was in the lock."

"I don't believe this to be true. You must leave now."

"We don't want to cause any trouble," said Henson. "We've seen all we need, I think."

Henson began climbing up. "This is a remarkable set of stairs," he said.

"Did you notice the swastikas?" said Esther, as if she'd just noticed them.

"The *Schutzstaffel* built it," the housekeeper said. "In the war."

"Too bad about the swastikas," said Henson, stopping directly in front of her.

"The cells were removed, but it is a strong stair. Why get rid of it?"

"Indeed," Henson said.

He studied the cellar space like a prospective buyer trying to imagine his furniture in place, and then, for a moment, Henson and the housekeeper stood eyeball to eyeball.

"Excuse me," he said.

Without expression, she stepped back. Esther and he quickly walked out to the Citroën. The housekeeper followed, then watched them from the front door. Esther rolled down the window. "We will contact Dr. Toorn later," she shouted. "Thank you."

The housekeeper stared until the car reached the bridge.

"Frau Blucher," said Henson, glancing in the rear-view mirror.

"Who?"

"Frau Blucher," he repeated. "You know." He neighed like a horse.

She did not respond.

"You need to get out more. Never mind. What do you think? Another dead end?"

"Toorn and his wife don't exactly make the ideal couple," she said.

"Anything that might suggest where he is?"

"There were several old boarding passes. He does a lot of traveling. Maybe he's in hell with Dr. Mengele."

"He'll get there pretty soon if he isn't already." Henson shifted gears and turned onto the road back to the highway. "All right now," he said. "What did we see? While it's fresh in our minds, what did we see?"

Esther stared at Martin, who was intensely watching the

road. This was a technique she had used in the Mossad: walk through a building casually and then repeat every observed detail as soon as possible. One agent she knew could meticulously sketch a room. Another had a precise sense of measurement: he was rarely ten centimeters wrong about the dimensions of things. Most people, like her, could develop the skill quite a bit after practice, but some rare individuals were astonishing.

She closed her eyes to visualize her trip through the house. She pictured the contents of the drawers, the objects on tables. Gradually she had the feeling something was wrong. It had something to do with the antique chair, the one that looked Spanish. Why? There wasn't anything unusual about it.

"Are you surprised at what's there?" said Henson.

"The apartment!" said Esther. "It isn't what's there. It's what *isn't* there."

"It looked to me like there was a lot of junk in the house. The apartment was pretty spare."

"That's exactly it," said Esther. "In that apartment in Amsterdam there were several expensive items. The Eames chair. The Chinese cabinet. The modernist painting."

"Maybe he stays there more and leaves his wife to rot."

"But think about it," she insisted. "He's an art historian. He's one of the world's great Van Gogh experts. What sign of it is there in his house?"

"His books. But you're right. Why would a person of that sensibility not have a single piece of significant art in his house?"

"Unless there was something valuable about that old pastoral painting over the fireplace."

"It looked like motel art to me."

"Me, too."

Henson drummed his fingers on the steering wheel. "He could be worried about theft. He could have stuff in vault storage."

"Maybe he's broke. Maintaining his wife's health. Just taking care of that property and an apartment in Amsterdam."

"Crap!" said Henson suddenly. "He's on the run. That's what it is. Maybe there were a few valuable pieces and he's run off with them."

"To Chile, maybe. Wasn't Manfred Stock's passport from Chile?"

"It's a place to start." Henson pointed to a small turnout beside the road. "I'll call Interpol. We'll see if we can find him on a flight to South America since he disappeared."

"Can we find out if he has secure storage someplace?"

"The Dutch police would know how to handle it," said Henson. The car leaned steeply as it came to a stop. Henson began to punch numbers into his cell phone. Esther stared out over the green field.

Her father was still the key, she was thinking. Meyer had to be Meyerbeer. He had looted art for the Nazis in Vichy. Toorn was a collaborator. They might have made a connection during the occupation, but it wasn't necessary. Meyerbeer somehow got possession of Minsky's Van Gogh and absconded with it to America, where he became Samuel Meyer. Maybe Toorn was afraid Meyer could identify him so he sent Stock to silence him. Maybe the painting from Meyer's house was a fake Toorn had made—the experts had not definitely pronounced it a Van Gogh, though they seemed close to it. But then why would Toorn declare it genuine? If Stock worked for Toorn, he went to Chicago to get the painting, but Esther was certain that Toorn was genuinely shocked when he saw the painting from her father's attic. She rubbed her temples. All this was dizzying.

"Yes," Henson was saying into the phone. "He would have to have traveled first class—he couldn't fit in an economy seat. Well, yes, I suppose he could have bought two seats. Uh-huh. If that doesn't work, try charter companies. Latin America anywhere, but especially Chile. Right."

Esther noticed a truck hurtling down the narrow road toward them, a European-size moving truck with the Mercedes symbol gleaming large on the radiator. Henson glanced up at it as it roared past, shaking their car.

Esther snapped her head around as it barreled and almost screamed. "Quick! Get off the phone! Now!"

The truck's tires ground into the gravel as it screeched to a stop.

"It's Stock!" she shouted.

Henson looked back over his shoulder as they heard the gears grind in the truck and the beep, beep of the backing warning began. "We need help here! Backup! Stock!"

Henson fumbled for the keys to restart the Citroën.

"Hurry!" The truck was gaining speed, wobbling slightly on the narrow road. They had no weapon, Esther knew, but Stock had always been armed.

The Citroën came to life and Henson slapped it into gear, but the truck was already on them. As the car's tires flung gravel and lurched into the road, the corner of the truck crunched into the rear quarter panel, shoving the car nearly perpendicular to the road. The big rear door of the truck blocked Henson and Esther's view and it seemed as if it were a giant aluminum bludgeon about to crush them.

Henson turned the steering wheel as far to the right as he could and accelerated. The smoke of the truck's and the car's tires swirled around them, but neither vehicle's tires could get purchase on the gravel and soil. The truck shifted gears, pulling forward. Esther vainly clutched at the door latch, not sure where it was, not sure she could get the door open in time. Henson shifted forward and back, rocking the car, but it was stuck in the same position across the road when the truck reversed and began to accelerate backward.

The car's rear tires caught as the truck closed in. The Citroën leaped several yards forward. It was too sharp a turn to make in one attempt, however, and the front tire on the driver's side slipped off the edge of the road. The car was hanging with its front tire spinning in the air over the irrigation ditch when the truck crashed into the rear. Metal screamed and the car, its engine still roaring, lurched and slid farther over the embankment. Just before it tilted to drop down toward the shallow water, Esther's door gave way and she rolled outward onto the gravel.

The rear of the truck, however, still loomed above her, and by the time she had raised herself to her bloody knees, she had to throw herself flat as the bed passed, barely missing her head.

The truck lurched to a stop. Beyond the differential, she saw a pair of shiny black shoes hit the ground as the driver dropped from the cab. He took a step toward the front, then hesitated and moved toward the back. He wasn't certain whether they were armed or not, she thought. She heard the unmistakable click of a semiautomatic pistol being primed. She slithered like a snake under the truck, feeling the heat of the exhaust system scorch her back.

"*Schnell!*" she heard someone bark. "*Haast!*"

The man was now at the back of the truck. Whoever had shouted had not gotten out. She rolled out on the side away from the ditch and crept close to the ground. When she edged past the rear tire, she could see the back of the man. Stock!

He glanced to see if anyone was coming up the road in either direction, then leveled his pistol and crept up toward the ditch.

Esther slowly raised herself and saw that the car had come to rest on its roof. Even in water only centimeters deep, if Martin was unconscious he could be drowning.

She remembered Yossi Lev had told Martin that unarmed she was usually the equal of any armed man. Flattery will get you dead, she thought, but she had nothing but gravel and grass to use as a weapon.

"Come out!" shouted Stock. "Come out or I will shoot!"

There was no reaction from the overturned car. Stock moved as if he might stick his gun in his belt. That would be the moment, she thought. But instead he switched it to his left hand and fired at the rear of the car.

He was trying to spark the gas tank.

One step, two steps across the gravel, and she launched herself feet first at Stock's back. He heard the movement and had half turned when her kick smashed under his armpit and drove him toppling onto the car. He struck it with a thump and bounced off the back end into the shallow water. It took him a few seconds before he stirred. Stunned, he tried to gather his senses, but he had lost his gun and was fighting to maintain his consciousness as oily, gasoline-coated water swirled around him.

"Martin!" Esther screamed. "Martin!"

She smelled the gas and jumped down the slope. Henson, covered with sparkling fragments of the windows, was pulling himself out of the narrow space between the roof and his side window.

The truck above them began to roar, and she heard the gears engage. "Hurry!" she said, tugging at his elbow. "There are two of them!"

The car creaked then, as if it were going to roll toward him and cut him in half. She planted herself in the slimy ditch and pushed hard to hold it up. Henson's hips emerged, then his legs and a shoeless foot. "Quick!" she said. "Quick!"

She frantically looked toward the truck and saw to her astonishment that it was pulling away, driving down the narrow road back toward the De Groot estate. When Henson was clear, she released her pressure on the car and it rolled only a few more inches before settling. She tugged and dragged him farther into the grasses as he mumbled something incoherent.

"Ha!" said Stock. He was standing unsteadily, coated with mud and oil at the far end of the overturned Citroën, his muddy, dripping pistol aimed at them.

"I won't make the same mistake a third time." He laughed. "Jew bitch!"

Henson's eyes cleared as he gradually understood where he was and the grim situation he was in. Esther searched frantically for any possibility of a weapon as she helped Martin stagger to his feet. Pressing her hand against Henson's chest to steady him, she felt his fountain pen in his jacket pocket. She wished it were a shoulder holster with a large caliber pistol. The field had been thoroughly cleared. The only stones were those used to build the berm, and they were huge. There were no branches. A chunk of the windshield. Some decorative strips from the car. The rear-view mirror. If Stock got close enough, perhaps she could get a handful of mud in his eyes. But he didn't have to get that close to shoot them.

"Everyone," Martin gasped, "is looking for you. You can't get away from everyone."

"I have more friends than you know, Mr. Henson. Many police."

"The best money can buy, I suppose," said Henson.

"At the highest levels," said Stock. "One or two are sympathetic."

"You can't buy my people," said Esther. "They have hunted bastards like you for more than half a century. And when they find you, you will die. I promise you that."

"Perhaps. But I don't think so. Enough of the pleasantries. Where is the list?"

"List?" Esther said.

"Samuel Meyer's list."

"My father had a list?" *So this is what it was all about,* she thought.

"Come, come. You force me to clichés. You can die in great agony, or you can die quickly." Stock grinned, enjoying his power, amused at his role as the killer. "It is your choice."

"We don't know anything about a list," said Henson. "What list?"

"He told her. That was why she was there."

"I was there to see my father," said Esther. "He was dying."

"And you will be dying soon. After your friend here."

"That's all right," said Henson. "If he fires, he'll blow his hand off. Let's get out of here." He took Esther's elbow and slowly turned her, as if he were guiding her to climb up to the road.

Stock's eyes widened as he straightened his aim. "You think a little water will jam it?" he said with a sneer.

Esther froze.

With a droll arch of his eyebrow, Henson pointed at Stock. "Mud in the barrel," he said.

Stock blinked, then slowly pulled back the pistol trying to keep an eye on his prisoners while seeing if Henson had lied. In that split second of his confusion, Henson bent down and snatched up a section of windshield, flinging it like a huge playing card. Henson and Esther dove in opposite directions. Stock ducked as the glass flopped harmless against the rear bumper, showering him with glittering pellets. In reflex he fired in Henson's direction, but in the split second that he swung the pistol toward Esther for a second shot, the gas tank in front of him exploded.

Blown backward, Stock splashed into the shallow water as orange flame spread across its surface. At the other end of the car, Esther churned mud to get farther away from the fire. When she stopped, she saw the pillar of black smoke curling and twisting high into the sky. The stench of the burning tires and the blasts of heat dizzied her, but she stared through watery eyes into the high grass trying to locate Henson.

"Martin! Martin!"

As she hoisted herself to the roadbed for a clearer view, she couldn't see the truck anywhere. But the smoke still confounded her when she tried to locate Henson. She grew more frantic trying to see through it, running from side to side until she decided to drop down on the opposite side of the road. She ran through the parallel ditch, around the burning car and clambered up to look past the rear. The smoke pursued her momentarily, and the view was even more obscure until a slight shift of the breeze, like a hand drawing back a black scrim, revealed Stock.

He was on his feet, covered with mud, his hair, jacket and shoulders smoking, lurching away from her like a Frankenstein monster. His pistol was extended out in front of him.

Martin Henson was moving on hands and knees, trying to avoid Stock's unsteady aim.

"Martin!" she screamed, scooping up a handful of gravel and flinging it with all the force she could muster. Only a few of the pellets struck Stock's back, but they got his attention.

He turned and she saw his face was burned and blackened. One eye was swollen shut. When he saw her, he smiled. There was blood on his teeth. She dropped prone on the road as the pistol cracked. She shimmied backward to drop behind the berm, but another shot kept her low, not moving quickly enough.

She heard a weird, wet scream—*Martin?*—and rolled off the road. She heard the sounds of a struggle and raised her head to see Henson riding Stock's back. The killer flailed and reared back, trying to get him off. He fired his gun over Henson's head, but Henson held on. He lifted his hand like a bronco rider, then brought it down hard into Stock's neck. When he pulled it back, blood spurted from Stock's carotid artery. Henson stabbed again and then again as Stock continued to struggle. Esther ran toward them and leaped into the ditch. Stock, still flailing to get Henson off his back, lurched backward, shuddered, and fell on him.

Esther dropped with both knees on his forearm and seized the pistol. Stock, however, had ceased to struggle. Henson's fountain pen was half buried in his gory neck.

Henson's eyes rolled and he groaned. Esther slipped the pistol into her belt and gripped Stock's shoulder with both hands. As she turned him off Henson, Stock exhaled, blood bubbling from his mouth and the holes in his neck.

Henson sat up, looked momentarily startled, then registered Esther in front of him. She held his face in her hands and watched his pupils widen and tighten as his consciousness stabilized. "Are you okay? Are you okay? You saved our lives."

He tried to look behind her.

"Stock's dead," she said. "I've got the pistol."

"Thanks for the tip." He coughed.

"Tip?"

"You patted the pen. In my pocket."

"That was all your doing, bubeleh. You saved our lives."

He blinked. "With a lot of help, lady." He groaned as she helped him to his feet. "Are you okay?" he asked her.

"Scraped, battered, and nearly fried," she said. "That was Toorn in the truck with him."

"I know," said Henson, pouring mud out of the shoe he fished out of the water. "Where are the cell phones?" he asked, tugging his shoe back on with a grimace. "We should call the Dutch police."

"In the car. Or the water. Who knows? I'm in the mood to get the bastard myself."

Henson didn't answer. He was looking down at Stock's neck. "My Montblanc."

"You can get those anywhere. I'll buy you a dozen if we get Toorn."

"My wife gave it to me," he said.

"Oh," she said. "Maybe we could—"

"Never mind," said Henson, snapping out of his reverie. "How many bullets are left in the clip?"

# EIGHTEEN

# The Collection

Toorn might have simply driven away, but the highway was in the opposite direction. He must have had the truck for a reason, and maybe it was to remove something from his house. Esther and Henson began supporting each other, limping as quickly as they could down the raised road, their wet shoes squishing in a syncopated rhythm. Their lungs ached. They knew that by the time they got to the estate Toorn could be long gone, his secrets safe forever. After a while they warmed up from their drenching in the cold water, and their stiff muscles grudgingly loosened. They also knew that they could be hobbling along as fast as they could into even more trouble. Manfred Stock might not be the only handyman in Toorn's employ.

After they'd gone about a mile down the road, the roof of the estate house became visible in the distance.

"What do you say we cut around through the trees and come up on the back?" said Henson, breathing hard.

"It will take longer. He'll know we're coming, regardless."

"He'll be expecting Stock, not us. I would."

"The woods would get us closer to the house and not give him a shot as soon, but he could simply escape out the front."

They lunged into the field.

"He could drive right past us," Henson said, splashing through a puddle.

"I'd put a bullet between his eyes."

"Dead men tell no tales," said Henson.

"You're right. That can't happen," said Esther. "We need answers."

They huffed across the field, watching for any motion in the direction of the house, but when the ground dropped even the roof disappeared. When they reached the line of trees, Henson grabbed a thick trunk, took several breaths, and then started toward the tall green wall of a neglected hedgerow just beyond. This area must have been a part of the estate once, or maybe it was where the school had stood. The trees stood at regular intervals and an old roadbed was visible in the brush. The hedgerow was so overgrown, it seemed impenetrable.

"What now?" Henson asked.

"Follow the old road," said Esther.

They went along the overgrown road in the direction of the house, and it turned into a narrow lane between two old hedgerows. The passageway was a bit claustrophobic, considering what they had been through, like being in a subway tunnel that might surprise them with an onrushing train from either direction. On the other hand, the delicate ferns and clusters of toadstools indicated that no one had been in the lane for some time.

"Bingo," Henson whispered, pointing to an opening in the hedgerow to their left. There had been an arch in the hedge that was now overgrown. Within the arch was a small iron gate well wrapped in spider webs and voracious weeds. Esther looked through and saw a long lawn enclosed by a semi-oval hedge wall. Within the area confined by the hedge were evenly spaced trees and a gravel walkway that had almost faded into the ground. Pedestals placed at regular intervals once would have been graced by statues—nymphs, gods hunting, Artemis, Flora—where the gentleman stroller could pause and contemplate his life or say something sprightly to his lady.

But that way of life was long gone. It had ended for certain when the SS had taken over the house.

"There's the garden enclosure," Esther said, pointing to the far end of the lawn.

"The windows are blocked by the trees," said Henson.

"From here," said Esther.

The gate hinges were frozen. Esther and Henson sprinted awkwardly from tree to tree, pausing behind each to see if their motion had caused any reaction. They neither heard nor saw anything suspicious. Time stretched and slowed until they flattened themselves against the brick wall.

"What now?" said Henson. "Do we try the door?" They had seen at the corner a heavy door studded with nails.

"I say up and over."

Henson looked up. It was about nine feet. "Can we?"

"I don't want to see if someone's waiting behind the door."

Henson nodded and laced his fingers to form a step with his hands, bracing himself to lift her.

"Learn that in the Boy Scouts?" said Esther.

He gave her a confused, then exasperated look.

"It's okay," she said. "It works."

She placed her muddy foot in the cradle formed by his hands and popped up to get a visual snapshot. Dropping back down, she said, "This is good." She then launched herself up, gripped the pitched bricks at the top of the wall and pulled herself up to lie flat on them.

"Come on," she said, stretching her arm out to him. Her hand clamped on his like a steel claw plucking up a junker. Almost instantly, Henson was lying across the wall as Esther dropped down and lifted Stock's pistol. Henson kicked his legs over and dropped down beside her, crumpling in a ball.

She glanced to see if he was okay. He nodded.

They had come down behind an ivy-covered trellis. There were five of them placed along the wall with urns on pedestals in front of them. Esther recognized that she and Henson were on the side of the conservatory. There were no doors into the house from this garden, just a grated iron door leading out to the rose garden. They had dropped right into a corner and couldn't be sure they hadn't been seen by someone inside the conservatory or behind the upper-story windows. They moved swiftly from trellis to trellis, then flattened themselves against the bricks on each side of the iron door.

A quick glance revealed Mrs. Toorn, her back to them, standing in front of her wheelchair. Beyond her, beyond the roses and the fields was the tower of black smoke from the burning Citroën. Esther tilted her head, and Henson lifted the iron latch. The door creaked open. They took another glance, then crossed the open patio to the old woman.

She did not acknowledge their presence on either side of her. Her pale eyes were fixed on the column of smoke.

"Mevrouw Toorn," said Esther gently.

"*Hij brandt,*" she said.

"*Pardon?*" said Esther in French, touching the old woman's elbow. Mrs. Toorn was trembling from the effort of standing.

Henson looked at Esther for an explanation.

Mrs. Toorn turned her head toward Esther. There was fear in her eyes, the same kind of fear that appeared in Rosa Goren's eyes when disconnected scraps of the past came back to her.

"*Hij brandt,*" she repeated, wobbling.

"I think it means 'he burns,'" said Esther, her unblinking gaze never shifting from Mrs. Toorn's. She handed Henson the pistol and gingerly took the older woman's arms. "*Asseyez-vous, madame. Calmez-vous. Tout c'est bien. Asseyez-vous.*"

Mrs. Toorn nodded and took her suggestion. She lowered her eyes as she settled into the wheelchair; then she looked up as if suddenly remembering the fire and stared at it. "*Manfred brandt. Meyer brandt.*"

"Meyer?" said Henson. "Meyerbeer?"

"'Manfred burns. Meyer burns,'" Esther translated.

There was a squeak, and Martin spun to see the housekeeper rushing at them.

"What are you doing? Why do you pester her? You are trespassing—" She saw the gun in his hand. She stopped in her tracks and raised her apron to her mouth.

"We are not here to hurt anyone," said Henson, holding the pistol sideways in his palm. "Where is Dr. Toorn?"

"In Amsterdam."

"No, he was here. Is the truck still here?"

"Truck?"

"He didn't come here," said Henson as much to himself as Esther. "That caps it."

"I go for the eggs," said the housekeeper, pointing toward

the rear. "I am only gone ten minutes. Fifteen, maybe."

Mrs. Toorn began speaking in Dutch. Her diction was a bit vague, but her speech did not sound incoherent. "Manfred" came out several times. Esther was struggling to understand her from her knowledge of German and Yiddish.

"Something about the burning, I think," she said.

"Come here," said Henson to the housekeeper. "Do you understand what Mevrouw Toorn is saying?"

The housekeeper did not move, still suspicious. Henson grabbed her by the arm and pulled her closer. "We are not here to hurt you. Or Mrs. Toorn."

The housekeeper listened. "She is saying that Willem weeps over the paintings, but she must weep in private."

"What does she mean by that?"

"She has spoken of SS Colonel Stock," said the housekeeper. "He was very kind to her, but he was burned, too. That is why she would cry."

"When you say 'kind,' you mean they were close?"

"She has told me the colonel was very mannerly. He brought her chocolates. She has a pin she said he once gave to her. It looked very expensive. I said the colonel was very generous, and she said he gave her much, much more."

"They had a romantic relationship. Is that what you're implying?" said Henson.

The housekeeper shrugged, but it was clear they were thinking along the same lines. "My own mother told me it was necessary to do many things during the war that would be unthinkable in other times."

Henson recalled what Toorn had said in his emotional monologue at the Rijksmuseum. "SS Colonel Stock was with the De Groot Van Gogh when it burned. Toorn described an Opel Blitz hitting a mine."

"She must have seen it," said Esther. Her face went pale. "In Amsterdam, Toorn mentioned slave-workers, the forced labor common in the war. Was Samuel Meyer the worker with Stock when the truck exploded?" *Did Meyerbeer steal the real Samuel Meyer's name?*

"Ask her," said Henson.

"It upsets her," said the housekeeper.

"Ask her if Meyer and Colonel Stock were in the truck carrying the Van Gogh."

The housekeeper knelt and adjusted Mrs. Toorn's shawl and gently spoke to her for several seconds. They heard the old woman mumble a few things, then say, "*Ja. Zij brandden . . .brandden.*"

Slowly, the story came out. The Allies were closing in. SS Colonel Stock, who had run an interrogation center in the De Groot house, had taken Meyer and a soldier to fill an Opel Blitz truck with the art stored in the carriage house behind the De Groot Museum just down the road. They hit a mine or were strafed by a fighter plane as they passed the house. All three were killed. British commandos began dropping from parachutes in the area, and then the Second Army moved through. No one could get to the truck before it was consumed. All that was left were bones.

"This is what Dr. Toorn saw," said Henson.

"But Meyer *could* have escaped," said Esther. "Can we be sure Samuel Meyer was killed?"

"If he wasn't, he stole the Van Gogh then," said Henson.

"How could he do that?" said Esther. "If it was a mine or a fighter?" *Or Meyerbeer stole it somehow and then stole Meyer's name as well.*

"Maybe he torched the truck himself, somehow," said Henson. "In the confusion, no one could be sure it had struck a mine."

"Then who is Manfred Stock?"

"SS Colonel Manfred Stock's son?"

"Stock must have escaped with Meyer. They were in it together."

"Does that make sense? An SS colonel and a forced laborer?"

Esther pushed back the obvious: that Stock was more likely to have conspired with Meyerbeer than Meyer. "Somehow," she said quickly, "they got separated, or Meyer took off with the Van Gogh. Stock went to South America."

Henson thought for a moment. "These are large inferences."

"My father conspired with a torturer to steal a Van Gogh?" Esther felt sick. "No wonder my mother left him."

"Let's not jump to conclusions," said Henson. "Why steal a Van Gogh simply to keep it in your attic?"

"Who are you?" said the housekeeper. "Please, Mevrouw Toorn is very old."

"Ask her about Meyer," said Henson.

"Please."

"Just ask her about Meyer, and we'll leave you in peace."

Esther paced along the roses, then drifted toward the gate leading to the front of the house. Henson watched. Her arms were crossed, and she stared at the ground.

After a few exchanges with Mrs. Toorn, the housekeeper said, "Meyer was a Jew. He was from the Rhineland or Lorraine or somewhere to the south, but he had fled to Beekberg a few years before. He needed work, and Dr. Toorn hired him to work at the museum. When the Germans rounded up the Jews, Dr. Toorn protected him."

"A regular Schindler," muttered Henson. "Why?"

The housekeeper said nothing.

"Ask her why Dr. Toorn protected Meyer."

Again the housekeeper questioned Mrs. Toorn. "She falls asleep," said the housekeeper.

"What did she say?"

"I didn't understand," she said. "He gave Dr. Toorn information."

"About what?"

"She didn't say."

Henson nodded. Was it plausible that an SS colonel would allow a man he knew to be a Jew to work around the De Groot estate and later conspire with him to steal the painting? Meyer must have been a traitor of some kind. That would have been enough reason for Rosa Goren to leave him. Maybe he wasn't Meyerbeer at all. Maybe Meyerbeer really was the man who had died in Switzerland. Henson was trying to absorb all this and make some sense of it, when Esther suddenly pointed out the gate.

"The truck!" she said. "In front!"

She was already looking in the driver's compartment when Henson got through the gate.

"The door was open," she said.

"It couldn't have gotten here without our hearing it," said Henson.

"Which means it went straight here."

"When the housekeeper was in the henhouse."

He readied Stock's pistol and quickly moved to the back of the truck. Esther flung up the rear door. It was empty except for a hand dolly.

Henson looked around. "We would have seen Toorn come out the back, don't you think?"

"Maybe," said Esther.

"Let's look inside."

Cautiously, they moved through the house, checking his study, the upstairs rooms, anywhere a man of his size could hide. They snapped back the door to the cellar. The iron staircase went down into exactly what they had seen before: Wine racks. The huge barrels.

Henson sat on Toorn's desk. "He's gone," he sighed. "Let's call Interpol."

The housekeeper appeared in the doorway. "Dr. Toorn?" she asked.

"Where is the telephone?" said Esther.

Henson remembered the housekeeper blocking his exit at the doorway.

"Wait," he said. "You said there were cells down there."

"They were taken out," said the woman.

"But where were they? Can you show me where they were?"

"I wasn't here," said the woman. "They were gone by—"

"But *where* were they!" said Esther.

"Exactly!" said Henson.

The housekeeper peered at them blankly as they climbed down the iron stair.

Henson banged on the end of one barrel and listened to the hollow sound. They moved back and forth, looking for any sign that the huge barrels somehow opened. Esther knelt to see if there were any circular marks on the floor. Henson squinted for a latch, a hinge, and felt for streams of air coming from any seam. Esther reached for the spigot in front of her and turned it. A hiss and a sour smell issued from it. A few drips of wine hit the floor.

Henson reached for the spigot at the bottom of his barrel and twisted.

A loud *clack* startled them.

Esther crouched. Henson spun, aiming the pistol. There were only the wine racks behind them.

One of them was out of line with the others.

They crept toward it. Esther pointed to an arc on the floor made by the rack's motion. She looked for Henson's assent.

"We could wait for backup," he said. "That would be the

sensible thing to do."

"And if there's another exit?"

He contemplated the pistol in his hand and offered it to her. "There are only four bullets, right?" he whispered. "You're the better shot."

"Four," she said, "and one in the chamber."

"You take it." He grabbed a bottle of wine by the neck, hefted it as a club, then grabbed the end of the rack with his fingers.

"One, two . . ."

The rack came forward easily, but the moving section was larger than Henson had realized. It slipped out of his grasp and crashed against the stationary one next to it. The bottles rattled and one slipped loose and skittered across the floor. A cool blast of air with a medicinal smell, like carbolic, swept out.

The corridor that lay before them was about three meters wide and at least thirty meters deep. Along each side were cell doors about two meters apart, six on each side. The entire corridor was unlit except for the light that spilled in from the basement. At the far end was a wider door at the top of two steps. It was covered in iron straps with a barred peep slot. The sliding door covering it was open slightly and a hazy blue light came from within.

They listened. There was a faint hum. An electrical device. A dripping in the three drains spaced between the cells.

Esther felt a chill, not from the oppressive humidity and temperature, but as if the ghosts of the dead were weeping in the cells, listening to the screams, waiting at the entrance of hell for the demons with death's heads on their collars to march from the room at the end and drag them to their torture. How much skin was scraped on the concrete? How much blood was washed down those drains?

She saw Henson wipe sweat from his upper lip. He took a deep breath and turned to go in. Esther grabbed his arm and pulled him back.

"Ladies first," she said.

She moved along the wall, easing up to each cell. Several of the doors were closed, but most were open at least a few inches. The hinges had rusted. A wooden bucket sagged in decay in one cell, but the others seemed empty.

Henson waited until she reached the end door. She tilted her head listening at the door, then waved him forward. He quickly went up to the opposite side. The door was open only a crack. Cold air poured out of the seam. He could see a bright, narrow spotlight raking the whitewashed wall in the chamber but nothing more. He spread his hands. Esther signaled him to step back.

She put a foot on the top step, then quickly spun past, catching a glimpse through the door slot, and landing beside Henson.

He widened his eyes with a silent question.

She shook her head.

"I'm high," he whispered, signaling with his hands. "You're low."

She nodded.

He positioned himself on the hinge side. She crouched on the other. He counted by raising fingers. One, two . . .

He shoved the heavy door with both hands. She whirled into the opening, prone on the floor and whipped the pistol to her left.

But it wasn't a man. It was the marble head of a Roman, or perhaps a saint, his blank eyes rolling skyward. The head sat upon a plain black pedestal under a large glass case, lit by a halogen spotlight hung from the ceiling.

A meter from the sculpture was a medieval cross with large, crudely polished garnets, and an etching of a Dutch sailing ship. Between them, beneath a Flemish wedding scene, a dehumidifier hummed. On the opposite wall was a large case containing an illuminated manuscript with Celtic ornamentation, a Torah wrapped in golden cloth, and several medieval chess pieces. Above it was a Rubens-style painting of a fleshy goddess being strewn with flowers by plump cherubs and serenaded by a trio of satyrs.

But in between the left and right walls was a semicircular alcove. In the center of the floor was a modernist eyeball chair with arms like gull wings.

Toorn slouched in it, his back to them, still wearing an overcoat, his right arm drooping toward the floor. He did not move. He seemed to be dead. Henson was going to feel for a pulse, but he looked up and froze.

Someone else was there, staring at them. In the end of the alcove, there were three spotlights. Their beams converged on a self-portrait of Vincent van Gogh.

"Is that the De Groot portrait?" asked Henson.

"Two buttons," said Esther. "As in the sketch."

Toorn broke the spell Vincent had cast, by expelling a stream of air, and Henson knelt to pick up a tiny bottle he had noticed on the floor.

"Nitroglycerin," he said, reading it.

"Is he dead?" asked Esther.

Henson looked down as Toorn's head moved. "Not quite."

"Get back from me," growled Toorn.

"You need a doctor," said Henson.

Esther stepped forward and saw that Toorn had a revolver in his meaty hand. She raised her own pistol and backed away. "Drop the gun! Drop it!"

Henson spread his fingers and slowly signaled the older man to lower the revolver. "Let's settle down, Dr. Toorn. Let's be calm now."

"Back up," said Toorn.

Henson raised his hands higher and took two steps back.

Keeping his revolver pointed at Henson, Toorn awkwardly shoved at the floor with his foot. The chair turned until he faced Esther. He blinked his oystery eyes.

"What are you going to do?" He chuckled. "Kill me?"

He coughed and rubbed his forehead with his sausagelike fingers.

"If you don't put down that gun."

"I'm a very old man," he said. "I've decided it would be azz good to die here azz anywhere."

"Here?" said Esther. "In a Nazi torture chamber?"

"I tortured no one. Here, under the eyezz of Vincent van Gogh." He took a breath. "He, who understood everything."

"We can get you a doctor," said Henson.

Toorn shook his head. "Just stay away from me. In a few moments, my heart will explode and I will save you the cost of a bullet."

"Do you even have a heart?" said Esther.

Toorn's face twisted. "So righteous you are. What would you have done in 1943? You have no right to judge me."

"I would likely have ended up here, and then in an oven," said Esther. "But I wouldn't have cooperated with them."

"*Ja, ja.* Sure. Like your father?"

"What about him?"

"He was a rat," said Toorn. "He would do anything to survive. You wouldn't exist if it weren't for me."

The pistol shook in Esther's hand.

Toorn smiled at Henson. "The truth hurts, eh? Poor Samuel

Meyer. Ha!"

"Was he Stéphane Meyerbeer?"

"Who?"

"Stéphane Meyerbeer, from Vichy."

Toorn squinted. "He was Samuel Meyer, a wanderer. He lived in Beekberg. He worked for a baker in the Jewish quarter until the wife flirted with him and the baker tossed him out in the street. Everyone in town laughed at him, threw him old crusts of bread like he was a stray dog. But where could he go? Anyone moving about without papers was in danger of being arrested. Although there was only an occasional presence of the German army in Beekberg until later, it was all over Holland. He knew what would happen to a wandering Jew, so he lived as he could. No one in Beekberg thought much of him after a while. They paid no attention to what he overheard. Yes, he got to know a lot of secrets lurking beneath windows! The old curator had been letting him clean up and sleep in the tool shed when the Germans decided to occupy Beekberg. I threatened to turn him in. He bribed me with enough to get in good with SS-Standartenführer Stock. Each time Meyer gave me information, I let him live a little longer."

"He betrayed his people?" said Esther.

"I know he lied sometimes. Very often he gave me the victims he thought I wanted, but the *Schutzstaffel* did not care. It doesn't matter that the real enemies are caught, only that a perpetual fear rains over the countryside in a steady drizzle. People were afraid of *me* for the first time in my life. I was made the De Groot Museum curator. I eliminated my superiors in the party. I married very well."

"I'm sure you cut quite a dashing figure," said Henson.

"I gave her no choice. Ha! My mother used to call me her 'little piggy.' Other people called me worse and laughed at me. They laughed at me no more. Miss De Groot had no choice. She became Mrs. Toorn."

*Meyer, "the Pig,"* thought Esther, *allied with Toorn, "the little piggy."* Her head was spinning.

He took several deep breaths. Again he massaged his forehead. "I am feeling somewhat better," he said. "Perhaps Vincent keeps me alive."

"You don't look better," said Henson. "You're white as a sheet. Let me get a doctor."

"No!" said Toorn. "I'll shoot you if you move. The last thing I want to see is my painting."

"It isn't your painting," said Esther, steadying her pistol with both hands.

"Whose then? No one other than me has seen it since 1944. I have cared for it like a mother cares for her child. I have sat here countless hours and communicated with it."

"Why did you identify the other painting as the De Groot Van Gogh?"

"Who would know? I thought it was the forgery I made. When I painted I could feel Van Gogh guiding my hand. When I painted self-portraits, I became him."

"You forged the De Groot to sell it to the Nazis?"

"No. To protect it. To keep it. Who knows what would have happened to it if they had taken it? And I knew they would take it, and every day the streams of bombers filled the sky. Berlin would be ashes, perhaps was already ashes. After Operation Anvil, two trainloads of art were evacuated here from the south. They were to be combined with the art being evacuated from here and sent to Bavaria. SS Colonel Stock was ordered to accomplish this. Then the British Second Army advanced ahead of schedule. I replaced the original here, which was already crated, with my forgery. When the truck burned, I thought my tracks were erased.

"Then, in Chicago, you brought that painting to me, and I

thought it was my forgery. It is embarrassing. The hand was not correct. I was so shaken I didn't recognize that until later. But I had already said it was genuine." He coughed again, cutting short a chuckle. "I was wrong, but I was right. I was imprezzed with the skill of my forgery, and then I knew it wasn't a forgery!" He looked at Esther. "When you are old, you, too, will understand weakness."

"And evil?" said Esther.

"It is in us if we pay attention. Vincent understood that."

"But why did you send Manfred Stock to kill Esther and blow up the painting?" Henson asked.

Toorn's eyes were closed, his breathing labored. When he spoke again, his voice was weak. "It was the list. Meyer said he had a list of the network. After all this time he said he was going to expose us. We escape for all these decades and then?" Toorn coughed. "We burned his house to destroy the list. I did not know about the painting. Then you came to me and I identified the painting as genuine. I thought it wasn't. Then I found out it was. I felt like a fool."

"And that's why he stopped?"

"Who? Manfred? The boy acted on his own. I told him he was as stupid as his father. I sent him to Chile as soon as I could."

"Sent him?"

"I should have kept him?"

"When?" asked Henson.

"As soon as I could. He was a child. Back then he was just innocent—not stupid."

"I understand," said Henson. "You're talking about when Manfred Stock was a boy. You sent him to his father even though he was your wife's son."

Toorn breathed heavily. "What could I have done during

the war? Challenged the colonel to a duel? How could she have refused Stock?" He chuckled. "She didn't want to refuse him. And what difference would it make? If the colonel found her attractive, that is his business. I was happy to accommodate him, eh? That is the crux of the matter."

Toorn closed his eyes again.

"When did you realize that the Van Gogh Meyer had concealed in his attic was not your forgery—that it was genuine?"

"I am the world's greatest expert on Van Gogh! I don't need X-rays and other witchcraft to know." Toorn shook his head. "If I had ever known that it was in that train from Marseille, I would have stolen it, not Meyer. They would both be hanging here now, side by side."

Toorn wheezed and his whole body moved as he breathed.

"You need a doctor," said Henson. He looked at the nitro bottle and saw there were no more tablets. "Is there more of this medicine? Let me get your medicine." Toorn looked at him for several seconds, then moved the gun. "Doctor," he said.

He lowered the gun and shoved the floor with his foot, staring at the Van Gogh.

"Hurry," said Esther, keeping Toorn in her sights.

Henson ran into the corridor, but even before he reached the wine rack, he heard Esther scream, "No!"

A deafening crack shattered the air behind him.

He skidded to a stop. Damn! Esther couldn't have, could she? When he leaped through the door, he slipped on blood, fell on one knee, and saw Esther, lying against the humidifier, her chest spattered in gore.

"Are you hurt? Where are you hit?"

"I'm not," she panted.

He looked back. The top of Toorn's head was blown off.

Henson turned slowly to Esther, then looked back again.

If she had shot Toorn, the blood would have sprayed in the other direction.

Toorn had rotated until he could stare into Vincent van Gogh's eyes, then, like the great master, had shot himself.

# NINETEEN

# The Secrets of Samuel Meyer

Three days later, the authorities were finished with their inquiries and Esther was free to go. She waited with her luggage in the tiny hotel lobby, lost in thought, when the door opened.

"Come on," said Henson.

"I've got a taxi coming," said Esther.

"Never mind," he said, holding out a twenty-euro note. "Leave the driver this tip. Are these your bags?"

"Oh no," she said. "I'm going to the airport. You're not going to waylay me again."

"I am taking you to the airport."

Esther crossed her arms.

"Scout's honor."

"Were you really a Boy Scout?"

"You thought I was just humoring you? There wasn't much to do in Welford. I liked it."

"So you helped old ladies across the streets of Welford, Kansas?"

"The street—singular. And there were about three old ladies."

"Straight to the airport," said Esther. "No recruiting pitch. I'm not in the mood."

"Scout's honor, but I do have some more information."

"I saw the press conference in the paper."

"More than that." He tilted her bag and headed for the door, snatching up her carry-on as he passed it. She gave a tip to the desk clerk and told him to apologize to the taxi driver for her.

Sitting next to him, she fastened her seat belt and said, "Straight to Schiphol. Don't get lost. My mother is having lung trouble. I need to be there."

"There is plenty of time," said Henson. He pulled away from the curb. As he turned the wheel, she noticed he was not wearing his wedding ring.

"The panel has verified that the Van Gogh found in your father's attic is genuine."

"I read that."

"Furthermore, their tests don't rule out that the alteration in the hand position is by Van Gogh, as well. There is a red pigment in the hand that began being manufactured at a certain point in mid-1888 and was available to him, so it gives them a rough date before which the alteration could not have been done."

Esther was silently watching two pedestrians who had drawn a small crowd by loudly arguing beside a canal.

"Furthermore, as additional confirmation, Dr. Crespi says the paint in the self-portrait of Toorn does not at all match the paint in either of the Van Goghs."

Esther remained silent. The pedestrians walked away in opposite directions. Esther looked down at her hands. "I think I may be able to forgive him someday. That's what I tell myself. But it tears at me."

"Your father did what he could to survive. It's hard to know what it was like then."

"I was thinking about the Sonderkommandos, those men in the concentration camps, the prisoners who carried the bodies out of the gas chambers and worked for the murderers. Some of them survived, too. I talked to one at my mother's rest home one time. I told him he did the right thing. I wasn't really sure. The pain in his face told me that he could never forgive himself. But at least he didn't turn people in."

"And now, somehow, you're blaming yourself. Think about it. Does that make sense? Retroactive guilt?"

"What do you mean? I don't know what you're talking about."

Henson pulled into a parking place.

She raised her arms in protest. "You said you were taking me directly—"

He turned sideways and grabbed her forearm. "Just be quiet a minute and listen."

She pulled it away but did not leave the car.

"You're alive because Samuel Meyer survived. You somehow feel that makes you guilty of his crimes, if we can call them crimes. Each person's soul is his own. You weren't born carrying the sins of your father. That's bull."

"That's fine for you to say," said Esther. "Your father was a nice wholesome farmer."

"Actually, he ran a grocery." Henson ran his fingers along the steering wheel, then looked her in the eyes. "And he wasn't entirely wholesome. In the 1970s he burned it for the insurance."

When Esther looked back at him, he turned away. He seemed to have startled himself by blurting it out.

"I'm not lying," he said. "That's what I think happened. He didn't get caught, but I'm sure that's what happened."

"But you at least had the chance to confront him with it."

"I didn't."

"Why not?"

"I didn't want to believe it. The store had been in our family since 1910. Later, after he died, I understood his entire life had been about protecting us, taking care of us. Welford was dying. We were going broke. I believe the sheriff must have known but looked the other way."

"You don't know that it's true, then."

Henson tapped his heart. Again she noticed he wasn't wearing his wedding ring. "I know it," he said. "We moved to Kansas City on the insurance, and I went to college on what was left. Sometimes I can convince myself that I have misinterpreted it all, but my heart tells me no. It was his way of loving us. I think he must have taken this crime upon himself only for us."

Esther thought for a moment. "That's one way to look at it, but, well, it's hardly the same thing."

"It was no better than theft. For whatever reason he did it."

"My father was helping the Nazis exterminate his own people!"

"Think about what you know. Samuel Meyer was a young man. They were rounding up the Jews. He tells Toorn some things that Toorn uses against people he was planning to get anyway. Toorn was holding Meyer's life in his sweaty palm. How do we know this? Toorn told us."

"Meyer survived, didn't he?"

"It doesn't mean that Toorn told us the truth."

"Meyer had the Van Gogh."

"He had Feodor Minsky's Van Gogh, which had come from Vichy France, looted by Stéphane Meyerbeer. He had to have taken it off one of the trains. Or perhaps SS Colonel Stock took it off the train and Meyer stole it from him. One of them, or both of them, burned the truck that everyone saw."

"So he helped Stock escape? How tidy that Stock's son should come back to try to kill me."

"Now, here's the thing," Henson continued. "The records have been searched. Meyer was rescued by American infantry. He was deloused and given new clothes. Could he have been carrying the Van Gogh? No one would notice that? He must have concealed it somewhere, perhaps even on the Toorn estate. In 1955, just after he was granted full American citizenship, he emptied his bank account to buy a Pan Am ticket to Europe and took a tour. I believe that he must have gotten the canvas then and smuggled it back to Chicago. Meanwhile, Stock got to Chile through the networks that spirited a number of former Nazi officers to safety in South America. I don't think Stock knew Meyer had the Van Gogh. Perhaps Meyer saw where Stock had hidden it, stole it, and secured it to wherever he picked it up in 1955."

"Perhaps! You think! What does all this prove? Nothing. If Stock didn't know Meyer had the painting, why did he send his son after it?"

Henson smiled. "That's what's really interesting. In 1966, when Immigration began to investigate your father, thinking he might be Stéphane Meyerbeer, the Wiesenthal group sent a young investigator to try to convince your father to come clean to get the burden of the past off, to help them locate other escaped war criminals, and, of course, to tell his story so that no one would ever forget what happened in the Third Reich."

"And?"

"He denied being Meyerbeer, and threatened the investigator, saying he knew what the man was trying to do." Henson paused. "The investigator pressed him, but Meyer merely told him he had nothing to say."

"The informer had given up informing? It's just fine to turn in your own people, but not to turn in escaped Nazis? He changed his mind about saving his sorry hide for some reason. I suppose you're going to tell me what that was."

"Perhaps because your mother had left him. Perhaps because he knew that what he could say would only make him look guilty."

"Perhaps, perhaps," said Esther.

"Perhaps to protect you and your mother from Stock and his ilk."

"That's hard to believe, Martin."

"Are you willing to listen to what I think happened?"

Esther shook her head. "I have run a hundred scenarios through my head. What makes you think your theory would be better? Take me to the airport."

"He wasn't *my* father," Henson said. "It makes no difference to me whether he was a war criminal or not. *That's* why I can think more clearly about it." He crossed his arms and sat back. He took a deep breath and spoke almost in a whisper. "Besides which, I have more facts than you know."

In the silence, a sputtering motor scooter rattled by.

"What are they?" said Esther.

"Will you hear me out?"

"Yes, but I don't have to accept your interpretations. You do have a motive. You're still trying to recruit me."

"Believe me, the task force will survive with or without you. The U.S. Supreme Court has opened the door to civil suits to recover looted art in other nations. There are a lot of Jacob Minskys and their families who have surfaced in the last few years and many pieces of looted art. Now, are you going to hear me out?"

Esther raised her hand quickly and dismissively. "Just be quick. I have a plane to catch."

"All right, then. First, the Minsky Van Gogh. That's easy. Meyerbeer looted it. It went north when Operation Anvil chased the Germans out of southern France. Meyer somehow got his hands on it and later got it to the States. What you don't know, however, is what Toorn knew. With his background, he might have known of the existence of the painting, but he never actually saw it until we brought it to him in the Palmer House. At first glance it looked like his own forgery to him. He nearly collapsed. He didn't know what to do. He was not young, he was in bad health, and his decisions weren't particularly sharp.

"Later, he remembered the detail about the hand. He placed several long-distance calls from the Palmer House trying to locate something he remembered from a Van Gogh letter that was in private hands. He did not find it until he returned to Europe. He had remembered it as a letter of Vincent's or his brother Theo's. In fact, the letter was by Dr. Gachet, another man who befriended Vincent. There are a couple of paintings of Dr. Gachet, including the one that set an auction record. Gachet did a bit of painting himself and may have done some imitation Van Gogh. Toorn eventually remembered a passing mention by Gachet to a cousin of his. Gachet wrote that Vincent had gotten very animated about

Oriental religion and gone on and on about it, and told him he intended to alter all of his paintings to reflect it. Probably, Vincent was in his cups again and he altered only one or two paintings before the impulse changed. You can bet, though, that the art experts will be looking very closely at other paintings from that period of his life. Joliette showed me some of Van Gogh's self-portraits in which he represents himself as a Japanese monk.

"It was a tiny detail in Dr. Gachet's letter, but Toorn remembered it. Given his ego, he saw a chance to prove his status among the experts. At the conclusion of the examination, when they had determined forensically the portrait was real, he would dramatically produce his written proof—the final element to remove all doubt and confirm his ability to spot a genuine Van Gogh at first sight.

"Why did he disappear so suddenly? He was trying to put together the money to buy the letter. Then he alone would be able to reveal it. But the Belgian owner was a crafty man who sensed Toorn's eagerness and wasn't willing to sell until he knew why Toorn wanted it so much."

"Much of Toorn's behavior remains inexplicable to me," said Esther.

"Why did Toorn come back to his country home with Stock?" Henson continued. "He realized the Minsky painting had passed through his hands during the war, without his knowledge. If the panel pursued a search for the painting's provenance, the old charges of his relationship to the Nazis might resurface and he would lose everything. He could be accused of authenticating the Minsky Van Gogh because he had known it from the period in which he was linked to the Nazi looting. He had to speed his collection, which would be a total proof of his illicit involvement, out of the country. He planned to join Stock in South America. I think he would have been willing to abandon everything else, except for the De Groot Van Gogh."

Esther blinked for a few moments. "Very well, then, but there is a flaw. If he didn't know of the existence of the Minsky Van Gogh, stolen by my father, why did he send Manfred Stock to get it from the house in Chicago?"

"That's the most interesting part." Henson smiled smugly and crossed his arms.

"The list!" said Esther.

"Exactly!"

When Manfred Stock had driven them off the road, he had demanded a "list." In all the chaos, they hadn't thought about it. "I didn't know what he meant," said Esther, "but I didn't have time to think about it."

"It bothered me, afterward. When I recognized it had nothing to do with the painting, a lightbulb went on."

"It was a list of looted artworks?"

"No," said Henson. "It was the Chicago Cubs of 1929."

She laughed. "They needed to know who played for Chicago in 1929? That must be easy enough to find out. The picture was looted from the Baseball Hall of Fame? What sense is that?"

"Just this: the names of the '29 Cubs *are* easy to look up, and guess what? The names on that picture in your father's house match only one real Cub about halfway through the list. Carl 'Driver' King, Ernie Brown, 'Spider' Woodsprite. These and several others are not the names of Cubs players."

"You must have a photographic memory."

"No, but I remember thinking it was odd that your father would have written a letter to the editor complaining about when Wrigley Field installed lights and would have kept a picture of the Cubs on his wall. Clearly, he was not a Cubs fan or a baseball fan."

"He called it a 'silly game,'" said Esther, "but that isn't what I meant. How could you have remembered all the names? That's incredible."

"I'd like to take credit for that, but I didn't," he said sheepishly. "You'll remember a couple of things were blown out the front window."

"The menorah."

"Which turns out to be a late seventeenth- to early eighteenth-century brass work from Trier, in Germany. It, too, was looted. And as luck would have it, the Cubs photo was blown out of the house along with it."

Esther nodded slowly as she remembered placing the two items together.

"But what do the baseball players have to do—"

"We checked the records. The Germans are very good record keepers. Among Stock's interrogation officers was a Karl König. *König* means 'king'—Carl King. König was in charge of the evacuation trucks at the point Stock was supposedly burned alive. 'Ernie Brown' matches up with a captain, Ernst Braun. Braun was caught in Algeria in 1949 and served the rest of his life in a West German jail. He, too, disappeared in Holland, but a festering wound in his hip made it impossible for him to travel well. He died in 1953. Braun was the chief torturer of several priests who assisted the Dutch underground. And so on with all the other names. As I said, only one of the names on the picture is a real Cubs player. And there are more names than there are players in the photograph: twenty-four in all."

"So my father had a list of vanished SS officers?"

"The most interesting of which is Spider Woodsprite. 'Woodsprite' in German is *waldteufel*. Ude Waldteufel was not among the officers in Stock's group. However, he was connected with a wealthy industrial family and managed to avoid being found until he was literally lying on an operating table in the 1960s. Lung cancer."

"He died, I hope. In great pain. And I hope no one let him out of sight while he was doing it. There was more than one false death among these war criminals."

"Well, we're certain the body released from the hospital was his. But the reason he was being sought was that he was a big suspect in the investigation of der Spinne, a network to hide former Nazis."

"And der Spinne means 'the spider,'" said Esther. "Spider Woodsprite."

"Immigration began investigating your father about the time Waldteufel was found."

"Waldteufel turned him in?"

"No, the records show that Waldteufel denied everything, but his capture was in the news. As was the inquiry about Meyer. There are records of international calls made to and from the house in Chicago just after the government began its investigation of Samuel Meyer."

"So my father was involved with them?"

"I think he threatened to expose them, perhaps in response to their threatening him."

" 'I have a list, if anything happens to me, I'll—' "

"Something like that."

"But why wouldn't they simply send one of their goons to take it from him?"

A moment later, Esther answered her own question. "They couldn't know where he hid it or who had it."

"Exactly. I would still urge you to consider that his real interest was in protecting you and your mother."

Esther thought. It was making some sense, though there

were still loose ends. "But why concoct these pseudonyms and hang the picture on his living room wall?"

"What better place to hide it?"

"But why do it at all if he had their names in his head?" She thought of her mother. Henson was about to speak, when she cut him off. "He was afraid he wouldn't remember them all. He wanted a written record."

"He may have come into contact with them only briefly, or heard their names only once or twice."

"And is Manfred Stock the Elder on the list?"

"I think he's 'Freddy Cain.' *Stock* can be translated to—"

"'Cane.'"

"Exactly," said Henson. "But maybe Meyer liked associating him with the Cain in the Bible."

"Maybe this nest of 'spiders' was heavy into art."

"That's what I suspect. He could inform on their thefts, as well as their identities. Basically, I think he blackmailed them to keep you and your mother safe."

"He was a cheap little informer according to Toorn."

"Maybe that's why they believed he would inform. Maybe—maybe he rose to the occasion for his daughter."

Esther choked up and bit her lower lip. "It's a good story. Hard to believe, but a good story. Give me one good reason he wouldn't simply turn the rats in."

Henson turned away from her. "I don't know," he said quickly. "But you know, it might be easier to believe than not to believe."

Esther cradled her head in her hands. "It's all maddening. How can we know? They left him alone from 1966 until he contacted me? That's hard to believe."

"If he revealed what he knew, it might reveal his own guilt. Maybe that's why he kept silent. He had contacted Toorn at almost the same time—well, just after he contacted you.

Again, it's in the phone records. It was no coincidence Toorn was in Chicago. He was coming to buy him off or kill him. Toorn's cell phone records indicate he called Stock in Chile. Stock sent his son, who, by the way, had been an undercover policeman under Augusto Pinochet."

"How could a man that looked like that be undercover?"

"It's a euphemism, I would think," Henson said drily.

"Where is the elder Stock?"

Henson shrugged. "He evaporated, but they have a lead on him in Paraguay. He's in his late nineties. All we can hope is that he was always looking over his shoulder and that the last few weeks have tormented him. He may be having a hot tea with Dr. Mengele and Heinrich Himmler."

Esther peered out the window. A young tourist couple had set their shopping bags at their feet and were kissing passionately. "I would feel better if we could prove some of this."

"You're welcome to help me try," said Henson.

"Oh, no. You made up this entire story to sucker me."

"I can prove every fact I mentioned. Phone records, German army records, all of it."

"But there are probably a dozen ways to interpret those facts."

"I don't think so," said Henson, "but look at it this way. Jacob Minsky recovered his uncle's painting. He isn't going to auction it, he says, much to the consternation of his lawyers. It's probably going to hang in the Rijksmuseum side by side with the De Groot self-portrait as an example of how Vincent did his work. The world gets two more Van Goghs. A little justice is restored. Maybe you found out something about your father, weak or strong as he may have been. Maybe you won't judge him so harshly."

Esther was weeping. Henson offered her a handkerchief, but she wiped her cheeks with her fingers.

"I need to go home," she said. "My mother needs me."

"I understand," said Henson.

He pulled the car away from the curb and joined the traffic. They were silent for many minutes, not even looking at each other.

Esther straightened herself. "You're not wearing your wedding ring."

Henson gave a little shrug. "I forgot it."

"I don't believe you."

He was silent for a few seconds, long enough for her to feel she had trampled on his feelings.

"I'm sorry," she said. "It's not my business."

"It was time," he said, and though she waited, he did not elaborate.

It wasn't until they had actually entered the airport grounds that she ceased staring through the window, took a deep breath, and spoke. "Listen, I have something to say, Mr. Henson."

"Tell me you'll come to work for us."

She shook her head.

"Uh-oh, you look grim."

"No, just serious. I want to thank you."

"Thank me?"

"For caring. You didn't have any reason to care about Samuel Meyer." She hesitated. "I mean caring about me, really. The problem of finding out what the story was with my father, it wasn't your problem and it certainly wasn't the problem of the Customs bureau."

"It was if he sneaked in illegally."

"Not after he died. You didn't have to keep me around, keep me involved."

"You were invaluable, lady," said Henson sardonically. "I credit you with saving my life a couple of times, you know."

"Maybe some of those situations wouldn't have come about if you weren't dragging me behind you."

"Who knows? You were there and that's all that mattered."

"No," Esther said. "What matters to me is that you tried to help me find out the truth about my father. I know you made some extra effort and I appreciate it."

"Well," said Henson, "if I helped, evidently I didn't help enough. You didn't get your answers. We don't know whether your father was a co-conspirator with Manfred Stock and Toorn. We really don't know for sure what happened with the Van Gogh."

She squeezed her hands together. "We don't even know for certain what it was that made my mother leave him," she said almost to herself. "I'll never know whether my father was a good man caught up in the circumstances of his time or a totally evil one."

"Maybe none of us ever knows that," said Henson.

"Oh, yes," said Esther, "I think they do. Don't you?"

He gave her a quizzical look but did not respond as he pulled the car up to the curb outside of the departure terminal. He stepped out to get her bag from the trunk.

She held out her hand. "It's good-bye then."

"Shalom," he said. He squeezed her thin fingers. "Look," he said, "I'll give you a card." She pulled away. "With a direct line. Be warned. If you don't find me soon, I'll find you. I am determined to convince you to join us."

"Your certainty amuses me," she said.

"It isn't certainty," he said, smiling. "It's confidence. Unadulterated, one hundred percent, pure Kansas Boy Scout confidence. We never give up."

She squeezed his arm. "Don't ever lose it," she said. "But be gracious in defeat, Boy Scout. My life is going in another direction."

He shrugged, still smiling.

She turned to get out, then suddenly turned back, took his cheeks in her hands and planted a kiss on his forehead. He was taken so much by surprise that he gaped.

"Shalom, Martin Henson," she said. "I'm going home."

Before he could say anything she was crossing the sidewalk into the terminal. It wasn't until he was halfway back to Amsterdam that he saw in the rear-view mirror the florid patch of lipstick on his forehead. Even after he wiped it off, he felt it there for days.

# TWENTY

# The Auction

Sotheby's new auction house is a modern white building on the Boelelaan just south of the A10 highway in southern Amsterdam. Henson overestimated how long the trip would take and arrived well ahead of time. He passed through security quickly and loitered in the lobby as news cameramen and reporters gathered in the patio area to stake out the most photogenic spots beside the planters.

The interest in this auction was worldwide. People anticipated a bidding record. The expert panel had confirmed that all the physical evidence supported, or at least did not contradict, the argument that the Van Gogh self-portrait found in

Samuel Meyer's attic in Chicago was indeed by the great artist. The paint, the brushstrokes, the canvas: all were consistent with the time period and the artist. Since the panel was still assembled, they also evaluated the portrait found in Toorn's secret collection, and it was authenticated as well: it was the De Groot self-portrait. For a short period of time art collectors hoped that both paintings would go on the market simultaneously. For the pair, the bidding would be astronomical, and the winner would become one of the most celebrated collectors of all time.

However, the records made it clear that the portrait found in Chicago was owned entirely by Jacob Minsky and the De Groot portrait's ownership was still in dispute. Possibly it belonged to the Sisters of Divine Mercy, but the general legal opinion was that the government of the Netherlands had become legal owner in the years after the war, when the assets of a number of defunct private schools had been shifted to the state. The German government was not pursuing the claim urged by one legislator that receipts existed indicating that the Third Reich had purchased the painting. One Dutch newspaper suggested that if such a case were pursued in the EU courts, the Netherlands should simply return the money that was supposedly paid, the equivalent of 2,000 euros—nothing compared to its current value.

A long, black limo pulled up in front of the auction house, and the photographers reacted as if a movie star had arrived. The driver opened the door, and Henson saw Jacob Minsky's attorney, Weston, climb out, obviously enjoying the attention. He turned and with the elegance of a Baroque courtier bent and assisted Minsky out of the back. Flashes barraged Minsky, and he waved an arm as if to bat them back. Watching through the window, Henson was reminded of Frankenstein's monster reacting to fire and chuckled. The chauffeur and Weston rescued Minsky and hustled him through the crush. As soon as they were inside, a waiter approached with a tray of champagne. "No thank you," Minsky said, spotting another waiter with sparkling water.

Henson observed the scene and then browsed the catalog. About twenty other artworks were to be auctioned as well as the Van Gogh, including two paintings by de Stijl artist Theo van Doesberg, three by George Vantongerloo, and several prints by Italian Futurists. Henson wasn't sure why he was attending, exactly, even though Sotheby's had sent him an invitation at Minsky's request. His work with the painting was over. There were many other artworks still missing from the lootings in World War II, let alone all of the various conflicts that had plagued the world afterward. Maybe it was just that the auction was a kind of ending. This was one time there had been a clear conclusion. Instead of dragging on for years as one nation's laws conflicted with another's, the art had been restored to its rightful owner. Perhaps he would celebrate with a glass of the champagne and a nice dinner and then feel energized for his trip to Belarus tomorrow to pursue a lead on some medieval reliquaries looted during the Soviet invasion of Slovakia.

The room had filled with bidders, many of whom seemed to know one another. There were a couple of men in sheiks' white robes and a large contingent of Japanese bowing to one another. "I'll getcha this time!" one man said in a Texas accent, pumping the hand of a wiry man who answered in that vague nonthreatening manner of the English upperclass. For a moment Henson thought the man was Prince Andrew, but he was much too old. Possibly he was related to the royal family.

"Young man! Young man!"

Minsky was pulling away from the group who had surrounded him and was headed toward Henson. "You made it! I'm glad. This is a great day, isn't it?" Minsky looked around, as if he'd misplaced something.

"You're going to be a very rich man by this afternoon, Mr. Minsky."

"Yes, well," said Minsky, "what can I do with money? Look at me. I could buy a better bed, but I can't buy a night's sleep, eh? I could get me a movie-star girlfriend like that Anna what's-her-name, but what then? Die in the saddle? It kind of takes the fun out of all that, if you know you're going to wake up dead. Not that I'm afraid of death, understand."

Henson smiled. "I thought you were going to keep it. I was a bit surprised to get the invitation."

"The insurance! You wouldn't believe! I'd have to live in a steel box. Vincent hung there in my uncle Feodor's room where anyone could enjoy it, learn from it. That's why I'm selling it. One condition of sale is that it must remain on permanent display. It doesn't belong to me. It belongs to the human race."

"You're a good man, Mr. Minsky."

Minsky swatted away the compliment as he had the flashes. "Ehnnn. Mr. Bigshot, my lawyer, says this might hurt the price. I say, What's a million or so? Phooey. He'll get his share." He grabbed Henson's lapel and pulled him close. "I'm going to donate to synagogues," he whispered. "You know, the ones with bad roofs and like that."

"That's great," said Henson.

"Mum's the word. They'll swarm like flies."

Henson made the motion of zippering his lips.

"So," said Minsky, "where's the beautiful Miss Goren?"

"She went back to Israel some months ago."

"I thought she worked with you."

"No. She had her own interests in the case, and then her mother was very ill."

"But I invited her, too."

"It all caused her a lot of pain."

Minsky nodded. He grabbed Henson's lapel again. "For her," he whispered, "I might consider dying in the saddle." He winked.

Henson smiled, cocked an eyebrow, and shrugged.

Minsky gave him a mock punch. "What's the matter with you, kid? Letting a nice Jewish girl like her get away?"

"You're probably right," said Henson.

"Of course I am!"

Weston approached with an elderly woman in a sable coat who had something to do with some kind of foundation. Weston gave Henson a brief handshake, but they were soon crowding Minsky.

*The swarming flies,* thought Henson. He drifted off, deciding a glass of champagne might be in order. Maybe he had missed his shot at Esther. Well, what was he supposed to do? He was trying to recruit her to work on the task force with him, not angling for a date. Four times since they had parted at Schiphol Airport, he had tried to call her. Once he got no answer. Three times he got her answering machine. The second time she had left a message that was forwarded by his secretary: "Miss Goren says to tell Mr. Henson that she appreciates the offer. It is very flattering, but she hasn't changed her mind."

Bidders were still arriving when a man in a tuxedo appeared in the door of the auction room. "Ladies and gentlemen, we will begin in fifteen minutes. We are expecting this to be a lengthy proceeding, so we would like to begin as punctually as possible." He then repeated the message in French and had begun in German when a hand in a brown driving glove touched the inside of Henson's elbow.

He knew instantly it was Esther. When he looked at her, her dark eyes were even more beautiful than he remembered.

"My God!" he said. "You came!"

She squeezed his arm, then pulled him close, a quick hard embrace. When it was over he still smelled the faint lemony cologne near her ear.

"It's so good to see you," said Henson. "Minsky was just asking about you."

"I didn't decide until the last minute."

"How is your mother?"

"She died about a month ago."

"I'm sorry."

Esther lowered her head slightly and said, "She did not suffer."

"I'm glad to hear that."

"We have to talk," she said, grabbing his arm again.

"What is it?"

"It has to be private. Is there a room?"

Henson looked around for one of the waiters. "I'll ask."

A few minutes later, a Sotheby's employee unlocked a consultation room for them in a side corridor, telling them to please exit the room to the right, that the rest of the building was off limits. Henson had implied that they needed privacy to discuss their bidding.

Esther, wearing tight black slacks and a brown leather coat, looked like she had rushed from the airport. She was carrying a leather portfolio, its strap over her arm. When she walked into the room, he could sense her tension and she spun as he closed the door, as if getting ready to defend herself.

"What is it?" he said. For a moment he thought maybe some of the people connected with Manfred Stock had surfaced and threatened her.

She dropped into a chair, slipping the portfolio from her arm. "You have to see this," she said.

She placed the portfolio on the table and unsnapped the brass latches. Reaching inside, she pulled out a worn, cloth-covered book. It was about the size of a mass-market paper-back. There were no words on the book's leather spine or anywhere on the cover. Scraps of paper with torn edges stuck out of the book, and the whole bundle was held together with a rubber band, which also held an envelope against the outside. Esther tugged it loose and handed it to Henson.

"What is it?" he asked.

"Just read it," she said.

On the envelope, in a cursive hand, were the words: "Please! PLEASE read this."

Henson looked at Esther in bewilderment. "Read it," she said.

I know that you hate me and nothing I say can break through that, but I must before I die tell you the whole story. Not for me. For you. So please read this. It is what I would have told you if you would have come to see me. I don't blame you for that, but it is why I am mailing this to you. I don't have much time left. The cancer is near my heart. They say I should go to the hospital, but I don't want to die there so I am staying here. I know I will never see you again. I deserve that. I have never lied to myself.

"It's your father," said Henson.

Esther began to say something but choked up, clenched her lips and nodded. Henson turned his chair to get more light on the paper.

Because I have at most only a few days, a couple of weeks maybe, I must soon set in motion a chain of events. Instead of giving you this diary face-to-face, I am shipping it to you. After I have safely handed it over, I will make a telephone call to take care of business that's some fifty years old. The fat bastard will be very surprised to know I am alive. I hope the shock kills him. What is more important is that the things you read in my diary must come to light. I know you will do the right thing.

" 'The fat bastard' must be Toorn," said Henson. "There was a phone record of the call."

"And then Toorn contacted Manfred Stock."

"Who sent his thug of a son."

"If only I had gone sooner . . ." Esther covered her face with her hands.

In the diary, you will find a full explanation of my behavior, for which your mother, the best woman God ever created, suffered greatly. You must understand that back then I thought I could not bear to have you both suffer so. They might have killed your mama. They might have killed you, just to spite me. These people were capable of anything. As a Jew you must know this. You know they are always there, hiding in crowds disguised as normal human beings.

There is so much I wish to say that I will never be

able to. Even if you were here, my heart is so full of regrets and memories and feelings that a thousand years of talking couldn't release them all. You were such a beautiful baby, my Esther Meyer! I know you turned out to be a beauty. I used to hold you and try to imagine you as a woman. You would look like your mother. For all the cruelty she suffered in her life, her beauty shined through. Nothing could take that away. And she was strong! So strong! Nothing could break her. And then I had to send you both away. I suffered. Night and day, awake and asleep I suffered, but I knew I had to be strong, as strong as my Rosa, as strong as I hoped my baby girl would be some day.

You might hate me for saying this, but I love you both as much, maybe more, than the day you left. Whether you believe it or not, it is true. I know I made some terrible mistakes and handled all this wrong, but I kept them away from you. You were unlucky in your choice of a father, princess, and I would do anything to make that right because I know how lucky I am to have you as a daughter, even if I only had you with me for a few months.

He had signed "Your Father" but crossed it out and wrote "Samuel Meyer."

"Wow," said Henson quietly. "How did you get this? When? Do you know it's from him?"

"I know," she said, taking a deep breath. "The diary proves it."

"But how did you get it? It was mailed to you? Why did it take so long?"

Esther pushed her hair back from her face. "My father didn't know I was coming until I called him from the airport. He had already mailed the package to me, care of Rosa Goren. It was forwarded to the nursing home, and the attendant must have put it in the closet or something. My mother died about six weeks after I left Amsterdam. They packed up all her things and put them in a box and I—well, I couldn't bring myself to look in the box for weeks. Months, actually. She owned nothing at the home. She had a"—she took a deep breath—"little glass horse, but someone took it, so all she had at the hospital was a picture of me and some clothes. I almost gave the box away. At the last moment I looked in it."

Henson nodded, set the letter on the table, and put both hands on Esther's shoulders. She turned up her palms and grasped his fingers. She did not speak or weep but stared into the space between her knees for some time.

"Can I see the diary?" he asked gently.

"It isn't really a diary," she said. "He wrote an account of his story just after coming to America. Then he added to it near the end of his life."

She continued to crush his fingers as she summarized the story of Samuel Meyer.

He had been born in Metz, but his father was a cook and young Samuel spent his early years in the French-occupied Rhineland. It was a contentious place between the wars, but Meyer's family remained there even after Germany took it back. Eventually, the Nazis went after the Jews and their property. As an able-bodied young man a little bigger than his age indicated, he was separated from his parents in order to be sent to forced labor. He escaped the train with another boy. They were shot at and pursued by dogs. When the other boy stumbled, Meyer looked down the hill and saw the policeman incite his dogs to rip out the boy's belly. He ran then for hours, until sunrise and nearly until the next sunset, when he collapsed in a field with nightmares of the sounds of bloody dogs.

He had escaped, however, and he wandered north into Belgium and eventually Holland. By the time he reached Beekberg, he wrote, he was 60 percent animal. He slept in ditches or under bridges. He stayed hidden in the days and moved through the night. He stole clothes off wash lines and ate chicken feed or roots or whatever he could find in garbage bins.

It was in this subhuman condition that two of the nuns of the Sisters of Divine Mercy found him asleep behind a stone fence. One spoke French. They gave him some biscuits they had with them and offered to take him in, but he had seen too much of what the Nazis could do and was afraid. He ran from them but came back to the same place the next day. They did not come, but he was drawn to the smell of cooking at the De Groot school, so, staying just out of sight, he waited until dark and approached it. He had been living as a hermit for many months. He had not spoken to anyone other than the two sisters, but they reawakened his need to be once again among people. Risking death, he began to accept the charity of the sisters and some local farmers. He eventually developed the courage to approach the curator of the De Groot Museum and ask for work to do.

The curator sometimes came out of the museum to bring him bread and cheese, or milk and a bit of rabbit. The Netherlands was now in the grip of the Third Reich, and the war was in full swing. No one was living well, but the curator shared what he could and warned Meyer that his assistant, young Gerrit Willem Toorn, was a member of the Dutch Nazi party. Toorn had seen Meyer now and again, but the curator had told him that Meyer was an idiot, the illegitimate son of a washerwoman who had lived harmlessly in the countryside for years. The curator thought Toorn was all bluster, a fat kid trying to prove he was a real man. He told Meyer that Toorn wasn't dangerous, but some of his friends were—not to mention their German allies.

The curator found out how dangerous Toorn could be when he himself was turned over to the Nazis because he had concealed the fact that his wife was part Jewish. He and all of his family disappeared forever into Bergen-Belsen. For the community, Toorn acted shocked that the curator had been arrested, as if he'd had nothing to do with it, though he never let the curator be mentioned without also mentioning his Jewish blood. The curator, in fact, was not Jewish, but many accepted that as the logical reason for his being "transported."

Meyer considered running away, but it was now much too difficult to move across the countryside. Toorn regularly threatened him with the same fate as the curator's—since he supposed him a mental defective—and threw scraps of food to him like a farmer feeding his pigs. The image of the dogs ripping up the boy who had escaped with him was always in his mind. Meyer continued his masquerade as an idiot, until Toorn discovered him reading a newspaper behind a hedge one afternoon. Desperately, Meyer begged him not to turn him in. He concocted the tale of how he was wanted in Vichy for stabbing the husband of his lover. He had understood Toorn correctly. The fat man liked to have control over people. He thought he had been given a whip with which to make Meyer leap through hoops.

He treated Meyer a little better at first, probably considering how he might use him. Then, drunk one night after having been insulted by one of his higher-ups in the local Nazis, he woke Meyer up in his place in the tool shed, his sweaty face looming out of the dark and ordered him to kill the man, one Piet Hoom.

"You know how to stab. Stab him. Make it look like the Jews or the Communists did it. Cut out Piet's tongue. Gouge out his eyes. Bring me his testicles. Yes, that's it."

Meyer agreed, but only to hold off Toorn for a while. He knew nothing about killing. But in the morning Toorn was still insistent, so Meyer pretended to know more about revenge than he did. He persuaded Toorn it would be sweeter revenge to have Piet Hoom disgraced, exposed as a traitor and dragged off by the Germans. If the man were murdered, Meyer said, it would make Hoom look like a hero or a martyr, and besides, there might always be suspicions about Toorn. At first Meyer thought he was arguing all this because he wasn't capable of committing a murder, but he knew if Toorn insisted, killing a man like Piet Hoom might be not only justice, but pleasure.

Toorn, however, nodded his head and complimented Meyer for "thinking like a Jew." They hid a radio in Hoom's barn loft. It was an old radio that no longer worked, but Meyer cleaned it up and placed it behind a row of harvesting crates. In front of his wife, Hoom was summarily shot by the squad that found it, begging for his life, insisting that he'd never seen the radio before and would never spy for the Allies. The wife and children were jailed for a while, then released. A few weeks later, Toorn (drunk again) thought he had been insulted by the new commander of his little group of Beekberg Fascists. An anonymous letter put that man into forced labor, though he survived the war.

It occurred to Meyer that a similar letter might get Toorn himself hauled away, but Toorn was also Meyer's protection.

Toorn was the devil to whom Meyer had sold his soul. Toorn might collect it at any time, but while Meyer was still useful Toorn would wait. Meyer hated himself. He had sunk so low that he had become, he thought, the sniveling servant who tends Dracula's coffin and feasts upon insects. And then the day came when Toorn thought it might be useful to his career to expose quietly more secret Jews. The SS had requisitioned the De Groot house and converted it into an interrogation center. Their intention was to purify the area and eliminate any traces of resistance. Toorn thought a few whispers would be much appreciated. Meyer fed him a couple of Communist partisans. They were teenagers and were killed in the public square, along with their fathers.

By now, the Allies were well established on the continent. Their planes passed over. German troops moved on the roads either going to or coming from France. Eventually, however, Meyer could wait no longer. He told Toorn about a man who had thrown a cobblestone at him when he was begging near a dairy. Meyer had now sold out a Jew, and his hatred of himself turned into a sleepless search for some way to get free, to hold Toorn in his power as he had been held by Toorn. Killing him might have been easy, but it would have exposed Meyer when it was only a matter of time before the Allies got there, or the Germans sued for peace as they had in the Great War. And anyway, a summary execution was too easy for someone as evil as Toorn.

One afternoon, a truckload of art arrived from the railway station. Rail service was regularly interrupted and constantly being rerouted. The De Groot Museum was to be a temporary holding facility until the art could be moved farther into Germany. SS Colonel Stock was initially suspicious of the creepy, dirty man who slept in the toolshed, but Toorn denied Meyer was a Jew, telling Stock that Meyer was an idiot who had always lived on the estate as a handyman. After a while, the Germans hardly noticed Meyer. He listened at keyholes and open windows. He soon understood that there was a conspiracy among several officers to divert much of the art. Field Marshal Göring, in particular, had planned a vast collection of looted art at the center of the new German empire. Heinrich Himmler intended to build a huge museum to a vanished race, the Jews, and include Torah arks, menorahs, and other valuable Judaica. The conspirators, including Stock, thought they could send enough to Germany that Berlin would never guess that some of the artworks had disappeared in transit.

Meyer scribbled down the names of the conspirators and hid the list in the lining of his jacket. Any time the art was open to view, he studied it.

Henson interrupted Esther's retelling. "These were the men listed on the photograph of the 1929 Cubs, correct?"

"Yes. These names are listed here in his diary."

"Is there any explanation for the numbers he wrote on the back?" Henson asked. "We've gone over and over them and come up with nothing. They might be Swiss bank accounts or who knows? One of our cryptographers suggested it might be a book code, but you need to know what book is the basis."

"I'm sorry," said Esther. "There is no explanation of it."

"All right, then. Does he mention the Van Gogh?"

Esther continued; she seemed to find this retelling a kind of comfort.

Although Colonel Stock and his men could easily have looted the De Groot, nothing was really notable in the museum except for the Van Gogh, and they were perhaps distracted by the masterpieces of earlier periods. Van Gogh, after all, was one of those "decadent" artists who had destroyed the art of painting and undermined Western civilization. Toorn, however, said that he was afraid the Allies might bomb the building or somehow gain possession of the painting. He suggested that the De Groot self-portrait might be sold to the Third Reich and he and Stock might share the proceeds. Meantime, he would replace the portrait in the museum with one of his own copies of it. For years he had been trying to paint like Van Gogh and was sure that one of his copies would pass to an untrained eye. It would have to be crated anyway to protect it from the war, so it might not be visible until the Allies were beaten back or a treaty was made. Meyer overheard these conversations and delighted that he might have created this idea in Toorn by frequently saying Van Gogh himself couldn't tell the difference between Toorn's facsimiles and the original. Stock didn't jump at the suggestion, but the idea germinated in him—perhaps he had no intention that Toorn would ever receive a pfennig for it—and eventually he acted as a go-between for the sale and contacted Berlin.

Meyer now hatched a scheme. Toorn and Stock placed the De Groot Van Gogh in a thin crate for shipping, but with the trains having problems from Allied bombing and partisans who levered up the rails, it would be a week before the next consignment could be loaded. The crates were stored in the old coach house.

Two days later, while most of the soldiers were distracted by the arrest of five partisans, Meyer slipped into the coach house. Crates were piled everywhere, and many of them were about the size that would have contained the De Groot Museum's self-portrait. Several truckloads of art from Paris and southern France had arrived in the last week. There were several reusable crates with latches and hinges, but many were simply nailed shut. When he touched one, however, he discovered the nails had already been loosened. Either Toorn or Stock, or maybe some of the soldiers, had been peeking inside. Meyer was astonished at the variety of paintings he saw and, despite the danger, he spent a long time in there. Eventually he saw a crate stacked against the wall with a paper label used as a seal on the side. He saw that it said, *"portrait V. Gogh, Arles."* His heart began to pound. Luck was with him. The label was already loosened by the damp of the carriage house. He peeled it off and switched the De Groot portrait in the crate for one of Toorn's facsimiles. He assumed that any expert of real merit would immediately spot the difference and Toorn would have been guilty of attempting to defraud the Third Reich.

He had the perfect hiding place for the authentic Van Gogh. Iron stanchions embedded in concrete flanked the steps leading up to the front of the house. These had once supported a set of gates and then had been used to tie horses. The caps were shaped like pineapples. Meyer worked one loose while painting it black. Inside, the pipe was dry and clean. He rolled up the painting in oilcloth and dropped it inside, set the cap back on top, and struck it on each side with a stone, tightening it. When he had finished his chore, the oil paint further acted as a glue. Nearly twenty years later, when he came back for it he had to use a sledgehammer to knock the cap off, but the Van Gogh was still safe inside. Not even dust had penetrated the pipe.

"Just a minute," said Henson. "The De Groot self-portrait never left Toorn's possession, though. The painting Meyer took from the stanchion years later was Feodor Minsky's."

Esther smiled. "Exactly. Samuel Meyer had opened the wrong crate."

"And replaced the Minsky self-portrait with one of Toorn's facsimiles."

"But then Toorn boxed up one of his other facsimiles in order to steal the De Groot self-portrait for himself."

"Both facsimiles were burned?"

"As unlikely as that seems . . ."

Henson snapped his fingers. "No! The Berlin receipts. Maybe they weren't false. Maybe the Germans thought the De Groot portrait—that is, Toorn's facsimile—made it to Berlin. After that it was lost, destroyed in the massive bombings or in the Russian siege of the city."

"Yes!" said Esther. "But Toorn thought it had been burned in Holland. Toorn never knew about the Minsky self-portrait."

"How many self-portraits did Van Gogh paint?" Henson asked. "Sheesh."

Stock received an order to personally escort the artworks to Berlin in two days, but his hands shook and he seemed distracted. The Allies were on the way. There were vivid tales coming from Germany about what Hitler had done to the men who conspired with Count Von Stauffenberg to assassinate the Führer and the recriminations had continued for some time as all treachery was being rooted out. Stock clearly didn't want to return to Berlin at that time, but why? He might have been part of the conspiracy to kill Hitler, but Meyer didn't believe that. Stock was too much of a true believer, he thought. Perhaps Stock had been stealing some of the art. Perhaps he was merely a friend or an old schoolmate of one of the plotters. That would have been sufficient for him to be on the list for punishment.

Whatever it was, Meyer never found out. He helped a sergeant fill the truck with the artworks, then was, to his surprise, ordered to get in the back. He had never accompanied the art to the station and assumed a bullet from Stock's sidearm waited at the end of the trip. He decided he would make a run for it when the truck passed a section of forest just beyond the open fields. There was a turn there and the Opel would slow. As they set out, they could hear fighting to the west. The British were moving in on Beekberg. Meyer cringed at the sound. His survival was only a few miles away, but he would most likely never reach it.

The truck set out fast on the dirt road, with Meyer sealed inside, the crates bouncing perilously against him. He managed to cling to the top of a coffinlike box holding a marble statue of Pan, which did not shift as quickly as the other crates.

The roar of the engine blocked almost all sound, and Meyer was considering how he might get the back door open when suddenly an even louder roar split the air. Holes appeared in the roof and wood splintered. His forearm was slashed and bleeding. They were being strafed. The roar of the fighter faded and Meyer crawled over the clashing boxes, hoping to kick the back door open. The truck, however, lurched from side to side and slowed. Meyer was almost to the door when the truck crashed hard, throwing him down and toward the front. The door popped open like the lid on a jack-in-the-box, and Meyer knew they had careened into one of the ditches beside the road. When he climbed up, he saw Stock lying in the road behind them. He had jumped or been thrown from the truck. Meyer saw him stir, rise slightly in an attempt to point his pistol, then fall back unconscious. Meyer jumped down and ran as he had when he had escaped from the train nearly two years earlier. When he finally collapsed in a patch of woods, he saw the column of black smoke from the truck burning.

His first instinct was to run for the British lines, but then, where the British or Americans were there would be a lot of German troops. He went south, almost the same journey he had made before, but continued on into Vichy France and ultimately found status as a refugee. He freely mixed truth and fabrications to achieve that, claiming, for example, that the nasty scar on his forearm was from his burning off the hated tattoo that would have revealed he was an escapee from a concentration camp.

"So he was never actually a survivor of the death camps?" asked Henson.

Esther shook her head. "But he never stopped believing they were looking for him. In the diary, he still says they are out there, rich with the gold and jewels and artworks they stole, slipping money to the enemies of Israel, financing secret Aryan movements, and so on. He covers nearly twenty pages ranting about these things. He saw signs of their conspiracies in all the major news events."

"He went paranoid, then?"

Esther flashed a defensive glare. "He had no reason?"

"He had more than enough reason. How could he not be paranoid?"

"Exactly," she said. "His mind was scarred. He trusted no one."

Henson nodded. "But he could have exposed them. Didn't he see the Nuremberg trials, and those of Eichmann and Klaus Barbie? How could he spend all those years remaining silent?"

"I've asked myself over and over, Martin. He says he once went to the federal courthouse in Chicago with the Van Gogh. He saw a man getting out of a cab. He knew he was being followed."

"But he lived in the same house for decades!"

"When you read his account, you will see it was all logical in his world. It wasn't logical in reality, but it was logical to him." Esther turned her head and stared into the tabletop.

Henson whistled. "What it must have done to him when the government accused him of being Meyerbeer!"

"It did exactly what you would expect," said Esther. "He thought the conspirators here were just trying to get him back over there."

"Why didn't he just go to Israel with your mother? Surely . . . no, that's the rational world. I don't know how things like that would have affected me." Henson thought for a moment. "Does he say why your mother left?"

Esther took a while to compose herself, then, after a deep breath, said, "He cut out his own heart, he says. He had to make sure he protected the woman he loved."

"He told her he was Meyerbeer."

"No," said Esther, "he told her the pregnancy had made her ugly. He told her that"—Esther choked up—"that he didn't want me. He told her he had a blonde woman who was pregnant with twins and that the whole Meyerbeer accusation was just a scheme by her husband to get even with him. He says he actually showed her the picture of a woman he didn't know."

Henson shook his head in disbelief. "Can all this be true? Do you think he is just writing for you?"

"She shouldn't have believed him, but she did. She went through worse things than he did, you know. Happiness, love, faith: all things like that were a question mark to her. She expected failure."

"I'll bet," said Henson, "there wasn't any question about happiness, love, and faith in you." He touched Esther's hand, expecting her to break down, but Esther held herself together for some time. Then he saw the tears sliding down her cheeks.

After several moments she wiped the tears away and said, "I think maybe he wanted to give me this account, maybe give me the Van Gogh so that I would be protected from *them*. When I refused to come to him, he decided to reveal what he knew and they sent Stock Junior."

"Maybe he wanted you to know who he really was."

"We shouldn't miss the auction," she said.

"Minsky asked about you. I think he's in love."

"Well, he's adorable"—she smiled—"but you have to look." She held out Meyer's account.

"I'll read it later," said Henson.

"No, look at the clippings."

Henson took off the rubber bands and lifted out a slip of glossy paper. Printed on it was a black-and-white photograph of a painting. A topless woman in puffy pants lay on her back. The cutline at the bottom said "*Odalisque in Red Pants*, Henri Matisse." He turned it over and saw from the partial text that the clipping had once been part of an art book or catalogue.

He took out another clipping, on much cheaper paper, black and white again. This time it was a typical Van Gogh: a vase of flowers. The artist's signature, "Vincent," was in the lower corner. "More of Toorn's work?" asked Henson.

"Keep looking," said Esther.

The next picture was a postcard, old and yellowed. A woman, sketched in pastels, with features that resembled Esther. On the back of the card it said "Edgar Degas, *Gabrielle Diot*, 1890." There were six or seven others, cut from books, newspapers, and even a 1935 calender. Henson glanced at Esther for an explanation, but the last one he lifted out stunned him. The picture wasn't good, the ink had faded through time, but it was still recognizable to Henson.

"This is a Matisse like the other one. This is the *Woman Seated in a Chair* from the Paul Rosenberg collection!"

"You've got it," said Esther. "You'll notice it is also 'P. 123.' "

"Plate 123 from whatever book— Holy mackerel! The numbers on the back of the picture."

"That's what I was thinking."

"This painting was stolen from Paul Rosenberg in Paris. He was one of the biggest collectors between the wars," Henson said. "We had a lead on this painting last year, but it didn't pan out. It's been missing since the Nazis took it."

"A couple of them are from the Bernheim Jeune collection, which was also looted. *Every one* of those clippings is a painting that disappeared during the war and has never been located. Meyer saw all of those paintings. He remembered them, and he cut these out for me."

"He must have rooted in some very dusty libraries."

"But he saw them in Beekberg during the war," Esther said. "My guess is that part of those batting averages on the back of his picture of the baseball players are the plate numbers and page numbers."

"The other numbers might encode names or initials corresponding to the 'players' on the front. This could open many a can of worms. Who knows where it might lead?"

"To more than just a Van Gogh conspiracy," said Esther.

Henson sat silent, staring at the clippings in astonishment. "I have to call Washington," he said, closing the book and replacing the rubber band. "But first, we are going to see Jacob Minsky. There aren't many from that time left, and I know it will be a reward if you join him."

"You pimp," she said. "Don't try to get rid of me. Without me, you'd never recover anything."